BROOM AND GLOOM

SQUEAKY CLEAN MYSTERIES, BOOK 9

CHRISTY BARRITT

COPYRIGHT:

Broom and Gloom: A Novel
Copyright 2014 by Christy Barritt

Published by River Heights Press

Cover design by The Killion Group

I GRIPPED the steering wheel of my economy-sized rental car and veered off the main highway, following the detour sign onto a small road through Oklahoma's backcountry. "On the Road Again" blared on the radio, and the deceitful sun shone brightly in the distance, making the day look much warmer than it actually felt.

A detour seemed a little too appropriate for my life. In fact, my life so far seemed to be defined by a series of setbacks.

Not anymore.

I'd just flown in from Norfolk, Virginia. At the airport, I'd picked up my rental car, and I'd hit the road. Before even checking into my hotel for the forensic conference I was attending, I'd decided to meet with my future stepbrother for dinner. I wasn't sure what my schedule would be like for the rest of the week, so I wanted to meet him now while I could.

His name was Trace Ryan, and he was an up-and-coming country singer. His mom, Teddi, was marrying my dad, and she'd insisted we meet. In an effort to keep the peace, I'd figured why not?

But right now I was in the middle of Nowhere, Oklahoma, hoping for the life of me my GPS wasn't leading me astray.

I looked down at the paper where I'd scribbled some backup directions and stopped at the end of a lane. A large aluminum-sided warehouse stood in front of me, six vehicles parked out front. There was nothing else around. No houses or barns or stores. Just flat land with a few sprigs of dry grass and a dead tree in the distance.

As soon as I stepped from my car, I could hear the whiny tunes of a steel guitar.

I glanced at my paper again. This was the address Trace had given me. I started across the dirt toward the warehouse, the air dry and cold around me. I pulled my canvas jacket closer, wishing I'd brought something heavier. Going out west, somehow I'd expected things to be warmer. They weren't. Of course, it was only March.

When I stepped into the building, a wave of loud

music hit me. I paused and spotted a cowboy onstage with a guitar strapped across his chest. I soaked everything in for a moment. The lights. The fog in the air. The loud music. Two rows of empty chairs in front of the stage.

"Can I help you?" A short man who exuded nervous energy stopped beside me. He had a hipster vibe with his shaved head, trim build, and chunky glasses. His head seemed too large for his body, which only added to his whole offbeat persona.

"I'm here to meet Trace Ryan," I said, nodding toward the stage.

"And you are . . . ?"

"His soon-to-be stepsister."

The man raised his eyebrows, staring at me like I was lying. "Is that right?"

"Talk to Trace. He'll confirm that I'm supposed to be here, Mr. . . . ?"

"I'm Jono, his manager. He would have certainly mentioned this to me." He looked back at the stage and scowled again. "We've had a stressful rehearsal, and I don't want to burden him any more before our big tour starts. This is make-or-break time, if you know what I mean."

"Is that you, Gabby?" Trace said from the stage, shielding his eyes from the spotlights.

"The one and only."

"Fantastic. A few more minutes and I'll be finished here. Jono, behave yourself. She's with me."

"Sorry," Jono murmured. "We get some people coming in here with crazy stories all the time. Can't be too careful."

As he walked away, I settled against the wall and listened to the band as they finished rehearsing. They had a good sound. Trace's voice was deep and not too twangy. Their songs were catchy, and their energy was infectious.

As the guitar and drums finished out a song, Trace pulled his guitar off. "That's a wrap, guys."

He hopped down from the stage and made his way toward me, a bit of Western swagger to his steps. I wondered if his walk reflected his attitude or if it was the boots and tight jeans that made him saunter that way.

As soon as he was close enough to reach me, he pulled me into a hug. "So good to finally meet you, Gabby."

"Same here." I patted his back, not expecting the warm greeting.

I'd never met the man before, nor had we even talked, other than to set up this meeting. I'd figured Trace felt just as obligated as I did to meet. After all, we were both adults. It wasn't like we'd ever live under the same roof or even spend a holiday together.

He turned back to the band. "Let's break for dinner and meet back here in two hours. Sound good?"

They all nodded and began to put away their instruments.

"I promise, I'll introduce you to everyone when we get back. Right now I'm starving." Trace put his hand on my elbow and led me toward the door. "I want to take you to this barbecue place not too far from here. It's Oklahoma dining at its finest. Sound okay?"

I nodded. "Of course."

Up close, Trace had that charisma that seemed necessary for celebrities to have in order to attain success. He had rugged good looks, eyes that were alive with mischief, a trim muscled body, and a voice that made women croon. His hair was light brown, he had a slight cleft in his chin, and he stood at least six feet tall.

After talking to Teddi, I'd formed the impression of him that he was a wannabe country star. He seemed like the real deal, though. He had an aura that garnered attention.

I climbed into his truck, an older-model pickup that looked like it had seen better days. Empty cans of energy drinks clanked at my feet, and dust kicked up behind us as we began traveling down the road.

"So your dad's the lucky man marrying my

mom, huh?" he said, glancing over at me. He had the perfect cowboy profile, especially with his oversized Stetson on. His shirt was a little too nice, too pressed and unstained to look like a real rancher, but I was sure women loved the image he portrayed.

"My dad's a very lucky man." My dad was a louse, and I still didn't see what Teddi saw in him. But the two of them seemed happy together. I didn't get it, but it wasn't my relationship, so I tried not to think too much about it.

"It's good to hear her happy again. After Dad died, I didn't know if my mom would ever be the same." We bumped down the road, a certain melancholy lingering in the air. "Has your conference started yet?"

"Tomorrow." The conference was my real reason for being here.

"Forensics, right?"

"You know it. It's a highly glamorous field. Just watch CSI sometime," I told him drily.

"Sounds interesting. Especially for a girl."

"What was that?" I jerked my head toward him, certain I'd heard him incorrectly.

A smile spread across his face, and he winked. "Just kidding. I like to give people a hard time. It's my love language. If we're going to be stepsiblings, you might as well get used to that."

"Good to know." I smiled, already liking Trace and glad that I'd come early to meet him.

As quickly as we'd started the journey to the restaurant, we pulled up to a stop at an old lodge-like building named the Tanglefoot Saloon. Trace followed my gaze, hunching to peer through the windshield at the restaurant.

He shrugged. "I know it's not much to look at it, but the barbecue is out of this world. It will have you licking your fingers and begging for more. You'll buy another plane ticket to Oklahoma just to eat here."

"You sound pretty sure of yourself. I never even said I liked barbecue."

"Heresy. Everyone likes barbecue."

As soon as I stepped inside the place, I was drawn back into the Old West. Everyone seemed to wear cowboy boots, drink oversized beers, and have cowboy hats perched atop their heads. The only thing that could have made it more perfect would be a piano man playing "Ragtime" and a group of cow rustlers and hustlers playing poker in the corner.

"A lot of the ranchers around here come in for dinner," Trace said, smiling as he watched my reaction. "It's great. I promise."

"A showdown outside after lunch would make this the perfect experience. Seriously. Even a fight between some farmers and cowmen. I'll take whatever I can get."

"Farmers and cowmen?"

"*Oklahoma*?" I reminded him.

His expression still looked blank.

"The musical? Please tell me you've seen it." It was the first musical I'd ever acted in, all the way back in middle school. It remained one of my favorites to this day.

"I was more into Garth Brooks than I was Andrew Lloyd Webber."

"Rodgers and Hammerstein," I corrected. "Webber did the music for *Phantom*."

"Well, I blame it all on my roots. They're more country and down home than they are cultured and refined."

"I'm sure you get by just fine."

He nodded hello to the voluptuous waitress, whose face instantly lit when she spotted Trace. She sashayed over and grinned. "Hey there, good looking. What brings you in here today?"

"I've got to introduce my sis to some of your barbecue."

"Your sister?" Her eyes turned to me, obviously assessing my worth as she looked me up and down. "I had no idea."

Something subconscious ignited in me, and I found myself hooking my thumbs through my belt loops. What could I say? When in Oklahoma, do as the Oklahomans. "I can't wait to try some of your ribs. They smell fabulous."

She smiled and then giggled. I must have gotten her approval.

"Well, come on back," she said. "I've got the perfect seat for you."

She led us to a corner table by the window. Peanut shells crunched underneath our feet, and the scent of something smoky and spicy lingered in the air, making my stomach growl.

The tables looked like wagon wheels with sheets of tempered glass atop them. The napkins were checkered, and all over the walls were memorabilia of the West—ox yokes, steer heads, black-and-white photos highlighting the past.

I couldn't help but smile. It was how I'd already dreamed Oklahoma would be. I half expected to see Gordon MacRae as Curly pull up in a surrey with fringe on the top. I'd been accused on more than one occasion of living in a musical, and I was okay with that.

After the waitress set down huge jars filled with sweet tea, Trace ordered ribs for both of us. That's when the first moment of silence fell.

"I hope you don't think it's strange that I wanted to meet with you. The truth is, I did have some ulterior motives." He cracked a peanut he'd taken from the silver bucket in the middle of the table.

"Did you?"

He nodded. "My mom likes to talk about you, so I've heard about your past."

Which part? I wondered. There was a long list to choose from—me almost being killed, my ex-fiancé almost being killed, my recent arrest. Take your pick.

Before he could explain, a woman ran up to the table and breathlessly stared at Trace. She was young with wide eyes, big hair, and a low-cut shirt.

"Trace Ryan?" she panted.

Trace grinned that million-dollar smile of his. "The one and only."

"I'm your biggest fan!"

Wow, his celebrity status had grown quickly. This man already had a well-established fan club and supporters who recognized him out in public. Kudos to him.

"I appreciate that. Would you like an autograph?"

"Would I ever!" she squealed. The squeal turned into a pout. "But I don't have any paper."

"Let me see your hand instead."

She happily obliged. He pulled a marker from his pocket—did he always keep one there for moments such as these?—and signed his name on the back of her hand.

The woman screamed again. "You just made my day!"

She continued giggling as she went back to her

gaggle of girlfriends sitting across the restaurant. Trace followed my gaze and winked at the onlookers. He seemed to be a regular Casanova.

Even stranger—either the woman hadn't noticed me at all or she'd chosen ignorant bliss and simply pretended I didn't exist.

Trace turned serious again as he turned back to our conversation. He cracked another peanut, and with the nuts still tucked into the shell, he tossed them back into his mouth like some people downed a shot of alcohol. "Sorry about that. All my fans expect this certain image. It's a lot to live up to sometimes."

"I can only imagine."

He wiped some crumbs into his hand and placed them on a napkin. "So, as I started to say, I need your help."

"What's going on?" I took a sip of my tea, curious now and feeling like I'd been swept up in a world that was entirely different from my own. My life was urban, brisk, and busy. Out here I actually felt like I could breathe. I had the urge to go all Rodgers and Hammerstein and burst into "Oh, What a Beautiful Mornin'."

"It's this lady." He pulled something out of his back pocket and shoved a picture toward me. A woman with hair so blonde it looked white, tanned skin, and a bikini-ready body stared at me from the photo.

"Pretty."

"Looks can be deceiving." He shook his head, a new tension seeming to wash over him. "She's making my life miserable."

"An ex?"

He shook his head. "I feel like a girl saying this, but I suppose she's more of a stalker."

Now this was getting interesting. "Really? Tell me more."

"About six months ago, I started getting fan letters from a woman named Georgia Dalton." He tapped the photo. "She started showing up at all my concerts and sneaking her way backstage to meet me. At first, she seemed like an overzealous fan with boundary issues."

"I have a feeling there's a 'but' in there."

He sighed. "Yes, there is. I quickly realized she was obsessed. I caught her outside of my home once. I still didn't think she was crazy at that point. But I was dating a girl named Caitlyn. One day, Caitlyn found her tires slashed. Then her apartment was broken into and her things ransacked."

"You think this woman is behind those things?" I studied the picture in front of me, wondering if a mentally unstable soul was behind those hazel eyes.

"Yes, I do. The problem is that I could never prove anything. The police could only file reports about the incidents, but there were no fingerprints or video surveillance or anything to point to Georgia."

"What happened to Caitlyn?"

"She couldn't take it anymore. We broke up, and she moved back home to Colorado with her family." His voice sounded earnestly sad as he said the words. "Honestly, I wasn't sure Georgia was behind it. Caitlyn also had an ex-boyfriend who was pretty controlling. I thought it could be him."

"I take it the story doesn't end there?" I took another drink of the sweetest iced tea ever. My teeth started rotting with every sip, yet my taste buds wouldn't let me stop. Maybe it wasn't a bad thing. The sugar was going straight into my bloodstream and making me overly alert.

He shook his head. "Then, two months later, I met Skye."

"Skye?" His life was like a regular soap opera. I was fascinated already.

"A teacher who had just moved here from Arizona for a fresh start. Her parents were killed in a car crash when she was only thirteen, and then her brother died, leaving her without anyone."

"Was she teaching here?"

He shook his head. "No, she said teaching wasn't for her. She was working as a customer service representative for a company. She worked out of her home, doing everything from her office there. It was pretty isolating, I suppose."

"How did the two of you meet?"

A soft smile pulled at his lips. "I was in this old, hole-in-the-wall music store checking out some CDs. The place is old and run down, and no one even knows it's there. Anyway, Skye was in there, and we just started talking about music. We really hit it off."

"Let me guess—that's when everything started going wrong?" I'd been around enough to know how the story usually played out.

"See, I was right. Girls can be good at this detective thing." He flashed a teasing grin that quickly faded. "Skye said she felt like someone was watching her. Then someone wiped her computer clean. Small things in her house kept being rearranged—but nothing that she could prove."

"But she thought someone had been in her home? She thought *Georgia* had been in her home?"

He nodded. "We threw the theory out there."

I shivered at the thought. Unfortunately, I could relate because I'd experienced something similar. "Did she ever call the cops?"

"Again, she couldn't prove anything. It was all a hunch, nothing concrete." He stared off in the distance for a moment. "I got back from a two-week tour. We'd talked several times while I was on the road, but I got back a day earlier than scheduled. I went to her house to surprise her, but she wasn't home."

"Could be a coincidence, especially since she didn't know you were coming."

"True. But I tried to call after that, and she didn't answer. After a day of not being able to get in touch with her, I got worried. Skye was always really good about calling me back in a timely manner."

"What happened next?"

"I managed to find the number for Skye's friend Darcy, but she hadn't heard from Skye in three days. I tried not to panic. I mean, we were at that weird place in our relationship where we'd only gone out a few times. We liked each other, but we didn't have enough time together to be serious. I couldn't say for sure if this was normal or not."

"You mean, maybe she was the type of girl who just liked to take off on a trip without telling anyone?"

"Exactly. She didn't have to answer to me. She's a big girl. Anyway, when I didn't hear anything for two days, I called the police. They got some information from me and did a little investigating. They called the company she worked for, and her boss said that Skye called in and requested time off. The police also said that they'd checked her apartment and there was no evidence of foul play. They came to the conclusion that she left on her own free will."

"But you think Georgia did something?" I leaned back, unsure if it was excitement over the case or my sugar high that made my blood zing.

"I do, but I have no way to prove it." He leaned across the table toward me. "Darcy did say that Skye seemed a bit of a gypsy, that she wasn't the type who wanted to settle down. If she left on her own, I certainly don't want to stalk her. But if something happened to her . . ."

"How long ago did this happen?"

His eyes crinkled with worry. "A month."

"You think every woman you get close to is a target for Georgia. She's some sort of femme fatale?"

"Exactly."

I grabbed a peanut and rubbed it between my fingers, suddenly starving. "What do you want me to do?"

Just in the nick of time, the waitress set our food in front of us and the tantalizing scent of barbecue ribs drifted upward. It wasn't until that moment I realized just how hungry I was, and I instantly wanted to inhale the entire plate of ribs, fries, coleslaw, and beans before me. Of course, I wouldn't, because that would be uncouth.

Trace took his hat off. "You mind if we pray before eating?"

It was refreshing to hear someone else ask that. "Please do."

As soon as he said "amen," I grabbed a fry and got back to the conversation. "So, please continue. I'm curious now."

"I really liked Skye, Gabby. My manager says I shouldn't become attached to anyone. Fans like the illusion that you're single and available to be the 'man of their dreams.'" He said the last four words in a mocking tone. "But I can't stop thinking about her. Not only about her smile but about the possibility that something happened to her."

"Your manager sounds like a pain in the chaps." I picked up a rib, realizing how messy this was going to be. I was willing to chance it.

"He is."

"When was the last time you saw this Georgia woman?"

He raised his fork but still didn't eat a bite. "That's the strange thing. I haven't seen her since Skye disappeared. The day I returned home from my tour, Georgia was waiting for me outside of the recording studio. I tried to brush her off."

"How did she respond?" I bit into the rib, and the meat nearly melted in my mouth.

"Not well. She got angry, and said we were meant to be together and that I'd eventually see it one day."

"Sounds scary."

He nodded. "You can say that again. But then she

left. It's been quiet. Too quiet, you know what I mean?"

I put the bone down and wiped my mouth with a napkin. Trace would never take me seriously with barbecue sauce on my face. I balled up the napkin and tried to look composed before addressing him. "What would you like for me to do, Trace? Find Skye? Track Georgia?"

He scooped up some coleslaw with his fork. "Jono keeps saying I need to let this go and get used to women doing crazy things in the name of having a celebrity crush. But if Georgia did something to Skye, then I feel responsible. I can't live with myself if she was hurt because of me. For a while, I even wondered if Jono might be behind it. I could see him as the type who might pay Skye off in order to ensure I'm single and unattached."

"He'd be a snake if he did that."

"I know. That's why I'd like for you to help me figure out what happened. See if you can locate Georgia and figure out what she's up to. Has she moved on to someone else? Did she have anything to do with Skye's disappearance? I need some answers."

"I understand."

"I know you have classes this week, but I figured you could snoop in the evenings. Maybe you could even stay in Oklahoma a little longer if you needed to? I could compensate you. What do you say?"

I stared at him a moment, at his green eyes as they pleaded with me. "I say, I'm just the girl who can't say no—to mysteries, of course. I'd love to help, but not for pay. We're family. Practically."

He grinned. "Thank you so much, Gabby. Now, eat those ribs. You're going to need your energy for this one."

AFTER DINNER, Trace drove me back to my car, dust kicking up behind his truck as we traveled down the lonely road. My mind spun with information as I tried to process everything he'd told me about Georgia and Skye. I needed to figure out the best place to start my investigation.

"We're going to rehearse some more tonight. Why don't you hang out?" Trace said, his hands casually draped on the steering wheel. "It will give you a chance to ask any questions. Plus, you could hear some of our music and meet the rest of the band."

"Really? I won't be in the way?"

"Nah, of course not. Family is never an inconvenience."

Funny, I'd never really felt that with my own flesh and blood. I was starting to like the idea of Trace becoming my stepbrother more and more. Maybe I could finally have the family I'd always dreamed about. "Tell me about this warehouse where you're playing. Do you own it?"

"It's just a space that we rent to set up before our tour so we can work out all the kinks before hitting the road."

"Is this old warehouse available anytime you need it?" I was trying to wrap my mind around how show business worked. I'd be lying if I said I wasn't fascinated.

"One of the label executives owns the space. He lets other bands use it, as well. We practiced at Wentworth's ranch for years. But then some fans found the place and kept interrupting. No one knows we're out here, and we like it that way."

"Sounds exciting." I was going to have fun immersing myself in this world this week. In my head, I could already hear Alan Jackson singing "Gone Country."

He draped one arm against the door. "It really is. I've worked my whole life for this, Gabby. I can't believe it's finally happening. We struggled for years to be noticed. Years. Finally, we hooked up with another band, and they liked our music. They invited us to tour with them as the opening act. Cowboy Blues, you ever heard of them?"

I nodded, impressed. "Cowboy Blues? As in, *the*

Cowboy Blues who sang 'With This Ring and Forever'?" I started singing and then abruptly stopped when I realized what I was doing. I cleared my throat. "My old college roommate used to listen to them all the time."

Trace grinned. "Nice voice, by the way. But yeah, Cowboy Blues are great guys. We would have probably never gotten this recording contract without them. And Jono, of course."

"So, you're going on tour next week?"

"That's right. This week we're having a soft launch. It's a release party for our new CD, and we wanted to have it at one of the places where we got our start. We'll have a real release party in Nashville next week. Reporters and label execs and everyone else will be there for that one."

This guy was the real deal. The way Teddi had described it, I figured he was playing at little honky-tonk bars and living in an apartment with four other guys who, when combined, still couldn't make rent and had to resort to delivering pizzas on the side.

Before I could say anything, he continued.

"We're playing at this festival the night after that. The organizer is a personal friend of mine, so I couldn't exactly say no. Jono wasn't too happy about it because we're supposed to be spending all our time concentrating on our upcoming tour. Anyway, it's a bunch of local bands, and we're headlining it. The whole thing is set up under tents, since it's still so cold outside. Should be fun."

"You sound busy."

"And this is nothing compared to what happens next. We continue with rehearsals this week, and then we have our official launch, appearances on *The Today Show*, 150 concert dates. It's going to be quite the ride."

"It doesn't sound like you have any time for dating."

He frowned and rubbed his chin. "No, it doesn't sound like that. But you make time for what's important."

"How did Skye feel about you being gone so much?" We pulled up to the warehouse, but Trace made no effort to get out.

"Skye wanted me to succeed. She was one of my biggest supporters, without being crazy." Trace shifted in his seat, turning to face me. "She even told me that this was my time to fly."

I chewed on his words as we both hopped out of the truck and walked toward the door. He'd had a changing point in his life. I supposed I'd had one—perhaps many—of them also, yet I'd remained in the same place. I prayed that being here this week would help me find some of the answers I was so desperately seeking—not only about Skye and Georgia but about my own life. I had to get off the treadmill I was on. I wanted to fly also.

Trace pulled his cowboy hat down lower, shielding his gaze from the setting sun in the distance. "How about this? Stick around and think about it. We'll talk again after rehearsal."

I nodded. "Sounds great."

We walked inside, and the band was having fun onstage, singing Aerosmith's "Walk This Way," only countrified. Their enthusiasm was infectious. They were all like little boys who'd just been given four-wheelers for Christmas.

"Guys, I'd like to introduce you all to my future sister!" Trace said, walking toward them.

The men onstage all paused.

With Trace's hand on my arm, he pulled me toward the foot of the stage.

"Everyone, this is Gabby. Gabby, this is everyone."

The guy playing guitar, a tall man with dark hair and eyes so blue I could see them from where I stood, nodded toward me. "I'm Wentworth. People call me Wentworth."

The rest of the guys chuckled.

"Wentworth and I have been best friends since sixth grade," Trace said. "We never dreamed this would actually become a reality."

"Music used to just be something we used to get

the girls." Wentworth grinned. With his model-like good looks, I was certain that he didn't need a guitar to help him get any dates.

"I'm Dudley," the drummer said. He was on the shorter side with long hair pulled into a ponytail and a brooding air about him. "People call me Dud, which, I assure you, is no reflection of my personality."

The guys all heckled him a moment.

"And I'm Leroy, the bassist. I have nothing clever to say, except watch out for these guys. It's always the smart mouths who get you in trouble." He was heavyset with a warm personality and a deep laugh.

"Great to meet you all," I started.

Trace turned toward me. "Make yourself at home, Gabby, and if these guys give you any trouble, you just let me know."

As I settled back to listen to the band, my mind drifted to life at home. I wondered how Chad was making out with the business today. We were the co-owners of Squeaky Clean Crime Scene Cleaning and Renovations. We were going through some growing pains right now, but Chad assured me he could handle the workload this week.

Meanwhile, my friend Garrett Mercer had taken off for Africa. He'd invited me to go along, but I'd felt like I needed to stay where I was and get my own affairs in order, no matter how tempting the idea might be. His trip was only supposed to last a month, but he'd already been gone six weeks. I took that to mean he was having a good time.

Then there was Riley. There was always Riley, whether I wanted him to be there or not. We'd been engaged, but a homicidal maniac had shot him in the head before we said, "I do." Long story short, he was recovering from a brain injury and had moved back home with his parents so they could help take care of him. I had to admit that hauling him to therapy every day had been exhausting, but I'd been willing to do it. He'd feared it was too much on me, though.

My heart had been twisted in knots since all of it happened, and I didn't know what I wanted anymore. My heart seemed to say I should wait for as long as it took for Riley to recover and see the light, so to speak. Logic dictated that I should move on. Every day I prayed about it and hoped to find the wisdom I needed for the future. Each day, I prayed for more grace for the journey. And, every day, I seemed to struggle.

"Here's some stuff you might want to look at." Jono appeared with a folder in his hands. "There's some pictures of Skye—Skye Flores is her full name—and other information. I put together some names and addresses. Stuff you may need to know, including some information about Georgia."

"You did?" I questioned.

He sighed and nodded. "I want to figure out what happened to this girl just as much as Trace does. He needs to have his head in the game, and until Skye is found, I'm not sure he will."

I flipped through a couple of papers and stopped at some scribbled notes about Georgia. "Just curious—how do you know Georgia's last name and address? I thought she was just a fan girl. Trace also had her picture in his wallet."

Jono shrugged. "It was pretty easy. She started an online fan club for Trace. Her name is right there. A quick Google search led me to her address. She sent Trace a picture, and—before you ask—I told him to put it in his wallet today, because I knew he was meeting with you. He doesn't normally carry it around."

"Do you know if Trace has ever been to Georgia's house before?" I asked carefully.

He shook his head. "Are you crazy? No way. After Skye disappeared, Trace wanted to track Stalker Girl down and demand answers. I told him that was a terrible idea. Besides, Georgia might get too much pleasure out of it, you know? She's messed up in the head, and I didn't want Trace to do anything that might feed her fantasies. I told Trace to call the police instead and let them handle it."

"And that's when the police concluded that Skye left on her own free will?"

"Exactly. They took an initial report but then closed the case."

"So you think that Georgia may be trying to eliminate any other woman from Trace's life."

"Simply said, yes. If there was foul play involved, I have no doubt that Georgia was behind it."

I wasn't sure I had a case, at all . . . unless someone had tried to cover up Skye's abduction by calling into her work and pretending to be Skye in order not to arouse any suspicions. If that were the case, then why not send a text to Trace also to further throw everyone off the scent?

"Gabby, I need you to find some answers for us. The tour starts in a week. This whole Skye thing could ruin Trace's chances of hitting it big. He needs to focus on his career right now."

Not to mention a woman's life could be on the line. Life was more important than a career.

Despite the icky feeling Jono gave me, I nodded. I would help—for Trace's sake. "I'll see what I can do."

"And you let me know if you have any more questions. Please."

As the band rehearsed, I flipped through the folder. I came across a picture of Skye. She was a pretty woman with long, dark hair that had natural-looking auburn highlights. The picture looked professional, based on the precise arrangement of all the elements.

She sat by a kitchen table, her legs crossed and cowboy boots showing beneath her jeans. Behind her, the sun streamed in through the window, and cheerful-looking flowers graced the kitchen table.

I sat there for a few minutes, reviewing all the information and trying to solidify the case in my mind. After an hour, I stretched and realized my back ached and my eyelids were getting heavy.

I needed to check into my hotel and get unpacked. I'd chew on the rest of this information at my hotel.

By the time I found my hotel, it was almost eight at night. I parked in the garage beside the convention center and then stepped into the lush establishment. A huge atrium stretched eight stories high in the center, complete with a fountain, live music, a restaurant, and a bar in the center. An employee greeted me from behind a granite-topped desk, got my information, and pointed me toward my temporary home away from home.

My suite had a nice sitting area at the front, a good-sized bathroom, and a bedroom with a king-sized bed. The place smelled a bit of overfragranced cleaners, and the heat was so dry my mouth and nose instantly felt arid. Still, the soft carpet and spa-like pillows made up for it.

I think I'm going to like it here.

I had to admit that I hadn't traveled very much by myself, so the change of pace was nice. Plus, it was good to be alone. I needed this time to sort out my thoughts about life.

The forensic conference began tomorrow. One hundred professionals from all over the country had flown in for the event. Some wanted to get in the training hours to keep their certifications current. Others just wanted to refresh certain skills, learn the latest technologies, or add to their continuing education. Experts were leading lectures on various topics relevant to the forensics community.

I'd decided I needed to come to both refresh my mind and get some direction for my career. I just couldn't keep cleaning crime scenes forever.

The conference lasted all week and ended with a main session where the Kirsh Award, named in honor of Robert Kirsh, a groundbreaking pioneer in the forensic world, would be bestowed upon one guest of honor.

I glanced around my hotel room with a contented sigh.

The last time I'd stayed at a hotel this nice had been for a law school reunion with Riley. My heart twisted with sadness at the thought. As much as I'd like to think I could write off our relationship and be over it in a few months, my emotions weren't cooperating. I wondered if there was a part of me that would always love Riley. Did that make me stupid or dedicated?

I deposited my suitcase in the bedroom, grabbed my laptop, and plopped down on the couch. I typed in crazy woman Georgia Dalton's name.

The first thing that came up was the website she'd set up for Trace. She certainly was obsessed with the man, typing in every sighting she'd had of him. Other fans posted pictures of him grocery shopping or posed with him at restaurants. The strange thing was that there hadn't been any new posts in two weeks. Coincidence? Probably not.

I ripped a piece of paper out of my notebook and began scribbling down questions for Trace like: Have you ever taken a restraining order out on her? Do you know where she's from? Where did she work?

Second, I searched for Skye Flores. There was no mention of her online. Was that because she was private, or was there more to it?

I flipped through Jono's notes and read that Skye had lived near Lawton. She'd left her career as an elementary school teacher four months ago, in the middle of the school year. That seemed strange within itself. Most teachers, unless they had good reason, at least waited until the school year was over.

Someone who quit midway through the school year might be a free spirit prone to following whims.

Maybe all of this was for nothing. Maybe Skye had just decided she needed a life change, and she'd taken off for a new adventure. I could see where the idea was tempting. It wasn't necessarily the right way to get a fresh start, but it was one way.

The final person I needed more information on was Caitlyn, Trace's girlfriend who'd moved back to Colorado. I actually had her phone number, and since she was one time zone behind me, I thought it was still early enough to call.

She answered on the first ring and sounded wide awake. Thank goodness.

I explained who I was. As soon as I mentioned Georgia, her voice changed from friendly to witchy.

"I hated to let her win. I really did. But what choice did I have?"

Her choice of words had me curious. "What do you mean 'win'?"

"I mean, she was trying to run me off, and she did. I left Oklahoma and came back home. I left everything behind me—my apartment, my career, my boyfriend, my life."

"Why did you give all of that up?"

"I thought that crazy lady would kill me! Nothing's worth that. I was tired of living in fear."

"So you feel confident that she was behind the

incidents that took place, like your car tires being slashed and your apartment ransacked?"

"I know she was. I just couldn't prove it. I went to the Laundromat one time, and she was there. She wasn't even doing laundry. She also showed up at the movies once when Trace and I were together. I looked behind me, and she was sitting about five rows back. Not watching the movie. Watching me."

I shivered at the thought. If what she was saying was true, then Georgia was messed up. As in psycho-chick crazy.

"I even thought I saw her here in Colorado one time."

That surprised me. "Really? Are you sure it was her?"

"No, that's the weird thing about her. She changes her look all the time. Sometimes she's a brunette, other times a blonde. She'll wear glasses, sunglasses, hats, change the way she dresses. She's creepy."

In other words, I could be looking for Georgia while I was here in Oklahoma and never even know I was staring right at the woman.

The thought wasn't comforting.

"One of the strangest things about her was that I could always tell when she'd been around because I found daisy petals," Caitlyn continued.

My spine stiffened. "What do you mean?"

"Whenever something happened, I found little

white petals in the vicinity. By my car. In my house. No one could ever prove it, but I felt certain Georgia had left them. It was the only thing that made sense, and the flowers only made her seem more messed up."

"I'd agree." Was it done in a "he loves me, he loves me not" moment? Wasn't that one reason why people picked petals off flowers?

"One last piece of advice," Caitlyn said.

"What's that?"

"If you see Georgia, run the other way."

CHAPTER
THREE

THE BLOOD spatter fanned out on the wall, drops of crimson that grew smaller as they traveled downward.

I leaned toward the display, examining each droplet and vying for the best position within the sea of onlookers. I quickly studied the pattern, looking only at the facts before me. The blood was an impact stain that appeared to have been projected through the air. Aside from the spatter, there were also some splashes, as well as an arterial spurt. I did a quick analysis based on the forward spatter, which would have come from an exit wound and was more of a fine mist. The spines, satellites, and elongation of the spatter told the grisly story of what had happened.

"The man was shot at close range," I said. "Even though it looks like the gun was fired from a distance due to the trail of blood, when you carefully examine the droplets, it's obvious that the gun used was high powered. It would explain the pattern of blood spatter here. At first glance, it's almost deceitful."

Everyone remained quiet, which surprised me. I'd expected an onslaught of opinions from my classmates. My stomach clenched as I looked back at them, waiting for their assessment of my assessment.

Only a new figure had entered our little semicircle, someone with an air of authority around him. His presence had shut everyone else up.

"Very good," the man said. He nodded approvingly at me. "I believe you will get the Student of the Day award, Ms. . . . ?"

My cheeks flushed. I'd arrived to class this afternoon, and there'd been a note on the marker board that we needed to examine the imitation blood left on the wall. A group of my classmates and I had gathered around to discuss it until the teacher arrived. Little had I known that the teacher *had* arrived. Little also had I known that the teacher was not Dr. Wilmette Perkins, as it said on our schedule.

The man staring at me now was Levi Stone, one of the world's leading authorities on blood spatter analysis. He'd been a guest lecturer during one of my courses in college, and I'd developed a big-time crush on him during that time. I never thought I'd see him again, yet here he was now.

I cleared my throat. "St. Claire. Gabby St. Claire." I really wasn't going for the James Bond effect. The words had just slipped out.

His eyes lingered on me a moment before he finally stepped back and looked at the red splotches on the wall. "Very good. Ms. St. Claire is correct. Blood behaves according to certain scientific principles, and we must draw conclusions based on what we see. Our job is to interpret the evidence that's been left behind and not to jump to conclusions. To the untrained eye, it would be easy to draw inaccurate assumptions about the pattern of this blood."

We all went to our seats, and I pulled out my notebook, ready to take notes and absorb all I could while here.

I couldn't help but marvel at Dr. Stone. Not only was he a leading expert in the field of forensics, but he'd authored several books about real-life crime. He consulted for various TV shows. He'd served as president for the American Forensic Association, and currently owned Stone Forensic Consulting, which, now that I thought about it, was based out of Oklahoma. He was a celebrity in the CSI world.

The man was handsome to boot. He was tall—well over six foot. He had ginger-colored hair, green eyes, and a well-defined body. A slight stubble covered the strong features of his cheeks and chin.

Despite the professional nature of the conference, he wore jeans, a button-up shirt, and cowboy boots.

I felt dazed as I listened to him from my seat in the conference room. Everyone else seemed to be on their best behavior as well, soaking in everything he had to say. Something close to fire ripped through my blood with every new fact, procedure, or technology I learned about.

Passion. That's what this was. I loved this stuff. I mean, I *really* loved it. I'd missed being immersed in this world of official law enforcement.

As Dr. Stone showed us slides from various case studies, I not only examined them for evidence; I also tried to figure out the best ways to remove the blood from the surfaces they'd stained. Years of being a crime scene cleaner had done this to me.

"What do you think, Ms. St. Claire?"

I turned my attention back to Dr. Stone, who stared at me. "I think you should clear any expectations from your mind. The less you know about the case before going in to examine the blood spatter, the more objective you're going to be."

He stared at me a moment longer. I waited for criticism, for him to call me on my bluff. Instead, he nodded. "Very good."

All too soon, the class ended. I gathered up my notes, stuffed them into my book bag, and started toward the door.

"Ms. St. Claire," a deep voice said before I was swept out the door by the flow of students.

I stopped, two people colliding into me from behind. As I turned, I saw Dr. Stone.

For some reason, nervous flutters rumbled through my stomach. It was like coming face-to-face with a crush from your childhood or a celebrity from your favorite boy band. Of course, mine happened to be a forensic specialist instead. I was a real nerd like that.

I pulled my bag up higher, waiting for the crowd to clear. Finally, the last of the students trickled out and I stood face-to-face with Dr. Stone.

"Yes, Dr. Stone?" My throat felt dry.

He studied me a moment. "Have we met before?"

He couldn't possibly remember me from my college days. "You were a guest lecturer in one of my college classes. But that was several years ago."

"Virginia, right?"

My cheeks flushed, and I hated myself for having this reaction. I was way too old to feel like this. I mean, I was twenty-eight and acting like I was thirteen. "Yes, I did go to college in Virginia."

He tapped his chin. "You were in my applied forensics class. Even back then, you were just as perceptive as you were today in class. We did that monthlong study where we assigned people to investigative roles and searched for answers on a real-life case. You were the only one in class who nailed it."

He had remembered! "You just made my day."

His eyes sparkled. "How could I forget someone with so much potential? Really, your work in examining that blood spatter today was amazing. This was from an actual case that I consulted on. Local law enforcement flubbed up the evidence and made a lot of improper assumptions that almost sent the wrong person to prison."

"Well, I love this stuff." I shrugged, acting as if his compliment was nothing, while in reality I was thrilled. Like, bouncing-off-the-walls thrilled.

He smiled. "Yeah, I can see that in your eyes."

We started walking down the hall together, and I noticed several people glance his way. He was like a rock star in the forensic world, and I was sure others would be clamoring for his attention. I'd take whatever time with him that I could get.

"I didn't realize you were going to be teaching this week," I started, tugging absently at one of my curls. I'd accidentally left my styling gel at home, which meant that my hair would turn into a frizzy mess faster than one could say "Superfreak."

"Dr. Perkins had something come up at the last minute, and the coordinator asked me to fill in. I, of course, said yes." He had this cool, detached tone to his voice. It was more than his inflection, for that matter. The way he carried himself also seemed aloof, like someone who didn't give a lot of credence to what other people thought.

I reminded myself to keep talking and not just stand there like a doofus. "You must live around here, then."

He nodded. "I do. Just about an hour out of town."

"Nice."

He pointed at my shirt. "You a Trace Ryan fan?"

I glanced down. I'd forgotten I was even wearing it. Trace had given it to me before we said goodbye last night. "You could say that. You like him?"

He nodded. "I do, actually. Their new single, 'Doom and Groom,' is really catchy. The radio stations around here won't stop playing it."

"Tonight's his release party for his new album with Ranchhand Records."

"Sounds like fun."

"Would you like to go?" As soon as the question popped out of my mouth, I wanted to snatch it back. What was I thinking? I waited for him to scoff, to say no, to make up an excuse as to why he had better things to do.

"Really? I'd love to. You really wouldn't mind if I came along for the ride?"

Being stuck in the car for an hour with a renowned forensic expert? I could think of worse things. "Not at all. Some company on the ride would be nice, especially someone who can help me navigate around these here parts."

"These here parts, huh? We're in Oklahoma, darlin', not the Deep South." He grinned, a dimple appearing in his left cheek.

I smiled. "Understood."

He checked his watch. "Let me just check on my kids; then I can meet you downstairs in the lobby. Does that work?"

I nodded. "Of course."

Kids? The man was probably ten years older than me, which would put him around forty years old. Most people his age had kids and a wife and a cute little house with a white picket fence.

And all of that was fine because I wasn't looking for love or romance or even a fling or a crush. Nope, nothing of the sort. I'd had my fill of romantic drama, enough to last a lifetime.

This was a time for me. No guys included. I had to figure out myself before I involved a man in my life, and that was that.

As he stepped away, imaginary spiders crawled over my skin. I had the distinct feeling that someone was watching me.

I looked up and down the hallway but saw no one.

Maybe I was being paranoid.

But usually, my instincts were dead on.

Could it be Georgia?

I brushed it off, but not until I scanned the hallway one more time and saw no one unusual.

Just in case, I'd stay on guard, because a girl never knew when trouble might pop up at the worst possible moment.

SPEARMINT. Dr. Stone smelled like spearmint as he sat beside me in the car, his frame entirely too big for the Fiat 500 that I'd rented. But he didn't complain, and a single apology from me when we'd first climbed inside seemed to be enough.

We didn't even begin to talk or have casual conversation as he directed me out of downtown Oklahoma City. Rush hour was in full force, and the last thing I wanted to do was seriously maim the man beside me because of my lousy driving. The forensic community would never forgive me.

Finally, I navigated out of the city and started north. Trace and his band were doing their "soft launch," as he'd called it, tonight. This would all be very interesting, even more so now that Dr. Stone was with me.

"So, what have you been up to? Where are you working?" Dr. Stone asked, leaning back but having nowhere else to go in the car. I knew I should have splurged for an upgrade, but how was I to know?

Any ego I had left deflated under his question. He expected me to tell him the name of a major police department. I wished that were the truth, and I had a glowing response that would be sure to impress him.

I gripped the steering wheel. "I'm a crime scene cleaner."

His eyebrows scrunched together. "What?"

I went through the story about how I'd dropped out of college, started my own crime scene cleaning business, finished my degree, started working for the medical examiner, lost that job due to budget cuts, and eventually gone back to crime scene cleaning.

In fact, by the time I finished, we'd pulled up to the Dusty Boots Café outside of Stillwater, and I put the car in park. I'd basically monopolized the entire hour on myself when I could have picked his brain—really, a term that was too literal for a crime scene cleaner—about the famous cases he'd worked.

"I want to talk to you more about your career later," he said, his hand on the door handle.

There wasn't much to say. I'd applied for other positions, but then Riley had been shot and I'd stuck around to help him out. He'd broken up with me on the advice of his therapist. I'd met another man who any woman would be lucky to be with, and I'd just turned down a trip to Africa with him in order to figure myself out, a task I would work on completing for the rest of my life, it seemed.

My life, at the moment, was complicated.

For that matter, my life always seemed complicated.

I grabbed my purse. "Let's go meet Trace."

I needed to promptly tell my future stepbrother that I'd gotten absolutely nothing accomplished in the investigation he hired me for.

Dr. Stone and I started across the dirt parking lot toward a nondescript building in the distance. It reminded me a bit of a biker bar, only there were no bikes outside. The place was in the middle of ranch country, and in the distance I could see a house, a barn, and miles and miles of fences.

A line of people stood outside waiting to get in, and I could already hear music coming from inside. Trace had told me that this was the place the band had gotten their start, so it only made sense to have their release party here as well.

"This is great," Dr. Stone said, crossing his arms beside me as a satisfied smile stretched across his face as we approached.

"A nice change of pace from looking at blood spatter?"

"You can say that again. Don't get me wrong—I

love what I do. But variety helps to keep things fresh. It helps life to stay interesting."

I had to admit that I'd never been to a CD release party before, and I didn't know exactly what to do. Wait in line? Go straight to the door? Trace had mentioned I was a VIP, so I was supposed to get certain privileges, right?

I decided to head toward the entrance, toward a large, oversized man who must be the bouncer. He glowered down at me as I approached.

"Can I help you?" His beefy arms made it clear he was not someone to be messed with.

I decided to act like I knew what I was doing. "My name should be on the list. Gabby St. Claire."

He uncrossed his arms for long enough to scan a clipboard. Finally, he grunted and nodded toward the interior of the building. "Go on in."

I turned toward Dr. Stone, not realizing he was so close, and I slammed into a solid wall of muscle. "Sorry . . ." I muttered, feeling like I'd just breached a professional boundary.

He grinned—though barely—and held the door. "No problem."

We slipped inside. The place was huge, much larger than I expected. In the center, there was a large open area. Probably for country line dancing, but right now it was full of people. Tables lined the sides, and a stage was at the front.

Trace and the band warmed up onstage. I quickly noted some members of the press—easily identifiable by their notepads and/or cameras. There were groupies huddled close to the stage. I even noticed a few other country music personalities lingering by one of the tables.

Just then, Trace hopped down from the stage and made his way toward me. "Gabby, glad you could make it."

"Thanks for inviting me." I turned toward Dr. Stone. "Trace, this is Dr. Stone. Dr. Stone, this is—"

"Please, Gabby. Call me Levi." He turned back to Trace. "And I'm well aware of who this is. I'm a big fan."

"Honored to hear that, and glad you could both make it," Trace said as the two men shook hands.

"It was an invitation I couldn't turn down," Levi said.

"Jody, can you come here for a minute!" Trace called across the floor.

A woman behind the merchandise booth came toward us, a bag in her hand. She flashed a smile at me during the handoff, like she knew something I didn't.

"Thanks, sweetheart," Trace told her.

I watched carefully, curious about what was going on.

Trace turned back to me, his eyes dancing with

light. "I've always wanted a sister. Have I said that yet? Mostly because I wanted someone to pick on, but that's beside the point. So, for that reason, I thought it was only fitting that you have this." He reached into the bag and pulled out a brown cowboy hat.

I stared at it a moment. Before I could even reach for it, Trace put it on my head. It felt snug and smelled like leather.

"What do you think?" Trace waited for my reaction.

I tugged on the brim, wishing there was a mirror nearby so I could get a better look. "I love it. Thank you."

"I can't have my sister standing out like a sore thumb here. You know? That's what family does. Family watches out for each other."

Something about his words warmed me. That's the kind of family I'd always wanted to have. For a moment, I felt like I did have it. I tugged the brim of the hat again and nodded my thanks. "I appreciate that."

"Now you look like a true country girl," Levi agreed.

"We just have to get you some boots next, right, little lady?" Trace said.

I started to correct him when I recognized the affection in his voice. I grinned instead. "Right, maybe I'll trade in my flip-flops for something with a little more country flair."

He took a step back and pointed to me. "A band is going to open for us, and then we're on. Sit back and enjoy yourselves. It should be a fun night."

With that, he bounded back onstage. I found a place with my back against the wall. Call me crazy, but ever since I'd been nearly murdered by a serial killer, I didn't like to have my back toward a crowd. It just felt too risky.

I was all ready to ask Dr. Stone—I meant, Levi—about forensics, when the opening band went onstage and started. The music was good, but loud, which made it impossible to talk. Levi was into the music, clapping and hooting and cheering.

Halfway through their set, which was longer than I'd anticipated, I started to feel a touch claustrophobic. The crowds felt like they were closing in, I was hot, and I couldn't seem to get a deep breath.

"I'm going to step outside a moment," I said in a loud whisper.

Levi nodded and kept clapping.

I went out the front door, by crowds of people who were gathered there, talking loudly and drinking. This must be the overflow lot for concertgoers. I quickly skirted around the building and paced around to the fence at the back.

A cow grazed in the distance. The outline of a

barn stood across the field. The peaceful scene was a stark contrast to the jostling crowds and loud music inside.

I leaned against the rough wood for a moment, marveling at how different my life was now than I'd anticipated. The same cycles seemed to repeat themselves over and over in my life. Even worse, I'd allowed myself to be at their mercy, nearly for my entire existence. That was going to change. Somehow, Oklahoma was going to be the place where all of that happened. I could feel it in my blood.

I closed my eyes and drew in a deep breath. I needed to get back inside, but I could still hear the sounds of the opening band blaring from the inside of the building. Maybe just a few more minutes out here.

Just then, a man walked around the side of the building, wiping his forehead with a white handkerchief. He froze when he saw me. "Sorry. I thought I'd be alone out here."

"Just getting some fresh air."

He hesitated a moment and then came to stand beside me at the fence. He tucked his handkerchief into the pocket of his brown leather jacket. "You a fan?"

"Something like that."

He nodded slowly. The man was probably in his late forties. I hated to notice only the obvious, but his most predominate feature was his ears, which stood out from his face considerably. His thin face only accentuated the feature, as did his skinny jeans, slim-fitting T-shirt, and tailored jacket.

"I used to be a fan," he muttered, his lips drawing into a tight line.

"Used to be? Then why are you here?"

He continued to stare straight ahead. "I thought I'd come and show my support. Then I realized it was a bad idea. Just another bad mistake that I've added to an already long list."

It sounded like there was a story there, but I didn't ask. "I'm sorry to hear that."

He wiped his mouth, and that's when I noticed he was still sweating. It wouldn't have been strange inside, where people were packed between the walls like cattle at auction. But out here it was probably thirty degrees. That's when I realized he wasn't sweating because it was hot. His heat was internal.

"I'm sorry to be pouring all of this out to you," he said. "I think I've had too many drinks. Don't worry. I called a taxi. It should be here any minute. I just couldn't take those giggling Ryan-ites at the door."

"Ryan-ites?"

"You haven't heard the term? Yeah, it's what the press is calling all the women who are in love with Trace."

"I take it there are a lot."

He let out a rumbling chuckle. "Yeah, to say the least. He's gotten himself into some real pickles."

The man sounded like he knew Trace. Interesting. "Has he?"

He shook his head, as if realizing he was talking too much. He turned, and his shoulders slumped. "Finally. My cab. Catch you around."

I realized it had gone silent inside. Trace must be getting ready to play. That meant I should get back to the concert.

I took my first step toward the door when I heard something that made me pause. My skin pricked as I waited to hear it again. It was a voice. At least, that's what it sounded like to me.

Finally, after several moments of silence, I let out a feeble laugh. I must have been hearing things. I took another step when I clearly heard it again.

"Help me!"

The voice had come from the direction of the field.

Had one of the Ryan-ites had too much to drink and wandered off?

I had no idea.

"Please! Help!" The voice rose in intensity and pitch.

I knew I had to do something.

"Hello?" I called. I gripped the rough wood of the fence, wishing I had someone to text or call. But Trace was now onstage, where he wouldn't hear his phone, and I didn't have Levi's phone number.

Besides, I should be able to handle this. There was nothing out here but wide, open spaces and a couple of trees. I'd programmed myself to overreact, to see danger in every situation. It was silly, a byproduct of the job.

"I'm over here. In the pasture. I was taking a walk and I sprained my ankle." She let out a moan.

My heart slowed. That seemed like a logical enough reason. She was just a woman with bad luck who needed a hand. I'd been there before.

I hated to miss Trace's set, but at least I'd been out here to help someone in need. Maybe God had placed me in the right place at just the right time.

"Keep talking. I'm coming." With a touch of reservation, I climbed over the fence. Just as I did so, the full moon above me disappeared behind a cloud. Chills washed over me as darkness hung heavier, blacker.

Quickly, I pulled up the flashlight on my phone to help light my steps.

There are just cows around here, I reminded myself. Harmless cows. Docile cows . . . right? I'd never been close to one before. Not really, at least. But based on all the *Far Side* cartoons I'd enjoyed growing up, I had nothing to worry about.

"I feel so stupid," the woman said. "All my friends are inside, though."

"Don't feel stupid. I've gotten myself into some strange situations before, also." Wasn't that the truth? By all reasonable explanations, I should be dead. I'd faced death on more than one occasion.

As I walked farther into the pasture, the scent of manure filled the air around me. The grass beneath my feet—what little of it there was—felt dry and crisp. The air was cold, and a steady breeze concealed any subtle noises.

"You're almost here."

I shone the light ahead but still didn't see anyone. I rounded a tree, certain I'd find the woman on the other side. Instead, no one was there. I paused. How strange.

Before I realized what was happening, something hit me on the back of the head. Then everything went black.

I AWOKE TO DARKNESS. With a pounding headache, I pushed myself up, something rough and prickly under my palms.

Where was I? What had happened?

As what appeared to be miles of nothing appeared around me, everything flashed back.

I'd been trying to help the girl who twisted her ankle. Someone hit me on the head, and now here I was. On the ground. Bristly grass beneath my fingers. A tree behind me, its roots rough under my hands.

I was still in the pasture, I realized. Why in the world had someone knocked me out?

I reached in my pocket and felt my wallet and keys. A quick survey of the ground, and I spotted my phone. I hadn't been robbed, but someone was definitely trying to send some kind of message.

After rubbing my head one more time and straightening my back, I glanced around. All the way around this time. In the distance, I saw the lights from the café. So maybe I hadn't been miles and miles away from civilization. But it had felt like it for a minute.

My fingers shook as I picked up my phone. I turned on the flashlight again. Using the beam to illuminate any cow patties I might encounter, I began my trek back to the CD release party.

How long had I been out? I couldn't remember what time it was when I'd come outside. A glance at my phone told me that it was already ten o'clock. Had anyone noticed I was missing?

I guessed that was the thing about being alone in a strange new place. There was no one to watch out for you. No one to notice when something was wrong. Not really.

Was this what Skye Flores felt like? Without a real sense of community around her or even roots, had she been an easy one to target? An easy one to disappear?

The thought made me sad, but also made me relate with her. I knew what it was like not to have a close family. My best friend was now married and expecting a baby. I was single. It just seemed like everything was changing. I had to change too to keep up.

I continued toward the lights in the distance, still perplexed over all of this.

Had Georgia called me out into the darkness and then clobbered me? The idea just seemed too absurd.

A rumbling noise sounded behind me, but I couldn't identify what would make that sound.

Tension stretched across my shoulders.

I pivoted, trying to see what was happening. But it was dark. So hard to see.

I raised my flashlight, and it caught the eyes of an approaching . . . animal?

What?

I sucked in a deep breath as the creature came closer. Suddenly, I realized exactly what was happening.

A bull was charging me.

Not just any bull. A huge one with long horns and red, glaring eyes.

I'd had many things happen to me in my life. But never, ever had I been chased by a bull. And definitely not by a bull with extremely long, painful-looking horns. Horns that could skewer me, impale me, or do any number of other unpleasant acts.

Nor had I ever been trained on how to handle a situation like this.

The trampling sound got louder and louder behind me as the bull quickly lessened the distance between us. I ran, moving as if death was chasing me. Because, essentially, it was.

I prayed I didn't sprain my ankle. That I didn't trip and fall. That my normally clumsy nature wouldn't kick in.

Finally, I stole a glance over my shoulder. The bull was only a few feet away!

But so was the fence. I just had to keep pressing ahead, despite the panic that wanted to freeze me.

My legs burned. My lungs tightened. My head swam—probably from the earlier blow to it.

I reached for the fence. The wood scraped my fingers just as I felt something nudge my leg.

I wasn't going to make it.

Panic clutched my heart, made my head swirl.

Before despair claimed me, strong arms reached around my waist. I flew into the air, my legs scraping against the fence. The next thing I knew, I was on the ground. Sore. Achy. Confused.

But safe.

Alive.

The bull snorted on the other side of the enclosure, staring at me like he'd exact revenge at the first possible moment. He pawed at the dirt and jabbed his horns into the wooden post.

"Have you lost your mind?"

I looked up and saw . . . none other than Levi

Stone. His hands were on his hips, and a look of outrage stained his eyes.

"I can explain."

"What in heaven's name gave you the idea of going walking in a cow pasture? Please don't tell me you were going cow tipping."

I shrugged, utterly exhausted, as I pushed myself up on my palms. I glanced around. It was just Levi and me out here, but I could still hear the music blaring inside the café. Thank goodness my former professor had been with me tonight.

"It seemed safe enough. They're cows, for goodness' sake. They just eat grass and moo."

He leered. "Bulls. They're territorial, and they don't like anyone in their space. You're obviously a city slicker. Hasn't anyone ever taught you how to act around livestock?"

I ignored the condescending tone in his voice, temporarily giving him the benefit of the doubt that maybe he was just concerned and had a funny way of expressing it. And for that matter, no, no one had ever taught me about livestock, because I'd never lived around livestock.

I scowled, stood—without his help—and brushed the dust off my jeans. "Someone called for my help. That's the only reason I crossed that fence."

He continued to stare. "Into the bull pasture?"

I nodded sheepishly, glancing at the field again.

The bull must have figured out he'd won the battle and strutted off. "It was a woman. She said she'd hurt her ankle. When I passed by that tree out there, she must have hit me over the head. Next thing I knew, I woke up and Toro over there charged at me."

His hands went to his hips, doubt evident in his body language and eyes. "So, you're saying this was a premeditated act of aggression toward you?"

"I don't know." My voice rose in pitch, right along with my emotions.

He stepped closer, glowering down at me. "Think, Gabby. You're an investigator. What do you believe happened?"

I sighed, still shaky and now irritated to boot. "Yes, I think someone lured me out there with the intention of harming me. Why? I have no idea."

His gaze softened some. "Did you see her? Do you remember anything about this woman?"

"I didn't see anyone. I only *heard* someone. It was a woman, and I'm guessing she was younger. I thought she was just being foolish and had too much to drink."

"Yet you're the one who ended up a fool."

My anger flared, and I threw my hands in the air. "I get it, okay? You can stop with the lecture anytime now."

I held my breath, unable to believe I'd just spoken

to Dr. Stone like that. He was someone I respected, whom the whole forensic community respected.

He stared at me, his arms crossed and an unreadable emotion in his eyes. "Do you want to call the police?"

"Look, I'm sorry. No, I don't want to call the police. Honestly, I just want to listen to Trace for a few more minutes and then get back to the hotel. Whoever called me is obviously long gone. Besides, a stampeding bull isn't a crime."

"Maybe we should have your head checked out."

Fearing I'd say the wrong thing again, I bit my tongue and started to walk away when he pulled me back.

"Look, I know you think I'm being rough on you. But I'm just trying to teach you the skills you need to be successful," Levi started. His gaze was intense on mine, and I could feel the fire blazing in my eyes as we stared off at each other.

I raised my chin. "I think I've been pretty successful so far, though it may not seem like it on the surface."

He lowered his chin, obviously not buying my explanation. "As a crime scene cleaner?"

My cheeks flushed. He'd hit a nerve. "Not to be rude, but you wouldn't understand."

"I do understand that you've let life dictate where you're going. If you continue on this path, you're never going to go anywhere. I don't want to see your talent go to waste."

It didn't matter that I'd essentially just given myself the same pep talk. From him, it sounded like a lecture. An uninvited one, at that.

"Can we just go listen to some music?" I hated to get huffy, especially with Dr. Stone, but I was done.

Not even songs about magical kisses and beat-up pickup trucks and eating watermelon on the banks of a river could cheer me up.

Why was I mad? I had the nagging suspicion it was because Levi was right, but I didn't want to admit that. Truth was, I could have made more out of my life. I could have been more focused. But being more focused would have meant not being there for the people I loved. How could I regret that?

"Excuse me for a minute," Levi muttered. He pushed through the crowd toward the bar. He lingered there, drinking and talking to the people around him.

I attempted to sit at an empty table, but my rump hurt from where I'd landed on the ground after Levi had pulled me to safety. My head also pounded, not only from the hit I'd taken over it, but also from the conversation I'd just had.

The rest of the concert was good, except for a couple of technical glitches—some feedback from the microphones, a guitar losing its amplification in the middle of the set, and a persistent hiss coming from the speakers. I could tell Trace was bothered by it, but he pressed forward, still putting on a great show.

As soon as the concert ended, the band sat down to autograph CDs. I pushed through the crowd and waved to Trace. "Good job, but I've got to go."

His eyes caught mine. "I wish your first concert wasn't full of glitches."

"What happened?"

He shook his head. "I guess that's what happens when you pick a small venue. On the road should be better because we'll bring our own equipment. Anyway, I'm doing that concert tomorrow night at the festival. Why don't you come and listen to how we sound without all things technical conspiring against us? Some of the other groupies will be there. Maybe they know how you can find Georgia."

"Text me directions?"

"Got it, sis." He looked behind me. "You come too, Levi."

I looked over my shoulder and saw that Levi had reappeared.

Levi smiled. "I'd love to."

I dreaded the ride home. I didn't want to hear Levi's opinions or his judgments, for that matter. But I didn't have much choice in the matter. I wasn't rude enough to tell him to find another mode of transportation.

So we climbed in my clown car and started back toward Oklahoma City.

Levi rubbed his hands on his jeans, not in what seemed to be a nervous gesture, but more out of exasperation. "Look, I'm sorry. Maybe I was rough on you back there."

I gripped the wheel, apparently still nursing a grudge. I figured it was better if I kept my mouth shut.

"I never did ask if you were okay."

How kind of you to actually show some concern. My bad mood was spiraling out of control. "My head is throbbing, but I'm fine."

"I don't like seeing innocent people get hurt, Gabby. That's my main concern. Whether you're a civilian or officially on the case, you can't be too trusting. It could get you hurt, or it could even ruin your career. I've seen it happen."

My hands tightened on the wheel again. "People don't usually accuse me of being too trusting. I had a lapse in judgment, I suppose, but it was all with good intentions. I thought someone was hurt."

"Well, I'm glad you're okay." He paused. "Maybe we should start over here. You were generous to invite me, and I can see that I've insulted you, and I apologize."

Some of the tension left me as I realized I was overreacting. "No, I'm sorry. I'm a little on edge. I'm hoping to receive some clarification on my future while I'm here this week. Sometimes you have to step back in order to see the whole picture."

"That's the spirit!"

Of course, that was easier to say than it was to carry out. Routines and habits became those things because they were easy and didn't require as much effort. Change took people out of their comfort zones.

"Can we just talk about country music or something now?" Earlier, I'd been anxious to pick his brain. Right now, I just needed to let all of that go for a minute.

I glanced in the rearview mirror and saw the same set of headlights had been behind me for the last fifteen minutes.

Coincidence? I couldn't be sure.

I wasn't going to bring it up to Levi right now, though. The last thing I wanted was more of his judgment. But I would keep an eye on the road behind me, just to be safe. Most likely, I was just reading too much into things.

CHAPTER
SIX

THE CAR TURNED from behind me onto a side street as I reached Oklahoma City. Coincidence? I couldn't be sure, but I'd already embarrassed myself, and I didn't want to sound paranoid, as well. At this point, I had no reason to think anyone had a reason to follow me . . . except for the whole bull incident.

I pulled up to the front of the hotel and put my car in park.

"It was fun, Gabby," Levi told me. "You sure you don't want me to walk with you?"

I nodded. "Yeah, I've got this." Even if I did hate parking garages.

After he climbed out, I parked my car and hurried up toward my room. I felt spent and done, and I just needed a few minutes of downtime.

As I hurried through the dark garage, listening

for any telltale signs of someone following me, I tried to narrow my thoughts.

I'd made very little progress on locating Skye or tracking down any information about her. I was only in Oklahoma for a limited time, and if I truly wanted to help out, I needed to kick this investigation into high gear.

Despite my efforts to focus, Levi's words echoed in my head as I stomped back up to my room. *I do understand that you've let life dictate where you're going. If you continue on this path, you're never going to go anywhere.*

Even more than being embarrassed, I felt angry at myself. What he'd said was true. I needed to stop settling for life and start taking more initiative.

As I approached my room, my cell phone rang. I recognized Teddi's number and answered. I unlocked my room and slipped inside, locking the door behind me.

"Did you meet Trace?" Teddi asked, a Texas drawl to her words. She'd lived most of her life there. When Trace moved to Oklahoma for college, she'd moved to Norfolk and gotten a job with the Department of Defense.

"I did. We met yesterday, and then I came to his release party tonight. He's very talented."

"Isn't he? I have to admit, I gave him a hard time and told him he should get a real career. I mean, I just wanted to make sure he could support himself. But look at him now. He's really on his way. I even heard his song on the radio here in Norfolk today."

"That's great." I dropped my purse and cowboy hat on the table by the couch before plopping down there myself and resting my throbbing head.

"Have you met his woman yet?"

I paused. "His woman?"

Her voice lilted with delight. "I got a text from her today. It was a picture of her and Trace together."

I tensed, leaning forward and suddenly alert. "Really?"

"Really. She's a pretty girl, but Trace has always had a thing for good-looking women. I texted her back, but she never responded."

"Can you forward the picture to me?" Something majorly wasn't fitting together here, and I didn't like it.

"It seems like a strange request, even from you, Gabby. But I suppose. Does that mean you haven't met this mystery woman?"

I unlocked my door. "I haven't met her yet, but I sure have heard a lot about her."

"I certainly wish my son had mentioned something to me first. But I suppose that's what happens when your kids grow up. You've got to let them go."

My dad had actually "let me go" before I was out of middle school. Our roles had been reversed for years. I'd been the one helping to take care of him for as long as I could remember. Up until the past several months, I'd even sent him money to help pay his bills. He did seem to be trying to improve lately. I only hoped the changes stuck.

"Okay, dear. I need to run. Your father and I have started watching *Hawaii Five-0*, and a new episode is coming on."

"Okay, can you send me that picture now? I've, uh, I've been dying to see what this girl looks like."

"Sure thing, darling. Have a good trip, you hear?"

"I will. Thank you." I hit end and closed my eyes.

As soon as I did, my phone buzzed. I glanced down and saw that Teddi had texted me. I pulled up the picture and gawked.

It wasn't Georgia, as I'd assumed.

It was Skye. Someone had texted Teddi a picture of Trace and Skye. The two stood on a sidewalk in an urban-looking area. It was dark, they both wore coats, and huge grins stretched across their faces.

Had Georgia abducted Skye and taken this photo from her phone? Was this Georgia's strange way of making a statement? Of letting people know that she wouldn't be second place to anyone else in Trace's life? I didn't know, but a shiver raced up my spine.

I decided to call Trace. He answered on the fourth ring, and I could still hear the sounds of a guitar ringing out in the background. "Gabby?" he shouted.

"It's me. Is this a bad time?"

"Uh . . . no, I guess not. Just listening to some music and hanging out here at the Dusty Boots Café."

"I just talked to your mom."

"You just found a soccer ball?" he repeated.

"What? No. I just talked to your mom," I said, my voice getting louder with each word.

"You just ate a new food, yum?"

"No! I just—"

"Wait a minute."

I heard rustling, and then finally some of the background noise faded. "Sorry. I can hear a little better now. What were you saying?"

"I talked to your mom tonight," I started, bringing my voice down. "She got a text today that I thought would interest you."

"From who?"

"She's not sure who it's from, but it was a picture of you and Skye."

"What? Who would send my mom that?" His voice rose in pitch.

"I was hoping you could tell me."

"I have no idea, Gabby. Skye was the only person who'd have any pictures of us, unless maybe a groupie took one. Do you have a copy?"

"As a matter of fact, I did ask your mom to forward it to me. I'm going to send it to you. One second." I pulled the phone from my ear and did just that. "Did you get it yet?"

He didn't respond for a moment. "Yeah, that's a picture of Skye and me on our second date. I took her to this restaurant in Tulsa. Skye wanted a picture, so she asked a random guy on the street to take it for us."

"Interesting. That means that either Skye sent it to your mom or . . ."

"Or Georgia has Skye's phone and sent it," Trace finished. "Maybe Georgia did it to send a message? One of those 'I'm watching you' type of things."

"That's what I wondered too. But how did Georgia get your mom's phone number?" There were so many details that didn't make sense.

He let out a long sigh. "You heard me say earlier that Skye used to think someone had broken into her home and riffled through stuff. What if Georgia broke into my place? What if she went through the contacts on my phone and found my mom's number? Maybe that's a long shot, but it's the only thing I can think of."

"I agree. It's outlandish, but it's one of the only options that make sense. The only thing is, don't you usually have your phone with you?"

"Unless I'm sleeping or in the shower."

I didn't voice my thought aloud, because it was too disturbing. But what if Georgia had snuck in and watched him while he was sleeping? If she'd gone through his things?

"Listen, you mentioned a friend of Skye's that you met once. Do you have her name and number?"

"You mean Darcy? Sure thing. As soon as we get off the phone, I'll text her information to you."

We hung up and he did. When Darcy's information came through, I gave her a call, and she agreed that she could meet me tomorrow for lunch in OKC.

This was perfect. I finally had a plan to move beyond the pallid quicksand that stalled me in this investigation. Now, if I only could say the same thing for the rest of my life.

THE NEXT MORNING, I was dressed and ready to head out the door to grab coffee before my first session when my cell phone rang. It was my best friend, Sierra. I considered ignoring the call and just getting back with her later because of the time crunch. But she was pregnant, and I wanted to make sure nothing was wrong.

I answered, dropping my hand from the door and pausing in my room.

"How's the conference going?" she asked.

I plopped on the couch for a moment. As soon as I did, my hindside ached. I guessed that's what happened when a girl nearly got made into a kabob by a bull. Not only that, but there was a knot on the back of my head. I'd only been in Oklahoma for a day and a half, and I was already a walking disaster. I had a talent for that.

"The conference doesn't start for five more minutes, but the trip has been interesting so far," I began.

I filled her in on Dr. Levi Stone, Trace, and the incident at Dusty Boots last night.

"Oh, Gabby, all of that sounds about on par for your life."

I frowned. Maybe my problem was that everything was always on par for my life: if one defined *on par* as a series of setbacks that occurred time and time again.

"You always find adventure," she finished.

Oh, so *that's* what she'd meant.

"There's a couple of things I thought you should know," Sierra said. "First, you have two flower arrangements from Garrett that came this week. They're really beautiful. I set them inside your apartment and really hope they'll last until you get back."

I smiled. Garrett was the man of every woman's dreams. I just wasn't sure the timing in which we'd met was ideal. At *all* ideal, for that matter. Right now, he was in Africa overseeing some water wells his company had built for the less fortunate there. What was there not to love about that? I hadn't actually told him that I was coming here this week. The whole trip had been a bit last minute. He texted me whenever he could, usually pictures of himself with kids in impoverished areas.

"I can't wait to see the arrangements," I told Sierra. I was sure they were expensive and gorgeous. Garrett had great taste.

"Also, Riley is in town. He was asking about you."

"Really?" I sat up a little straighter. The flowers hadn't surprised me. Riley being in town had. "Tell me more."

"He seems different, Gabby."

My throat clenched, and I knew my emotional state for the rest of the day very well could hinge on what she said. That wasn't a good thing, and I knew that. "Different good or different bad?"

"Different good. I keep trying to put my finger on what has changed. Riley has always been determined and driven, but now he just seems even more confident about what he wants. I can't describe it. But we had a good talk. I guess his therapist is nearly ready to sign him off. She said he's progressed very quickly."

"That's great." It was only too bad he'd started his own life up in DC instead of in Norfolk, where I lived. For too long, I'd held on to the hope that he might move back, and we'd pick up where we'd left off. I had to let it go. "What is he doing in town?"

"My impression is that he came down to see you. He didn't realize you were at the conference."

"You're just saying that."

"No, I'm not. He was asking when you'd be back and how you were doing. He seemed anxious to talk to you, for that matter. Anyway," Sierra continued. "Once he found out you were out of town, he cut his trip short."

I wondered what that was all about. There was no need to speculate. I should have learned my lesson by now about doing things like that. "Enough about Riley. How are you feeling, Sierra? How's the baby?"

"Moving all the time." Her voice lightened. "I'm already counting down the days until he comes."

"That's wonderful. How much longer is it?" Like I didn't know. It was only sixty-six days until her due date. That meant I only had sixty-six days—a little more than two months—before I officially became Aunt Gabby.

"Sixty-six days," she said. "We miss you around here. Chad is doing okay. Clarice and Braxton have been pitching in."

I glanced at the time and saw my class started five minutes ago. So much for that coffee. "I hate to cut this short, but I've got to run, Sierra. It was good chatting, though."

"You too, Gabby. Talk soon. And stay out of trouble!"

I tapped my pencil on the table, doing my best to concentrate on the lecture being presented about advances in fingerprinting techniques. For some reason, I couldn't stop thinking about Skye and Georgia, nor could I stop looking over my shoulder.

Behind me, there were probably thirty other students, most of them with their gazes fastened either on the lecturer or on their notepads or laptops. Four rows of tables served as desks. At the back of the room there was a door with a glass window and a table with water and plastic cups.

The guy behind me scowled every time I turned. I knew I was a distraction, and I regretted that. But was someone leering into the classroom? Or was my imagination just going crazy?

I really hoped that when I talked to Skye's friend today, I'd get some insight.

As soon as my class was over, I hurried downstairs, out the front door of the conference center, and across the street to a little deli where I'd arranged to meet Darcy. I walked inside and saw a line of mostly businessmen and -women standing at the counter, hollering their sandwich orders to the workers on the other side of the glass case displaying meats and cheeses. Most of the customers were checking their phones, glancing at watches, or talking into headsets.

I spotted Darcy right away—she was the only woman sitting by herself with her eyes fixed on the door. She was a brunette with blonde highlights, soft feminine features, and a wide smile. She stood when our eyes connected.

"You must be Gabby," she said as I approached.

"Darcy?" I shook her hand.

"That's me. I already ordered a tuna on rye with a side of fruit. Hope that's okay."

"It's just fine. I appreciate you meeting me." I glanced once again at the line and decided to bypass eating. Otherwise, all our time would be up before we even talked. Instead, I slid into the booth across from her.

She studied me for a minute, not trying to hide her scrutiny in the least. "Trace hired you?"

I nodded, trying to ignore the tantalizing scent of toasted bread and bubbly cheese. "That's right. He's concerned about Skye."

She crossed her arms and leaned back with a thump. "So am I. I just wish more people were. The police seem to think she just up and left."

"You don't believe that?" I watched her, trying to get a good read on her. We sat by the window near the door, and people passed on the sidewalk outside, each one looking brisk and focused.

Darcy frowned. "No, I don't. Something suspicious happened, and I'd really like some answers."

"How did you know Skye? I understand she lived by herself and worked from her home. I also heard she'd just moved here about four months before she disappeared and didn't have any family."

She pursed her cotton-candy-pink lips as if impressed. "You're thorough. All those things are true. Aside from me and Trace, she pretty much stayed to herself. She was kind of quiet like that. The two of us met because, at the time, I worked at her favorite coffee shop. I guess all of us have our vices, even loners. She couldn't resist a good cup of coffee. She came in every morning, and we started talking. Eventually we got together for a couple of movies and went out to dinner a few times."

"What was Skye like?" I shivered. Every time the door opened, a burst of cold air filled the space. I pulled my jacket closer.

She shrugged. "She was sweet. I could tell she was a little off balance being here all alone. She was still trying to find her place." A worker delivered Darcy's sandwich, and she glanced up at me with apology in her eyes. "Hope you don't mind if I dig in. I have to be back at work in forty minutes. I'm working as an administrative assistant now. Better pay but not nearly as fun."

"Please, dig in. You don't mind if I keep talking and asking questions while you eat, do you?"

"Please do." She raised her sandwich and took a bite.

"Why did Skye give up teaching and move here? Did she ever say?"

Darcy raised a hand over her mouth to block my view of her half-emulsified food. "She said she just wanted a change. I didn't question her too much. She said teaching wasn't what she thought it would be. There was too much paperwork, too much trying to please administrators, and not enough time to invest in the students. She wasn't keen on staying with her new job either, but she was hoping to keep it until she figured out what else she might want to do."

Smelling her sandwich made my stomach grumble. Maybe I was hungrier than I'd thought, I realized, as visions of a ham and cheese on Italian bread danced in my head. I pushed aside those thoughts. "Did she ever mention the name of her school or where it was located?"

"She didn't talk about it much, but she used to bring her own coffee mug into the coffeehouse. It said Arrowhead Central Elementary School, Second Grade. I think she was from somewhere in Arizona? I'm not sure, though."

I stored away that information. "What did she think of Trace?"

"She was in love with him. Couldn't believe someone like him would be with someone like her.

Her eyes just took on a new light every time she talked about him."

"Did you like the two of them together?"

She thought about it a moment and gave a half-hearted shrug and nod. "I guess so. I mean, I was only around the two of them together maybe once. It's funny, though, because they met in a music store. I didn't even know the girl liked music, other than what she could get in an MP3 format, so I still marveled at the way they met. She said she'd just stumbled upon the place. What timing, huh?"

"Why do you think people haven't rallied to find her?"

Darcy wiped her mouth with a stiff paper napkin. "I know, right? Some people go missing and the whole country hears about it. They're usually young, white, pretty, come from some kind of affluence. Skye was most of those things, except affluent. But there's no reason why this shouldn't have gotten more attention."

If it had, would she have been found by now? Was this just further proof that life wasn't fair? I kept my thoughts silent.

"I heard she called into work before she disappeared," I said instead. "I guess all of that made authorities believe she left on her own free will."

Darcy nodded. "It's true. She even sent me a text

just saying she needed to get away for a while and not to worry about her."

"You weren't convinced?"

Darcy pushed her half-eaten sandwich away, suddenly appearing too distraught to finish. "Why would someone just leave everything, including a hot, famous boyfriend, behind?"

"It sounds like she could have had a history of doing that."

Darcy let out a sigh and stared off into the distance for a moment. "I suppose you're correct. But still, something just doesn't add up. I always thought it strange that Trace didn't take to the airwaves to plead for her return."

I tilted my head. I hadn't thought about that, but she raised a good point. Trace had some clout, but he apparently hadn't used any of it. "Did you ever ask him?"

"Oh, no. Like I said, I only met him once. Skye and I were strictly coffee-and-occasional-girl's-night-out friends. If Trace was in town or close enough that she could drive to his concert, she was there. I was only a fill-in friend. I got that, though. She was in love with the man. Something in her eyes changed whenever she talked about him."

"Any theories about what happened to her?"

Darcy let out another sigh. "I did have one other idea. I know it might sound crazy."

"I'll take crazy to nothing." The door opened again and I shivered.

Darcy leaned closer and lowered her voice. "Skye was in credit card debt up to her ears. I heard her talking on the phone to some collectors. I have wondered on occasion if maybe she disappeared on purpose just to get those people off her back."

"You really think that's a possibility?"

She nodded. "I do."

I nodded, letting the idea settle. Was I just wasting my time looking into this?

That remained to be seen. But I wasn't giving up. Not yet, at least.

CHAPTER
EIGHT

THE WORKSHOP after lunch left me exhausted. It wasn't that I didn't think a whole session on light sources at crime scenes wasn't interesting. I did. It was simply that I was tired, and I kept on thinking about Darcy's tuna salad sandwich. I'd missed my coffee this morning and my lunch this afternoon. I was going to run out of fuel soon.

That's why I decided that, even if it meant being late for my next class, I was grabbing something to eat at the little gift shop downstairs right after this workshop ended.

After what seemed like hours, the lecturer dismissed us. I was the first one out of the door. As soon as I stepped into the hall, heaving my bag higher on my shoulder, I paused. The skin on my neck crawled.

There was that feeling again—the feeling of someone watching me.

I paused and turned, scanning the wide, plush hallway of the hotel for a sign of someone. Mostly, though, scanning for Georgia.

All I saw were conferees with laptop bags slung over their shoulders or notepads in hand walking from one workshop to another. People a lot like me. No one suspicious.

"How are you feeling today?" someone asked behind me.

I nearly jumped out of my skin. As I turned and saw Levi there, I let out a small laugh. "You caught me going off into my own little world." I patted my heart, feeling foolish. Being around Levi had a tendency to make me feel that way. "I'm sore but fine."

"You heading out to meet Trace after class?" He began walking with me.

"I'm planning on it."

"Mind if I ride with you?"

I cut him a sharp glance. "You really want to go?"

He shrugged. "I *was* invited and all. Of course, if it's a problem with you, I won't go."

He'd surprised me. I didn't know him that well, and there were professional boundaries in place still. Despite my overreaction to him yesterday, I still had to acknowledge that the man was brilliant. When would I ever have the chance to hang out with someone of his caliber of expertise again? I could push aside a bruised ego for that.

"Of course you can ride with me. I just assumed you wouldn't have the time."

"I can't turn down an invitation to hang out with one of my favorite singers. Besides, I still need to talk to you about your future."

"Let's meet outside after the last workshop, then," I told him.

When he walked away, I paused to scan the hallway once more. A vaguely familiar figure appeared in the distance. My muscles tightened. Where had I seen that face before? Was it Georgia in one of her disguises?

"Gabby St. Claire?" the woman asked.

I squinted, trying to place her. She was tall and thin, and had dark hair that was pulled back in a severe bun. She wore a black suit with a gray shirt, which gave her a bit of a vampire vibe. I guessed her to be my age. "Yes?"

"It's Evie Manson. We were in freshman biology together."

Realization dawned on me. No wonder she looked familiar. "That's right. It's been years."

She nodded without a smile or an ounce of warmth to her voice. "I transferred to Yale after freshman year, so it's been a long time. Good to see you again. I thought I'd spotted you in the hotel yesterday, but I didn't have a chance to say hello."

So she was the set of eyes I'd felt on me. Not Georgia. I mentally laughed at myself. "What are you doing now?"

"I'm a forensic psychologist." She stared at me, but I couldn't read the look in her eyes. She'd stopped me, yet she didn't seem prepared to make conversation.

"Good for you. Sounds impressive."

She continued staring, her eyes pensive, judging. "You?"

Did I have to go here again? There was something a little humiliating about admitting among people who should be my colleagues that I was still crime scene cleaning. I shrugged. "I'm looking for a new position in forensics."

"I see." She nodded in the direction of Levi. "You're hanging out with Dr. Spatter, I see."

Dr. Spatter? What an awful nickname.

"Purely professional," I assured her.

She stared at me, something I couldn't read in her gaze. "Sure."

My defenses started to rise. "No, really. That's all it is."

She took a step backward, still not looking convinced. She raised her eyebrows as if she knew better than I did. "Well, we should catch up while we're both here. Perhaps lunch one day?"

"That would be great, Evie."

Or not. Not great at all. Why would I want to hang out with someone who acted like I was beneath her? The old Gabby would have blurted that very thought out. The new Gabby was trying harder to watch what she said.

With that, Evie turned and walked away. She'd always been a strange bird. We'd been in a study group together, and needless to say, I hadn't forgotten her. She'd always been so logical and analytical that she seemed to lack empathy and personality.

I hadn't thought about her in years. Years.

A glance at the time on my phone reminded me that I needed to get to class.

Right after I grabbed something to eat.

The lecturer for the workshop on "Bridging the Relationship Between Science and Policing" had a monotone voice that nearly put me to sleep. For that reason, I took out my cell phone and tucked it under the desk where no one could see it. I pulled up the Internet and did a search for Arrowhead Central Elementary in Arizona.

To my delight and surprise, there was only one school listed in the state with that name.

Bingo!

Not only that, but the school had a great website. I was able to click on second grade teachers and a list of eight people came up, complete with pictures and email addresses. Things usually didn't happen this easily for me, but I certainly didn't complain when they did.

I scrolled through the photos and found another teacher who seemed to be close to Skye's age. The bio for Melissa Edwards said she'd been at the school for three years, which would put her there when Skye was. On a whim, I emailed her and told her I was a friend of Skye's and that I had a couple of questions. I hit send, unsure if anything would come of it.

Less than five minutes later, my phone buzzed. Melissa Edwards had emailed me back already. I marveled at my luck and quickly clicked on the message.

I know Skye. I'd be happy to talk. Is everything okay with her? I haven't heard from her since she left. You can call me at three, which is when my students leave.

I glanced at my watch. That was only thirty minutes away.

I did my best to listen for the remaining workshop. But, as soon as I could, I slipped out, found a semiprivate spot beside the fountain in the atrium, and called Melissa. She answered on the first ring.

"Hi, Melissa. It's Gabby. Thanks for the quick response."

"No problem," she said, her voice high pitched and tiny. "I've been thinking about Skye lately, so I was glad to get your email. Is she doing okay?"

"No one has actually seen her for about a month. That's why I'm contacting more people who know her. We're trying to make sure she's okay."

"Oh, wow. A whole month? That doesn't sound good. No one knows where she is?"

"That's correct."

"I'll be there in one minute!" Melissa called to someone in the background. "Sorry. We're having an impromptu grade-level meeting. That means I only have a few minutes, so fire away with any questions. I want to do whatever I can to help."

"What can you tell me about Skye? We're having trouble tracking down information on her background."

She drew in a long breath. "I don't know what to say. She was private, even more so after her brother died. That really seemed to be a defining moment for her. She withdrew a lot after that happened. I think it was one of the reasons she decided she needed a life change. Sometimes people deal with grief in ways that seem strange to others, but I think starting fresh was one of her coping mechanisms."

"So, you really think that's why she moved?" Interesting. I hadn't thought about that.

"Well, that and some guy."

"Some guy?" A group of conferees started past, loud and boisterous. I put one finger over my other ear so I could hear. This was one piece of information I didn't want to miss.

"She never said any names, but that was my impression. Said there was someone she'd met out in Oklahoma. She wanted to explore the relationship and see where it led."

"Did she ever give you a name?"

"No, I can't say she did. I didn't know anything about him, not even that she'd met someone, until right before she moved. All she said was that maybe life would start looking up."

I definitely needed to dig into that more. "I know this is a wide-open question that draws on a lot of assumptions, but I'm looking for anything. Can you think of any reason she might disappear?"

Melissa drew in a deep breath, as if the question burdened her. "I don't know what to say. She did seem like someone with no roots, you know? I mean, she had her brother. But when he was gone, she had no one else. I think—don't quote me on this—but I think she grew up in New

Mexico, went to college in Texas, and then taught here in Arizona. She was kind of all over the place."

"What about debt? Did she ever mention any debt to you?" I remembered what Darcy had said about Skye and money. What if Skye had taken off to avoid paying her debts?

"You know, she did mention that she had some student loans once. You know how it is with teachers. Administrators barely pay us enough to live on. Add college loans on top of that, and we're underwater a lot."

"I've heard that before."

"Listen, I'd love to talk more, but my meeting is starting," Melissa said. "Let me know if you have any more questions, okay? You've got my number."

I thanked her and hung up. Skye moved here for a boy? Who? I needed to ask Trace about that. Because if she moved here for someone else, that meant I had another lead I needed to track down.

I stepped outside and onto the sidewalk after my last class, wanting a quick breath of fresh air before meeting with Levi. I had to admit that I enjoyed the bustle of the busy streets. Sitting in a class for eight hours a day was difficult for me, and the fluidity of the city—of horns honking and people hurrying and buildings looming—awoke my senses.

I decided to stretch my legs and started down the block. It had actually warmed up some since lunch, something I wouldn't complain about. The sun felt toasty on my shoulders.

Someone yelling on the street corner caught my eye. My head swerved toward the man before my thoughts skidded to a halt.

"Repent now! The day of reckoning is upon us!" The man held a sign proclaiming, "The End Is Near" as he paced the sidewalk. He had greasy hair and a wrinkled and scruffy face, and wore layers of clothing.

Was he a sidewalk prophet using the scare tactic of hell to convince people to be saved? I supposed God could use those methods just as well as He could use any. My style was probably more personal and conversational and less in your face.

I tried to look away before the man caught my eye and trapped me into a conversation, but it was too late.

"Do you know Christ, young lady?" he called. His gaze pierced mine.

"I do." I started to walk away, to turn on my heel, but the man kept talking.

"Have you accepted Him as your personal Lord and Savior?"

I froze, drawing in a hesitant breath. "I have."

He leaned closer, his eyes sharp enough to cut through me. "But have you really?"

"Yes, really."

"Are you sure?" His breath hit me like the stench from a sewer pipe might. This man's heart might be good, but he definitely had some issues.

Before I could defend myself again, someone grabbed my elbow and led me away. "Ignore him."

I glanced up. It was Levi. Just Levi. My heart rate slowed.

"He's been there every day this week." He led me toward the parking garage. "He's a little wacko."

"His methods leave something to be desired."

"More than his methods."

I stiffened as we continued to walk briskly across the street. "What do you mean?"

He glanced at me. "Come on, all this 'the end is near' garbage. Religion is just people trying to scare other people into embracing their moral code."

My first instinct was to be offended. I breathed in a quick prayer and tried to have an open conversation instead. James 3:17 came to mind. "The wisdom that comes from heaven is first of all pure; then peace-loving, considerate, submissive, full of mercy and good fruit, impartial and sincere." I prayed for that wisdom. "Maybe that's what religion is. But God is more than that."

Levi scrunched his eyebrows together as he directed me to a stairway inside the parking garage. How did he know where I'd parked?

"You really believe that?"

I nodded. "I do. I believe there are greater powers at work in this world."

"I do too. I call it karma."

"I take it you're an atheist?" I didn't know why it surprised me. I mean, scientists weren't exactly known to be God-fearing people.

When I'd first started in the field, I hadn't been sure about God. But God and my faith in Him had helped me to get through some pretty dark days. I was taking baby steps, but God was molding me into a better person, one who put the needs of others first. Every once in a while, I took steps backward. My emotions tried to control my actions, and my lack of faith stupefied me. But every day I tried to do my best and live out the life I knew that God wanted.

"I believe all the latest surveys would label me a 'none,'" Levi continued. "I have no religious beliefs or affiliations. I put all my faith in science."

I almost told him I was sorry to hear that, but I didn't want to sound judgmental or insincere. So I nodded instead. "I see."

"Hey, how about if I drive this time?" He changed the subject as quickly as a car switching lanes.

"Really?"

He grinned, that cool, aloof smile that made me wonder. "Yeah, really."

"Sure thing." I couldn't think of a reason for him not to.

"Great, then follow me."

We rounded the corner, and he stopped beside a . . . motorcycle.

"This?" I stared at the oversized Harley. I didn't know much about Harleys, but based on the shiny chrome, the flawless paint job, and the lush leather seat, I had a feeling that this bike was top of the line.

He nodded, almost appearing satisfied. "It warmed up enough today that I could ride, and it's only supposed to get warmer as a front comes in. You okay with it?"

"Sure, as long as I have a helmet."

He unlocked a slick black one that was hooked on the bike and tossed it to me. "Here you go."

I pushed aside my doubts and pulled my hat off—yes, I was wearing my cowboy hat. I thought I might be developing a new addiction to it. I put it in my backpack and pulled the helmet on. "Don't you need a helmet?"

"I'll be okay. Every once in a while I like to live dangerously." Levi climbed on first and then nodded behind him as he slid some aviator sunglasses on. "Let's get going."

I swung my leg over the bike, realizing just how

close I was to the man. Even though there was nothing romantic between us, it just felt weird to be this near to someone who used to be my professor.

"This is not time to be shy—put your arms around my waist."

I'd never been accused of being shy, but I felt out of sorts around this man. I held on to his midsection, flushing at our nearness. I was being ridiculous. I was out of my comfort zone, and it was making me feel off balance. Not good.

As we pulled out of the parking lot, I glanced over and saw Evie standing outside the conference center. Her calculating gaze followed us down the street.

Something twisted in my gut. I wasn't sure what it was, but I tried to shove the emotion down and stop thinking the worst about situations. My gut seemed to be trying to tell me that a storm was looming in the distance, though.

For the first time in a long time, I prayed my gut was wrong.

CHAPTER
NINE

WE ARRIVED EARLY to the fairgrounds where the music festival was taking place, and I almost hated that the motorcycle ride was over. There was something invigorating about the wind sweeping through my hair and nothing but open road around us. It all gave me an adrenaline surge and made me feel revived.

However, I was freezing cold and wondered what the chances were that I could get some coffee somewhere. Slim to none, if I had to guess.

I paused as I took off my helmet, resisting the urge to shake my hair free like every woman on TV did. Instead I ran my hand through my curly locks, hoping my strands hadn't frizzed too much.

Most of all, I felt relieved that I didn't have to touch Levi anymore or smell his spearmint scent.

Something about it just seemed too intimate—at least, more intimate than I wanted it to be.

I glanced around. There were three tents in front of me, various trailers lined up behind them, and a field full of cars. A long line snaked its way toward the front door of the largest tent.

I climbed off the Harley, stretched my legs, and noticed Levi glance over at me. He made no effort to hide his curiosity. "How was it?"

"It was great. I have to admit it, I was skeptical, but there was something freeing about riding."

Something close to satisfaction lingered in his gaze. "I agree." He pointed across the field. "This is where we're supposed to be?"

"That's what I understand."

I bypassed the crowds just as Trace had told me to do and approached a heavyset man standing at the entrance of the tent. This was a different heavyset man than the one at Dusty Boots, yet the two men seemed eerily similar. I told him my name, and he checked a clipboard and then nodded approval.

The place was cool right now, but as soon as people packed inside, it would warm up. The music was loud and pounded in my chest. The scent of dirt and plastic mingled near my nose, a mix of the dry floor and the thick plastic wall behind me.

I took my place against the edge, soaking everything in for a minute. I needed to keep an eye out for anyone acting suspiciously. I also wanted to talk to at least one of Trace's groupies. I needed to find out if anyone else had seen Georgia around lately.

I looked up at Levi, who stood beside me, his gaze focused on the stage area where techs straightened cords and adjusted lights. In my mind all those years ago, he'd been much kinder and more sensitive, while still being tough and masculine. Guys had big shoes to fill, especially after women got their fixes of romantic movies. I wasn't giving up on that dream to find my soul mate, though, despite how many times my heart had been hurt.

Again, Riley and Garrett's faces tangoed in my head. Two men. Two different sets of intentions. And one heart—that would be mine—that was torn.

That wasn't even including a mind that wondered if I should just start from scratch. An ache deep inside that sometimes wanted to give up completely on love.

I cleared my throat, realizing I was wasting time when I could be talking to one of the world's foremost authorities about my investigation. "Do you know anyone with the Lawton Police Department, by chance?"

He glanced down at me, his expression unreadable. "Lots of people. Why?"

"Do you think I could look at some evidence that

was collected in a missing woman's case? Especially if the police have already closed the case."

"Doubtful. Why do you ask?"

I let out a long breath. I'd known it was a long shot, but I'd kick myself if I didn't exhaust every possibility—every ethical possibility, at least. "Trace's girlfriend disappeared. The police believe she left on her own accord; Trace doesn't. I told him I'd help, but I'm running into dead ends."

Levi eyed me, an unreadable emotion flashing in his gaze. "You think you can do something law enforcement can't?"

I raised my chin. "Law enforcement is over-worked. There are cases that slide by. Even though I hate to say it, it's true that the squeaky wheel gets the grease."

That smile appeared again. "I see. What evidence is there that malicious intent was involved?"

"That's what I'm trying to figure out. This woman would be the perfect victim. She had no family. She'd just moved here. She worked at home by herself and hardly had any friends."

"Still doesn't mean she is a victim."

"What if I told you that Trace had a stalker who keeps running off his girlfriends?"

He nodded slowly as realization rolled over his features. "Maybe that's the person who tried to make you a rodeo clown last night."

"I've thought of that," I admitted. "Anyway, the police think she left on her own free will. Her friend even thought she could have had some debt collectors after her, so she disappeared. That said, there may not be a case at all."

"Wrong. There may not be a *crime*. Any way you look at it, a woman is missing. You should start with her inner circle and work out."

"The problem is that her inner circle is only two people. She was pretty reclusive."

"It sounds like you have two likely suspects, then."

I cut him a sharp glance. That would mean that Trace could be guilty. But he had no motive for abduction or, even worse, murder. Nor could I imagine Darcy as a suspect. I didn't know her well enough to form an educated opinion, but I just didn't see her as malicious. "I don't see that."

"And that's your first problem. You're making assumptions and letting them guide you."

I scowled. This man could really get under my skin and make me feel more insecure than nearly anyone I knew. Yet, at the same time, I knew he was right. I had to take my blinders off.

"Have you tried to locate this woman?" He crossed his very defined arms across his very solid chest. I only knew how solid it was because of that motorcycle ride.

I shoved my hands into my back pockets, already anticipating his judgment. "No, I haven't. I haven't had time, not with classes."

"You'll have to decide what your priorities are, then. What's more important to you, Gabby? Finding a missing woman who may have disappeared on her own free will—to avoid creditors, right? Or furthering your education?"

I pressed my lips together. "They're both important."

"Then it's just a matter of deciding what you're going to put your mind toward."

"What would you do?"

He shrugged, staring at the stage for a moment. "I like picking and choosing my cases and deciding what's important. That's why I started my own company. Ask yourself what's going to take you further—this wild goose chase or actually taking your career seriously?"

I bit back a retort because part of me wondered if he was right. Sidetracked. Set back. Delayed.

Most of those issues were of my own doing, and sometimes change was so hard.

I STOOD on the edge of the festival, the back of the tent against my back. Mostly, I was looking for Georgia, though after talking to Caitlyn, I wondered if I would even recognize her. If the woman really did change her looks that often, then spotting her might be a challenge.

The room had filled with people the instant the doors opened. Men, women, children flooded inside. Quite a few of the ladies screamed. Some held up signs asking Trace to marry them. There were lots of cowboy hats, and plaid shirts, and smiles.

About the time the band was supposed to start, I saw Jono walk onstage and talk to various tech engineers, looking even more tense than usual. Something about the way he walked made me question what was going on. The concert was supposed to start anytime now, and so far no one was onstage.

"Excuse me a minute," I mumbled to Levi.

He didn't say anything, just surveyed the space. I pushed my way through the crowd and approached the security guards against the stage. Of course, they immediately stopped me.

"What's going on? Something's wrong."

The man stared at me and grunted.

"Please, Trace is my brother. I need to know if he's okay." At once I had visions of Georgia finding him and deciding to exact her revenge on Trace instead of his love interests. I really hoped that wasn't the case.

The guard continued to stare. Finally, I gave up, realizing I'd get nothing from him, and crept along the edge of the stage toward the back exit. I glanced to my left and right to make sure no one was looking. I was about to slip out when a hand grabbed my arm.

I looked up and saw Levi standing there. "Everything all right?"

I swallowed. "Yes. I'm just . . . just concerned, I suppose."

He glanced behind him quickly and then followed me outside. "I want to help," he admitted.

For a moment, I felt comradery with the man. I needed to mark that one down for the books. On a hunch, I started toward the back of the property.

"I think Trace's trailer is back here. I just want to make sure everything is okay."

"Your spidey sense is tingling?"

I couldn't help but smile, even though part of me wondered if he was being condescending. So much for that comradery. "I suppose."

A small crowd had gathered in the distance in front of one of the trailers. I saw Jono approaching them from the opposite direction, and I quickened my steps. Sure enough, Trace was in the middle of the group.

"Has anyone seen Dud?" he asked.

Everyone mumbled no.

"We can't start without him. What do you want us to do?" Trace said, turning to a short, balding man beside him.

"I'll stall for as long as I can," the man said before taking off.

Trace spotted me and waved me over. "Our drummer is missing," he explained.

"*Missing* missing or just wandered off?"

He rubbed his chin. "We don't know. It's not like him to disappear like this. He knew how important this concert is."

"You checked his trailer?" Levi slid his sunglasses on.

Trace's head flicked toward him, something dark clouding his gaze. "Of course. First thing we did. We don't know what's going on. This just isn't like Dud, though."

"When did you last see him?" I asked, shielding my eyes against the setting sun.

"We rehearsed two hours ago and then took a break," Trace said. "No one's seen him since then. As you heard, Todd—he's the festival coordinator—is going to try and buy some time until we can find Dud."

"We can help look," I offered, hoping Levi didn't mind. I looked back at him, and he nodded.

Trace rubbed his hands on his jeans, looking more anxious by the moment. "That would be great. Should we call the police?"

"If there's any chance foul play could be involved, then you'll want to call the authorities sooner rather than later," Levi said.

Jono already had his cell to his ear.

Levi and I took off down a row of trailers. I jiggled the door of each of them, and they were all locked. I glanced at Levi and noticed he surveyed everything around him with quiet, purposeful motions.

"What's going on in those other tents?" Levi asked.

I shook my head. "I think concerts take place there at various times. It can't hurt to take a look now, right?"

We skirted around the perimeter of the property, past several vehicles that we peered inside of, and finally reached the first tent.

The door—really just a flap—was closed, and the security guard stood beside a truck talking to a pretty girl. He stretched to full attention when he spotted us trying to get inside.

"Anyone in here?" Levi said, an air of authority about him.

I supposed when you'd consulted on major cases where your name had made national headlines, you had that option.

The guard, who appeared young and cocky—yet something still told me he was unreliable—strode toward us. "Of course. I've been here the whole time."

"Any other ways to get inside?" Levi asked, his hands on his hips and an overall imposing air about him.

"There's a door around back. That's where the band goes in. But—"

Before he could finish, Levi headed toward that area. The security guard was on his heels, quivering like a toddler trying to convince his dad not to punish him.

"What are you doing? You can't go in there!"

"Someone's missing," Levi muttered, still charging forward and not acting the least bit ruffled.

"We need to check every possible place where this man might be. His truck is still here, his trailer is empty, and his band is waiting for him before they can go onstage."

The security guard still scrambled to keep up. "And who are you?"

"I'm a police consultant. No, I'm not official right now, but when someone's missing, every moment counts. Capisce?" He still didn't slow, didn't even look back at the man.

"Capisce." The guard frowned. "But I've been at this tent for the last three hours. No one's in there. There's no concert there until tomorrow night."

Levi stopped and turned on his heel, coming face-to-face with the security guard. "Then you won't mind if we look inside?"

The guard swallowed so hard that his Adam's apple bobbed up and back down. "No . . . no. I guess not."

He pulled the door open. I stayed close, remaining silent—unusual for me, but I wanted to soak in everything. I wanted to see how Levi handled situations like these.

"Where are the lights to this place?" Levi asked, stepping into the dark, enclosed space. A concert hall —or tent—without a band, lights, and an audience almost felt like some kind of music graveyard.

"Right over here, sir." The security guard hurried

across the back of the tent, and I could hear him fumbling with something.

I had to admit that I truly stood in awe of the respect that Levi commanded. Was he cocky? Maybe. But even more than that, he came across as authoritative, like someone who knew what he was doing.

The lights popped on and the smaller, arena-like tent came into focus. After gathering my surroundings for a moment, I opened my mouth, about to suggest splitting up. Levi beat me to it.

"Gabby, you go that way. I'll make my way behind stage. Let's see if we can find Dud anywhere."

I nodded. "Took the words out of my mouth."

Slowly, I walked along the rows of chairs. I realized with a touch of dread that the method of my searching indicated I didn't think I would find Dud alive and well. I was looking for a body.

My throat tightened at the thought. I was probably overreacting. I'd just seen too many crimes, so many that my mind instantly went to devious explanations instead of simple ones.

That thought calmed me for a moment. I had to stop seeing malice wherever I went. My life would be much easier when I did that.

Row by row, I searched. Row by row, I only saw chairs.

"Gabby, over here!" Levi shouted.

My nerves returned in an instant. I sprinted toward the backstage area, instantly putting on my brakes when I found Levi.

A few feet away, I saw someone lying on the ground, unmoving and in an unnatural position. Blood surrounded him.

"You know what this means, don't you?" Levi asked.

I nodded. "It means that poor Dud is dead."

CHAPTER
ELEVEN

FIFTEEN MINUTES LATER, the police showed up. Those fifteen minutes afforded me the opportunity to survey the scene. I tried to be subtle as I pulled out my phone and snapped some photos of bloody handprints and some footprints at the scene. There were definitely two sets, and they seemed to indicate a scuffle.

The Locard Theory, I remembered. *Every contact leaves its trace.* Those footprints would let investigators know the height, weight, and sometimes even social class of the person wearing those shoes. Also interesting, I'd learned this week that Nike shoes were the ones most commonly worn at crime scenes.

The question for me was: Were these footprints there before Dud even came back here? It was hard to tell.

The detective who took charge of the scene was short and stout and had only a fringe of hair. A coffee stain graced the front of his button-up shirt, and his khakis looked a little too tight.

"Dr. Stone, didn't expect to see you here," Detective Brooks said, his gaze skimming over us as he pulled on some plastic gloves.

"Didn't expect to stumble on a crime scene." Levi stepped back. "Detective Brooks, this is my colleague, Gabby St. Claire. She works in the Norfolk, Virginia, area."

I wanted to add, "As a crime scene cleaner." But instead I lived with the illusion that I did something more, at least for the moment.

He nodded his acknowledgment before stepping toward Dud. "What do we have here?"

Levi explained to him everything that had happened from the time we arrived until we found the man with a gunshot wound to his chest. Levi and I had guarded the area, making sure no one else came inside to contaminate any potential evidence.

I followed his gaze to the grisly scene behind me. The bullet had taken off part of Dud's face. Right now, blood and brain particulates slid down the otherwise white walls of the tent and down the black speakers, and were spread across the grassy, dusty ground.

I'd seen a lot of awful scenes. Truly awful ones. But this one would haunt me.

The detective began inspecting the area just as the crime scene unit came in, set out markers, and began taking photos. They started with the broad scene and narrowed their photos down to the minute details.

I knew exactly what they were doing. It's what I was supposed to be doing: officially working cases rather than inserting myself into them.

Instead I came up with ways to remove all evidence that the crime ever happened by scrubbing blood away and picking out bones from walls and scrubbing other . . . unmentionable parts of the human body . . . from surfaces. I was feeling the reality of my decisions now more than ever.

I stood on the side, by the door, and watched everyone as they worked. Levi chatted with the detective, pointed to various blood spatter patterns, and otherwise acted like he owned the place. The ME showed up to eventually take the body away for an official autopsy.

Just then, Trace came running in the door beside me. The police officer stationed there held him back. But Trace still remained in the entry, his eyes darting around, desperation, fear, and worry mingling in their depths.

Finally, his gaze fell on me. "What's going on? I heard the police were here."

"I'm sorry, Trace," I started. I didn't want to say too much, since the information wasn't mine to release. Still, my heart clutched with anguish.

"Did you find Dud?"

I didn't say anything, which seemed to be answer enough.

"Oh, no. Not Dud." He lunged toward the tent again, but just like before, the officer stopped him.

"Sir, you can't go in there. It's an active crime scene."

"Is it my drummer? Can you just tell me that?"

The detective exchanged a look with the officer, something silent passing between them, and finally the detective nodded. He stepped toward the doorway. "The body appears to be that of Dud Larson."

Trace let out a moan. I slipped past the guard and put my arms around him, trying to offer what little comfort I could. He felt too tight and wound up to be comforted, though. I stepped back, keeping one hand on his arm.

"Not Dud. No, no, no. What happened?" His eyes looked haggard as he dragged them up to meet mine.

"He was shot," the detective said behind me, his voice laced with compassion.

"Can I see him?" Trace took an eager step forward.

The man didn't realize what he was asking. I put

my hand on his arm. "You don't want to see him, Trace. You don't want to remember him like that."

Trace closed his eyes, squeezed the skin at the bridge of his nose. "Who would do something like this?"

The detective's hawk-like eyes soaked in every movement, every expression, every nonverbal exchange. "We intend to try to figure that out, Mr. Ryan. Did Dud have any enemies?"

Trace remained silent a moment, staring straight ahead as if in thought. "There was our old manager. He and Dud didn't see eye to eye on a lot of things. It was part of the reason we let Lenny go. Dud was a good guy. There was nothing not to like about him."

"What else can you tell us about him?" the detective continued.

"He's twenty-six, from Austin, Texas. He's single, a great drummer, and he always joked about how he used to be a rodeo clown before he made enough money as a musician. Dud hasn't even been with the band for a year, but he fit right in."

Detective Brooks nodded. "We'll need to contact next of kin for Dud. Do you have that information?"

"I don't, but Jono does. He's our manager."

"Thank you." The detective put away his notepad. "You'll be around if we have any more questions?"

"I'm in Oklahoma for the rest of the week. Then we're supposed to go on a 150-city tour."

I walked Trace outside. Crowds had formed on the other side of the police line. Most likely there were concertgoers who'd gotten wind that something was going on.

"What can I do for you?" I asked Trace.

"Figure out who did this." He shook his head, his neck muscles bulging and veins popping out on his temples. "I just can't believe this. Dud still had so much more of life to live."

We started walking back toward the trailers, away from the crowds displaying their cell phones and snapping what they hoped would be the Twitter photo of the day. They couldn't possibly realize the grim reality of finding someone who should be full of life suddenly only an empty vessel.

"I know it has to be quite a shock, especially since there was violence involved." I dangled my hands in my pockets, adjusting my cowboy hat so the sun wouldn't hit my eyes. You said you'd just seen him two hours ago?"

"That's right. We finished rehearsal, and we were all having some downtime until the concert started. It's important that we conserve our energy before a big show. I thought he was in his trailer, probably playing the Xbox. It was one of his favorite ways to unwind."

"Is there anything else you can remember? Anything at all that might be a clue as to what happened to him?"

"I really don't know, Gabby." He pulled his hat off and wiped his hand through his thick, light brown hair. "Nothing seems clear right now, to be honest."

Jono rushed over to us. "What's going on? I've been trying to find out something and searching all over this place for Dud. Then I heard that someone found a body. Is it true?"

"Dud is dead, Jono," Trace said, his voice strained and tight.

Jono blinked. He took his glasses off, ran his hands under his eyes, and then slid his spectacles back on. "Dead? He can't be dead. We just saw him."

Trace nodded. "He's been shot. Gabby and Levi found him in one of the concert tents."

Jono started pacing. "I can't believe this. We need to come up with a plan. Put together a press release."

Trace's gaze went cold. "Jono, Dud is dead. I don't care about the concert or public relations or even the tour."

"Well, someone's got to be the one who worries about these things. This is what you pay me for. I'm deeply sorry about Dud, but I'm trying to think of the bigger picture here!"

Trace's jaw flexed. "We can't go on without Dud. I won't do it."

In the distance, someone squealed. "Trace Ryan, I love you!"

A woman started toward him, but a ring of police officers stopped her before she crossed the police line.

It was a zoo around here. Just give it another hour, and the press would join this circus. I felt as if I'd been swept up in some Western version of Hollywood with red carpets and stardom and crazy fans.

"Jono, why don't you take Trace back to his trailer and talk about things. Out here in the open isn't the place to do it," I told him.

As they nodded and walked toward the sunset, I paused and glanced around. I needed to seize the opportunity to do some snooping. From here on out, I was taking this investigation by the horns.

I lingered at the crime scene for a few minutes. Somehow I'd still been given the clearance to stick around while the police did their work. I guessed that's what happened when you had a world-renowned forensic expert with you.

The concert had been canceled, and everyone had been cleared out about an hour ago. Since then, it had been relatively quiet outside. Trace and the remaining members of the band had been sequestered to their trailers, and I planned to check on him before I left.

I watched for a moment as Levi measured the blood spatter, as he observed it from different angles, as he recorded the size of every drop in every location.

I knew my time was whittling away, so I paced toward the back of the tent.

From the corner of my eye, I saw the young security guard who'd supposedly been guarding this tent pacing in the distance. He was a younger guy, probably in his early twenties. Though he was small, he seemed fit. He had light brown hair that was cropped close, and something about him screamed that he was street smart. Maybe it was the way he walked or the way his hair was trimmed or the look in his eyes. I couldn't exactly put my finger on it.

What I did recognize was that he looked nervous. But why? I needed to find out.

Trying to look casual, I stuffed my hands into my pockets and approached him. He stopped pacing when he saw me and straightened, as if he feared his body language would give too much away.

"Horrible what happened, isn't it?" I asked.

He nodded. "Yeah, more than horrible."

"You had no idea he was in here?" I asked. "How did he manage to slip inside, then?"

He shook his head. "I dunno."

"You have no guesses, even?"

He shook his head again. "No guesses."

"That's strange. Somehow he got by you."

He rubbed his neck. "He must have sneaked in through another entrance somewhere. I don't know. It doesn't make sense. I keep running it through in my mind."

I had a feeling Dud could have easily sneaked in while this security guard was flirting with attractive concertgoers.

"Did you see anything?"

He shifted uncomfortably. "I did see Dud walking around here earlier. He said he was stretching his legs before the concert."

"Was he by himself?"

He shook his head, more sweat forming on his forehead. "There was a girl with him."

"What did she look like?"

"She was a brunette. She had curly hair. Soft curls, you know? Not like those tight ones. She was medium height, thin. That's all I could see. I didn't get a close look at her."

Interesting. That girl might have been the last person Dud was seen alive with. That made her the number one suspect.

"Have you told the police that?" I asked him.

"Not yet. They told me to wait here."

"You're going to tell them, right?"

He rubbed his neck again. "Yes, of course."

"Great."

Despite his seeming willingness, I had the strange feeling there was something he wasn't telling me.

CHAPTER
TWELVE

I SLIPPED AWAY from the crime scene and made my way toward the band's trailers. On a whim, I went toward the trailer next to Trace's and rapped on the door.

Wentworth answered. "Gabby. What's going on?" His voice sounded subdued, as it should after finding out someone who'd been your friend and band mate had died.

"I need your help."

"Come right in."

I stepped inside and spotted Leroy, the bass player, lingering in the background, his feet propped up on what was probably the kitchen table. The news blared on a small TV set high in the corner, and the entire place reeked of potato chips and dirty socks.

Wentworth sighed and pushed some magazines

off a small bench seat. "Have a seat. And excuse the mess. We weren't expecting company."

I lowered myself there, careful not to get too comfortable.

Wentworth sat at the kitchen table and frowned. "We don't know what to do. I just can't believe what happened to Dud . . ."

"I know. It's terrible," I agreed.

"You found him?" Wentworth asked.

I nodded. "I'm sorry. Can I ask you a few questions?"

"What do you need to know?"

"I need to know who Dud was dating."

Wentworth leaned back. "I think her name was Jody."

"Jody from merchandising?" I remembered the woman who'd brought me the cowboy hat.

Wentworth nodded. "That's the one. She sells our albums, T-shirts, photographs. She just started a couple of weeks ago."

If I remembered Jody correctly, she was tall with blonde hair, and nothing at all like the woman the security guard had described as being with Dud. "Is she here now?"

"She stays with the merchandise, so if I had to guess, she's probably packing up T-shirts right now."

"Has she heard about Dud yet?"

He shrugged. "I doubt it. Jono sent us all to our

trailers, probably to keep us away from the press. I have no idea who knows what."

I stood to leave but paused. A picture on the table caught my eye. "Who is that?" I pointed to a tall man with a thin face and oversized ears.

"It's our old manager, Lenny. We were going through some old candid photos for an article. That's why all those old snapshots are out. Why?"

I stared at the photo. "Because I saw him at your release party at the Dusty Boots Café."

He was the man I'd been talking to right before being lured into the bull's territory and nearly gored to death.

"Really?" Wentworth said. "I figured he'd stay far away. He and Trace didn't exactly see eye to eye."

"There was bad blood between the two of them?"

He nodded. "I'd say. Lenny didn't appreciate getting fired. But Jono has really taken us so much further in our careers. It was a good choice. Jono had connections and a go-get-'em attitude. Lenny was still trying to find his way, and we were just meandering along behind him."

I thanked them and then started toward the tent where the band's merchandise was sold. I weaseled my way past the guards at the door. That's when I saw a woman packing up things from a table in the distance.

Just as I thought, she was a honey blonde, exceptionally tall, and more curvy than thin.

"Can I help you?" she asked as she placed another stack of T-shirts into a box.

"I'm sorry to intrude right now. I was hoping to ask you some questions, though."

"You're Trace's stepsister, right?"

"Future stepsister."

She shrugged. "Close enough. What can I do for you?"

"It's about Dud."

She nodded nonchalantly. "What about him?"

Something about the way she said it made me realize that she didn't know he was dead.

After a moment of silence, she paused. "Don't tell me he's in trouble. Is that why the police are here?"

"You don't know?"

"Jono just told me to start packing up and that the concert was canceled."

"Is it true that you and Dud were dating?" I shifted, praying my words were compassionate and wise. This wasn't the way I wanted her to find out about her boyfriend.

"Where did you hear that?"

I offered a half shrug. "Word gets around."

She rubbed her palms on her jeans before continuing to pack. "We weren't exactly dating. But we were together, if that makes sense. He wasn't the type to commit, but he wasn't the type who wanted to be alone either."

I got her meaning loud and clear. "Did you see him today?"

She shrugged. "I saw him earlier. We haven't spoken."

"Was he seeing anyone else?"

She shrugged again. "I don't know. We just started hanging out. We hadn't talked about being exclusive or anything. But I liked him. Where are you going with all of this?" Suddenly, her face fell and she went eerily still. "It was Dud that the police found dead, wasn't it?"

I didn't know what to say, and at once, I regretted my spontaneity.

My silence seemed to be answer enough for her.

She let out a gasp and stumbled backward. Before I could swoop in and catch her, she passed out.

Two hours later, Levi walked my way, motorcycle helmet caught between his waist and arm. "You ready to head back?"

I nodded, figuring I'd already talked to everyone I wanted. "Yeah, I guess our work here is done."

Jody was fine and being cared for by a paramedic and some other coworkers from merchandising.

Trace was sequestered in his trailer. And Jono was managing everyone else.

We started across the lot toward his motorcycle.

"You did well back there." Levi nodded toward the tent where we'd found Dud.

"Thank you. You weren't too shabby yourself."

A half smile clipped his lips. "You mind if I show you something before we go back to the hotel? It's just a little detour."

I shrugged, intrigued. "Sure."

He tossed me a helmet, and I traded my cowboy hat in for a less fashionable but way safer piece of headwear. Then I climbed on the back of the motor-cycle and wrapped my arms around his waist again. I had to admit—it still felt a little weird. But Dr. Stone —I meant, Levi—was a professional.

We took off down the street, but instead of heading back toward Oklahoma City, he turned and headed down more barren roads. The sky above twinkled brightly with pinprick stars laid out on a velvety black backdrop. I didn't have a view like this where I lived in Virginia. Out here, everything just seemed clearer. I hoped that would apply to my thoughts as well.

The air was brisk around us, but it felt invigorat-ing. Being on the motorcycle made my senses feel alive. With anyone else behind the wheel, I might have been nervous. But Levi seemed so in control, like he knew what he was doing. He seemed like that in every area of his life.

We rode for what seemed like hours, although I assumed it had been maybe twenty minutes. As the wind rushed over us, my mind drifted to today. Dud was dead. He'd been seen near the tent with a girl he wasn't dating. He was the newest band member. He seemed well liked. So why had someone killed him?

Now I had two mysteries I'd encountered since coming to Oklahoma. First, I had to figure out what had happened to Skye. Second, I wanted to figure out who killed Dud. This was all on top of taking the classes I'd paid for and really my whole purpose of being here in Oklahoma. I really needed to learn how to multitask better.

Levi slowed as we approached a rugged wooden fence. It was too dark to see details—if there was cacti or tumbleweed or anything else hinting of this very different landscape. He turned up a drive before finally pulling to a stop in front of a sprawling ranch home. He cut the engine and turned toward me.

"What do you think?"

I wasn't sure where I was or what I was supposed to say. "It's . . . a house."

He raised an eyebrow. "Astute."

"So I've been told."

He nodded toward the house. "Let's go inside for a minute and take a load off."

He probably just wanted to talk about the case. Maybe ask me about my future. Probably even offer me some direction for my career.

I pushed down a nudge of anxiety that wiggled inside me and climbed off. The darkness felt deeper than what I was used to as I looked around me. A momentary chill washed over me as I realized I was out in the middle of nowhere, in a place where no one knew where I was, and there wasn't a soul who'd miss me within sixteen hours of here—unless Trace was included.

This was one of the perfect scenarios for disappearing. Being too trusting had never been one of my problems, but my sensibilities were in question at the moment.

Was that how Skye had felt? Had she trusted the wrong person? Moved out here to Oklahoma where she didn't know anybody, found herself in a bad situation, and had no one she could turn to for help? Trace had been on the road when she disappeared, so it had just been Skye out here, alone in a big world.

"Come on." Levi started toward the front door. As he did, his hand went to my waist, not in a friendly nudge. It lingered there, too low to be professional, too gripping to be an accident.

In an effort to avoid an awkward situation, I twirled and looked up, pretending to be fascinated and preoccupied with nature around me. "I love the stars here."

"As far as flaming masses of gas go, they're nice." There wasn't much emotion behind the words, almost as if he'd agreed just to placate me.

Or was it that I saw nature as one who appreciated the Creator, while he simply saw life as happenstance?

He sauntered ahead, unlocked the door, and then waited for me to catch up. With a touch of trepidation, I followed him inside.

He was former law enforcement. Respected by thousands. Called up for the toughest of cases.

I was overreacting here. There was no reason to feel off balance.

I stepped inside and rubbed my arms, suddenly chilly as I lingered in the entryway. I glanced around the massive house, complete with oversized rooms, high ceilings, and an entire wall of windows across the way. The scent of cedar and leather and maybe even pine drifted up to me.

"This is my paradise." He took my helmet and set it on a table by the door. "Let me get you a drink."

He strode ahead, and by the time I reached the kitchen, he'd already pulled out two beer bottles and popped the top on both. He handed me one, but I shook my head.

"I don't drink."

"More of a wine girl?"

"Not particularly."

"Alcoholic?" he asked, taking a long sip.

"Not me, but I've been around enough other people who are." I shoved my hip against the counter and crossed my arms, wishing I was anywhere but here at the moment.

"Understood. Two for me, I guess." He took another long swig.

"Dr.—I mean, Levi—if you don't mind me asking, why are we here?"

"Thought you might want to see my place." He shrugged like it was no big deal.

"It's almost midnight."

His gaze lingered on me a moment. "I thought we could talk about the case while it's still fresh in our minds. We could talk at the hotel, but there too many rumors might start up. We wouldn't want that."

"I see."

He walked from the kitchen, down several steps, and into a sunken living room. I lifted a quick prayer before following him. The room itself was nice, with a grand, two-story fireplace made with what looked like river rock. The walls of the room were made of logs, and animal skin rugs were on the wood floor. It was like an oversized man cave. Nowhere was there even a hint of a woman's touch, which seemed to indicate to me that his ex-wife had never lived here.

He made himself comfortable on a leather couch and patted the space beside him. "Come. Let's talk and compare notes."

I approached the couch, but sat one cushion away from him—a comfortable distance to chat. Somehow, my youthful fantasies about the man were fading fast from my mind.

He took a long sip of his beer. "Best way to unwind after a hard day on the field."

I didn't say anything. I'd actually found time with good friends and in prayer to be the best medication, but if I said that, I'd sound self-righteous.

He glanced over at me, one arm stretched across the back of the couch. "So, please tell me you're going to pursue a career in forensics and not just settle for crime scene cleaning."

I nodded slowly. "I'm looking for the right job opening. But crime scene cleaning really isn't that bad. It helps me pay the bills, keeps me connected with crime scenes, and makes me feel like I'm making a difference in the lives of the people left behind."

"Your skills are being underutilized. You need to be out on the field."

"You really think?" It felt good to hear his affirmation.

He nodded. "I really think so. I saw you today actually in the field. You handle yourself very well.

You're perceptive, you think outside of the box, and you've got a good head on your shoulders." He took another long sip of his beer.

I drew my legs beneath me, trying to relax. "What would you do if you were in my shoes?"

He put his head back and let out a long sigh. After a moment of thought, he sat up again. "Honestly, I'd start applying for positions and grab up anything you can find just so you could get your foot in the door. In the meantime, I'd also get some more education."

"A master's?"

"Even higher if you want to stay on top." He raised his hand above his head as if to illustrate his point. "You might as well get your PhD. You're going to go a lot further with it, and the additional education will be good for you."

"It's something to think about." I'd never once considered it, even. I knew more and more people were maxing out their education and degrees, which did make the job field tougher.

"Once you have experience and education, you can start consulting."

"Why would I want to do that?"

"Because then you get to pick the cases that are interesting to you. You can still be on retainer with your place of employment. But the real money is in consulting, lecturing, writing books."

Something zipped through my blood as I pictured myself traveling the United States and giving my opinion on various crime scenes. It would be a great opportunity to make a difference, to really focus on the cases with the most impact. The thought had me dreaming big, but why shouldn't I dream big?

"I'd choose a specialty if I were you, as well. Mine, of course, is blood spatter. But there's also demand for fingerprint experts, forensic anthropologists, linguists, even people with a specialty in the fine arts. The possibilities are vast." He set his bottle down and grabbed the second one.

With every sip he took, I could see him loosening up more and letting down some of his guard. "Are there any specialties that are really hot right now?"

"You follow your heart, not what's popular. If you follow what's popular, you'll only end up unhappy." He scooted closer. "You have something in your hair."

I tensed as he reached over and picked something out, his hand brushing my jaw.

"There you go. Just a little gnat." He flicked it away before his warm gaze fell on me again. "You know, maybe you could even come work for me."

"Really?" My heart sped a beat. "You would consider that?"

He nodded, a little too hard. "Of course I would. I'm always looking for interns and assistants. This job isn't a one-person show, even if I do get all the glory."

I imagined myself working under him. There was so much I could learn. The experience would be phenomenal.

He leaned closer. "I could really take you places, you know."

Alarms sounded in my head. Was he hitting on me? My throat went dry. "So, tell me about your kids."

I tried to get his focus on something other than my neck, which was where his eyes kept going. I tugged up my shirt, which wasn't low cut. But I felt like it was at the moment.

"Why talk about them? I only get to see them once a month. End of the story." His gaze lingered on my chest. "There are other things we could chat about."

I scooted back, suddenly very uncomfortable. "Like forensics?"

He grinned suggestively. "Yeah, forensics."

I recognized that look in his eyes. It was desire.

I stood and yawned, trying to make it clear that I was tired and ready to go. "We should probably be getting back."

He stood also and stepped closer, his whole body leaning into me. "You in a hurry?"

"I figured you would be, since you have to teach

tomorrow and all." I wanted to back up, but my legs hit the side of the sectional and stopped me in my tracks.

His fingers brushed my cheek. "You can stop pretending, Gabby."

"Stop pretending what? That there was a possibility you were a decent person?"

"I can see it in your eyes. You're attracted to me. It's okay. You're not in college anymore. We're both consenting adults."

I heard the suggestion in his voice and leaned away. "I don't know what to say." In fact, socking him across the jaw seemed way more effective than words at the moment.

"Let's not say anything." His arms circled my waist.

I pushed him back. "Dr.—I mean, Levi. I don't think this is a good idea."

His lips trailed my neck.

"I'm not that kind of girl. I don't have flings like this." I tried to take a step back but felt trapped.

His hands tightened on my waist. "Maybe you should live a little."

"Levi, this is a bad idea, on so many levels." I gave him a firm push.

With that, his hands dropped and he stepped back. Something changed in his eyes. His body language went cold, hostile even. "I see."

A flash of guilt was immediately followed by outrage. "You've got to understand, of all the people in the forensic field, I probably admire you the most. I've looked up to you for years."

"I gave you a chance to do something with your life, Gabby, and get out of this hole you're in."

A sick feeling gurgled in my gut as I realized the implications of his words. "You're saying if I had a relationship with you, you could help my career advance?"

"Not a *relationship*." He made air quotes around the word. "Although, if it made you feel better, we could call it that."

I held up my hand again, disgusted with a man who'd once been my idol. How could I have been so stupid? "I like to make my own way. I'm not the type who will sleep my way to the top, if that's what you're implying."

He let out a quick, demeaning breath and shook his head. "You've got to stop being so rigid."

My frustration reached its boiling point. "I can't believe I was so wrong about you."

His gaze frosted. "There are plenty of women who would love to be with me right now, Gabby. They'd give up everything to be in this position."

"So, I guess I should feel honored." Sarcasm dripped from my words, and I didn't even try to hide it.

"You're not doing yourself any favors. I can tell you that you won't be getting any recommendations from me. Maybe just the opposite."

My mouth gaped open. "You're telling me that you would ruin me professionally just because I wouldn't sleep with you?"

"You're a wannabe investigator. Read between the lines."

It was probably better that he'd cut me off before I said anything I regretted.

He shook his head and stepped away. "Good night."

"Good night? How am I going to get back to the hotel?"

"You're resourceful. Figure something out."

With that, he sauntered out of the room and down the hallway. I heard a door slam and knew I was on my own.

CHAPTER
THIRTEEN

I WAS FUMING INSIDE. Absolutely fuming. More than frustrated, more than panicked, I was madder than a grave robber surrounded by urns.

How could someone I'd looked up to and respected for so long be such a jerk? The idea of sleeping my way to the top absolutely repulsed me. I wasn't the type. I never would be. I couldn't respect anyone who did.

Besides that, Levi himself had warned me not to be too trusting. All along, he was the one I shouldn't have trusted. He had a lot of nerve.

I shook my head. The other fact remained that I wasn't usually so naïve. How had I gotten myself in this situation? Even more: How would I get out of it? Not with my dignity intact, that was for sure.

The only person I knew and could even think of

as a possibility of whom to call was Trace. I had his number and he was fairly close. I really had no choice here.

The problem remained that I had no idea where I was, though.

I might as well be stranded in the desert.

With Levi out of sight, I let out one more huff and decided to search his house. Certainly he had a piece of mail somewhere that listed his address. Right?

I started down the opposite hallway from the one that Levi had gone down. With a touch of hesitation, I pushed open the first door. On the other side was an entertainment room, complete with two rows of recliners and giant-screen TV. The next room contained weight machines and a treadmill. I couldn't imagine finding his address in there.

The next room was a child's room.

Levi's child's room.

There were toy airplanes hanging from the ceiling, colorful books on the shelves, and stuffed animals arranged behind a wooden headboard. The warmth of the room contradicted everything I felt about Levi Stone.

What would someone who was such a jerk be like as a father? Didn't parenthood usually set people straight, make people better? And how sad was it that he only saw his child once a month?

I closed the door. As I started toward the next

room, unable to merge the image of Levi the Jerk with Levi the Father, a chill suddenly washed over me. I glanced down the hallway, but there was no one there.

At once, the darkness seemed more ominous and my seclusion out here felt even more isolated. Anxiety crept into my psyche.

With my back against the wall, I continued creeping down the hallway, feeling like the idiot walking into danger instead of running away from it.

The lights. That's what was always missing in those movies. Why didn't people just turn on some lights? Why didn't *I* just turn on some lights?

I felt along the plaster until I found the switch. But as I flicked the lever upward, nothing happened.

I flipped it a couple more times, but still nothing happened. No light drove away the darkness.

Great. Was the electricity out? What were the odds?

I'd go get Levi and ask for his help here, but the last thing I needed to do was knock on his bedroom door. No way would I set myself up for that one.

Tears burned at my eyes for a moment as another lurking thought emerged. Had Levi said all those nice things about me and my talent just because he had ulterior motives? Had he not meant a word of it? I'd felt so reaffirmed in my calling to do forensics. What if it had all been a lie?

A creak sounded behind me. I twirled around, expecting to see someone there.

The hallway was empty.

Outside, the wind picked up, and I shivered. That had probably been it. The wind had made the noise, maybe even knocked out the power.

I wanted to get out of this house. Now. I hadn't asked to come here. Hadn't asked to be in this position.

After a moment of hesitation, I opened the next door and saw an office. An office.

Thank goodness. This was the natural place for him to keep his mail. I needed to find an address —now!

I pulled up the flashlight on my phone. Man, did I love that feature. I scanned the light over the room and didn't see anything suspicious. With that in mind, I crept forward.

My hands trembled by the time I reached his desk, which, of course, was clear of anything other than a desk calendar. Pushing away any guilt—I wouldn't be doing this right now if Levi hadn't been such a jerk—I pulled open the top drawer. A pile of papers was there, and I began to flip through them. At the bottom, I spotted some envelopes.

His address was right there. Mission accomplished.

I paused as I saw the return address. It was from a

law firm, and the mail was marked certified, though it hadn't been opened yet. Interesting. I wondered what that was about.

Of course, all I cared about at the moment was getting out of here.

My fingers were still quivery as I found Trace's number and dialed. He answered on the second ring.

"It's Gabby, and I need your help."

"Sure thing. What's going on, sis?"

"It's a long story, but can you pick me up? It's an emergency."

"I'll be right there."

"Being right there" translated into thirty minutes of me pacing by the front door. Finally, I saw headlights pull into the driveway. Once I confirmed it was Trace, I hurried outside, feeling a touch humiliated at everything that had transpired. I knew that Trace deserved an explanation after coming to get me at two in the morning.

I climbed into the passenger side seat and slammed the door. As I watched Levi's house disappear in the side view mirror, I realized I would be content if I never saw that place again . . . or if I never saw Levi Stone again, for that matter.

"You okay? You seem a little shaky," Trace said, giving me a curious glance.

"Levi was much less of a gentleman than I'd hoped." I held my hands up to the warm air pouring from the vent, finding immense comfort in such a small thing. But I felt safe here with Trace, and feeling safe wasn't something to be taken lightly.

His jaw tightened. "One of those guys, huh?"

"Yeah, one of those guys. I have enough guy problems, and I don't want to add any more to my list." I shook my head as a tremble shook me. "Sorry I had to wake you."

"I wasn't asleep. I have a musician's schedule anyway—up all night, sleep all day. Of course, anytime you need me and I'm close, just let me know and I'm there."

"Thanks, Trace. How are you doing with everything?"

"I can't stop thinking about Dud."

"Any updates?"

He shook his head, the moonlight hitting the side of his face. Seriously, he looked like he could be filming a country music video at the moment. A sad one, unfortunately.

"Not that I've been told," Trace said. "I called and told Dud's family what happened. One of the hardest phone calls I've ever had to make."

"I can imagine. I'm sorry."

"I just can't comprehend who would do this." He grimaced. "Dud's family is coming into town. I'm thinking the funeral will be early next week, provided the body is released by then. Jono's not happy with me, but I can't see starting the tour next week without Dud."

"It sounds really tough."

"Plus, on a purely logical level, we'll have to get a new drummer. It's going to take more rehearsals to get used to playing with someone new. We can't launch our tour and make mistakes." He shook his head and glanced over at me. "That sounds callous, doesn't it? I mean, part of me doesn't even care if we go on tour. But contractually, we're obligated to our record label. Plus, I know Dud would want us to go on. He was living his dreams, making a living making music."

I shifted in my seat to better see Trace. "Trace, someone told me that Dud had been seeing Jody from merchandising. But the woman who was described as last seen with Dud didn't look anything like Jody."

He frowned. "Really? Dud was usually pretty loyal. I can't see him fooling around, despite the reputation musicians might have."

"Was there any tension in the band?"

He half shrugged, half shook his head. "Not really. Just the usual stuff. There's always going to be some creative pressure. Sometimes egos get in the way. But really the band gets along great." He paused. "I suppose there *was* some strain with our drummer."

"Dud?"

"Sorry, I should have clarified. Our *first* drummer. He committed suicide last year. He had a lot of issues, and he was dragging all of us down with him. We didn't want to cut him loose, but he was unreliable and unpredictable. We had suspicions that he was doing drugs. Anyway, he didn't take it well. One of his friends found him in his apartment. He'd ODed."

"I'm sorry to hear that. That's got to be tough."

"Absolutely. I never wished harm on him. I really didn't. I was hoping getting cut from the band would be a wake-up call for him and that he'd get his life together." He shook his head. "It didn't work out that way."

"What about Jono?"

"What about him?" He looked at me again, a clueless expression in his eyes.

"I heard there was some tension after you fired your first manager and hired Jono."

He readjusted his hat. "That's just business. It's not fun. I wish I didn't have to deal with it. But Lenny had been with us for years and taken us nowhere. We needed someone with connections and a proven track record."

"How did Lenny handle that news?"

Trace shrugged. "About as well as you can imagine. He wasn't happy. He said we'd never succeed without him."

Was he willing to make sure the band failed by killing Dud and sabotaging the beginning of their year-long tour? It seemed pretty desperate, but I wanted to keep my mind open to all the possibilities here.

"He was at your release party, Trace."

Trace jerked his head toward me, crinkles at his eyes. "What? No . . ."

I nodded. "He was. I spoke with him. I didn't realize who he was until I saw his photo in Wentworth's trailer."

"Why would he come to the party? What sense does it make? He hasn't spoken to me for months."

"And I guess he didn't speak to you while he was at the release?"

Trace's grip on the steering wheel tightened as he readjusted his hands. "No, I had no idea he was there, even."

"Did he know about Georgia?"

Trace was silent for a moment before nodding. "No, but Lenny gets around. I think he and Leroy might still talk. They were pretty good friends. I suppose Lenny could have heard about Georgia from him."

Then he could know to frame the things that had happened on her.

"Is he working with another band yet?"

"Not that I know of. You think he could be guilty?" He cast a fleeting glance my way.

"I'm not assuming anything. But I want to examine every possibility."

Because someone wouldn't have lured me into a bull pasture for no reason. Something was going on, and I would figure out what.

TRACE PULLED to a stop in front of a small house in a middle-class neighborhood. "You mind camping out here tonight? I promise to drive you back to the conference in the morning. I've got a radio interview in an hour."

"In the middle of the night?"

"It's for a morning show over in Britain. I don't want to come across as ungentlemanly-like, such as Levi did. Not all of us Oklahomans are jerks."

"You don't give me that vibe, and I really just appreciate the help." I didn't feel unease at his suggestion like I did when Levi had pulled up to his place. I should have trusted my gut all along.

We walked inside. The place was a bachelor pad, but all around were mementos of country music and the rodeo. There were framed records, and pictures of

Trace with his favorite stars—Garth Brooks, George Strait, Brooks and Dunn. "You really do love this stuff, don't you?"

He hung his hands on his belt. "Sure do. It's what I've wanted to do forever. I just can't believe I'm finally here. It's a dream come true. And it all happened because of a breakup."

"A breakup?" Now this was a story I wanted to hear.

"I dated a girl for two years. Thought we'd get married. But she broke up with me—totally blindsided me—and I wrote 'Doom and Groom' as a result. I never expected it would become a hit."

"Funny the way things work out like that."

He walked into the kitchen. "Would you like some water?" He held out a bottle.

I took it from him and twisted off the top. Then I plopped down on the couch and stretched out, grateful to finally be able to breathe again. I glanced in the corner across from me and raised my eyebrows in surprise at the cage I saw.

I stepped closer. "Is that a . . . bunny?"

He let out a chuckle and raised his water bottle. "Yeah, what can I say? I'm on the road too much to have a dog, and I'm not much of a cat person. I figured I could take a rabbit with me on the road. Bugs and I are always there for each other."

Terrible visions filled my head. I tried to push the images away.

"What's wrong?"

I opened my eyes and stared at him. He was being sincere. "You have a bunny."

Still nothing registered in his gaze.

"Bunny boilers?" I hinted.

No reaction.

"Come on, you have to have seen *Fatal Attraction,* one of the top femme fatale movies of all time. And now you have a stalker *and* a bunny."

"Oh yeah. I never thought about that—and I really don't want to." He plopped down beside me. "So, Gabby, tell me about the man my mom is going to marry."

Any feelings of relaxation I'd felt instantly disappeared. The last thing I wanted to talk to Trace about was my father, mostly because I didn't want to be honest. I didn't want to skirt around the truth. But I didn't want to alarm Trace either, or ruin one of the best things that had happened to my dad in the last decade.

"My dad has . . . he's turned a lot of corners," I finally settled on saying. That was putting it nicely.

"Oh yeah?" He stared at me, obviously waiting for more.

"I don't want to lie, Trace. My dad was messed up for a long time. I longed for a father for most of my life, and he never stepped up to the plate. Instead, he turned to alcohol to numb the pain after my brother disappeared." My words sound melodramatic, but they were true. I decided to end on a positive note, though. "But your mom has turned him around."

"I appreciate that, Gabby. I have to say, that pretty much echoes what Teddi said about him."

My eyes widened. "Did she?" I'd always thought Teddi was blind to my father. I had no idea she was aware of my dad's past.

"My mom may have a heart of gold, but she's not too trusting. My dad worked hard in the oil business as a blue-collar worker for a long time until the cancer got the best of him. She believes in second chances."

"We all need someone in our lives who believes in second chances, don't we?"

"We absolutely do." He glanced at his watch. "Look, I'd love to talk more, but I've got to prep for this interview. You going to be okay?"

"I am. I just appreciate you doing this. Thank you."

He opened the closet and pulled out a pillow and Sooners blanket. "Make yourself comfortable. I wish I could offer you more."

"I assure you, this is plenty."

As he disappeared, I leaned back and tried to relax for a moment. Of course, my mind was racing a million miles a minute with more questions than answers.

I plucked a piece of paper from the end table. Perhaps it was nosiness, or maybe even boredom. But I began reading the words there, scribbled in a sloppy scrawl on a piece of yellow legal paper.

I just want to tell you

I know you feel broken

I know life ain't always easy

Pain is easily awoken

Good times roll by too fast

But I assure you

You'll be whole again one day

Every night that's what I pray

Because the sun still rises in the east

And the rain still falls in the spring

Life goes on

And so must you.

Because there's one thing I know for sure

You're a survivor

Something about the lyrics hit me, and tears popped into my eyes.

So much for not being mopey.

But I felt like these lyrics could have been written for me. My life, in some ways, seemed like it was in a constant state of flux. Yet, in other ways, the things I wanted to change stayed the same. I desperately wanted to be whole again, and I knew the only way to do that was through fully trusting in God in every aspect of my life.

I closed my eyes. "Lord, give me wisdom and guidance. Show me Your path as I press on toward what You've called me to do. Help me run this race without growing weary."

Suddenly, a verse came to mind. *And it came to pass.*

Wasn't that the truth? Problems were like the tide. They came and went. As I closed my eyes, I felt like God was speaking to me.

Press on. Bad things will pass on. Good things, too. But the one constant in your life will always be there: Me.

Just then, my phone buzzed. I pulled it out, and a text message from Riley popped up.

Just wanted to let you know that I've been thinking about you.

Great. What timing. Here I was having my spiritual breakthrough moment, and Riley contacts me.

This was where I had to put action to my words. It was one thing to make silent resolves. It was a whole different story to live them out. To live out my trust in God.

So, what did it mean that Riley was "thinking about me"? Was he jerking me around? I'd basically come to the conclusion that his "My therapist told me to do it" was the equivalent of "The devil made me do it." But what if he really was trying to do what was best for me and our relationship? I hadn't seriously considered that possibility since all of this happened.

Getting away was a good thing because it gave me space and distance from all the changes in my life. Sometimes, emotions clouded judgment, no matter how hard we tried to make it not happen that way.

I stared at the text another moment, considering how to respond. Finally, I settled on, *Hope they're all good thoughts.*

Lame, Gabby, I scolded myself as soon as I hit send.

I held my breath as I waited to see if he'd respond.

He did, with: *Of course. What else would there be?*

I nibbled my bottom lip for a moment, trying to think of something witty. Instead, I wrote: *Hope you're doing well, Riley.*

Instead of dwelling on what I'd like to say, I put the pillow down, spread out the blanket, and switched the lamp off. I needed some rest if I was going to get through class tomorrow, as well as try to help Trace.

My mind drifted to his story about "Doom and Groom." An amazingly bad experience in his life had turned into his success. I knew that was the way life worked sometimes, but I had to wonder how God might turn around things for me. Was there any way He could take my brokenness and my heartache and turn it into something to use for His good?

Could I change what had become a doom-and-gloom outlook into a vision for the future? I knew I could. Something was changing inside of me. I could feel it.

This was me. Gabby St. Claire. I was single. Independent. Well on my way to achieving success in the forensic world. One day, I'd look back on everything that had happened over the past year—even longer, if I started when my mom died—and I'd see that everything was working together for the good of those who were called in Christ Jesus.

I let out a long breath and tried to close my eyes. Only I realized I wasn't sleepy.

I pulled my eyes back open.

When I glanced at the window, I saw someone there staring inside at me.

IN WHAT MAY HAVE BEEN one of my dumbest moves ever—also known as HMS (Horror Movie Stupid)—I darted toward the door. I threw it open and darted outside onto the porch just in time to see a blue sedan squeal away down the street. I would have darted into my car and chased the Peeping Tom, if I'd actually *had* a car.

I tried to read the plates, but it was useless. It was too rainy and dark outside. Instead, I stomped my foot onto the cement, as if that would make anything better. How frustrating was it to be that close to answers, only to have the person I was looking for slip away?

"Gabby?"

I turned toward Trace. He held a phone in his

hands. He must have just gotten finished with his interview.

I pointed down the street. "Someone was just peering in your window. She drove off before I got here."

His face went pale. "A woman?"

I nodded. "I can't be sure, but it could have been Georgia. It all happened so fast."

He sighed and leaned against the doorframe. At once, he looked totally exhausted. "I was hoping she was gone for good, but I figured that was too good to be true."

"Trace, I'd like to look into Georgia some more. How would you feel if I dropped you off with the band and borrowed your truck? I'd like to stop by her house this morning. I doubt she'll be there, but at least I can question her neighbors and see what I can find out."

"Don't you have classes?"

I nodded, remembering a workshop about ballistics that I really wanted to attend. However, as Dr. Stone had reminded me, life was all about making decisions. Right now, I was deciding to focus on this case, especially since I wondered if Skye's disappearance had any connections with Dud's death. "I can miss just once. I'm only in town for a little while. I don't want to leave without any answers."

He stared at me a moment before nodding.

"You're a big girl. You make your own choices. But I don't want you doing this out of any obligation to me."

"No obligation. I'm just following my instincts."

He nodded. "Okay, then. You should probably try to grab a few hours of sleep first."

My body wanted rest, but my mind was racing a mile a minute. Despite that, Trace was right. I needed to get some shut-eye if I wanted to keep a clear head and sound mind. "Sounds good."

I stepped inside and Trace locked the door.

"Gabby." He turned toward me, worry in his gaze. "I hope I just didn't put you in danger. If that was Georgia, she might think you're competition, not family."

I bit down. That same thought had crossed my mind as well.

After a few hours of restless sleep, I pulled myself off the couch and stretched. My muscles were tight and sore. I felt like I hadn't rested at all, yet I remembered some vivid dreams that assured me I had drifted off.

I borrowed a toothbrush from Trace—an unopened one he'd gotten at the dentist—and did my best to clean up without any new clothes or makeup. Thankfully, the cowboy hat Trace had given me would conceal my frizzy hair.

Trace talked me into eating breakfast with him before heading out, and I agreed. He drove down the street to a hole-in-the-wall diner with a faded vinyl floor, sparkly tabletops, and waitresses who all looked like they should be retired.

Trace took a long sip of his coffee and leaned back in his vinyl chair. "So, that professor guy was a jerk, huh? You want me to go beat him up?"

I let out a chuckle at the thought of having a big brother come to my rescue. At my age, the thought was just humorous. Plus, I was pretty sure I was older than Trace.

"I think I can handle this myself. I was just so blindsided by how he acted. I've looked up to him for years. *Years.* Nowhere in any of my thoughts was he a jerk."

Trace frowned. "Guys can be like that. Sorry you had to go through it, though. You don't have anyone special waiting for you back home?"

My heart twisted at the thought. "I was kind of dating this guy named Garrett Mercer—"

"Of Global Coffee Initiative?" Trace's eyebrows shot up in recognition.

I smiled, forgetting how popular the man was. He'd graced magazine covers, been featured on national news shows, and even been invited to movie premiers. "Yes, the one and only."

"I love their coffee. Go on, though."

Just then, the waitress—who, no joke, was named Flo—set two big plates in front of us. I'd splurged. My breakfast feast consisted of bacon, eggs, home fries, and toast. Thankfully, I had no aspirations of being a supermodel, so I was going to enjoy every glorious, fattening bite.

I glanced at Trace's western omelet, complete with cheese, peppers, onions, sausage, and ham. He'd probably work all of that off just in rehearsal.

We bowed our heads and offered thanks before digging in.

"So, anyway, tell me about Garrett Mercer." Trace raised his fork. "You've heard all about my life—and my problems. I want to hear more about you."

"He invited me to Africa with him."

"Africa? On a safari or something?"

I shook my head. "No, he's touring the area where his company has built wells for the less fortunate."

"Sounds like the opportunity of a lifetime."

"I said no." I stabbed one of my potatoes. "I felt like I needed to stay around and try to get focused instead of bouncing from whim to whim. Especially after everything that happened with Riley."

"Is Riley the man who was shot by Scum?"

I nodded, my gut still twisting when I heard the nickname of the notorious serial killer. He'd turned my life upside down. I'd survived, yet pieces of me had died in the process. "I guess your mom told you about that?"

Teddi had also been abducted by the man, all in a revenge plot to get back at Riley and me. It was only by God's grace that we'd come out alive.

"She did. It sounded tragic for everyone involved. I was in Brazil when it happened. I know it's hard to believe, but we're actually pretty popular down there. When I got within cell phone range, I got the messages about what had happened. By that time, Teddi was back at home and safe. She told me not to come, that she was fine."

"She's a strong woman." She was. At first, I thought I'd resent it if my dad dated anyone else. After all, there was no one like my mom. But Teddi was truly sweet, and she was so good for my dad. She'd never be my mom, but I'd be honored to have her as a stepmom.

"Tell me about Riley."

Sadness pressed on my heart. "I was supposed to marry him. I was picking out my wedding dress with Teddi when I got the news that he'd been shot. Life hasn't been the same since then. I try not to feel sorry for myself, but it's difficult when a homicidal maniac changes the course of your life. I have to accept that everything happens for a purpose, even something as tragic as what Riley went through."

"Is he out of your life now?"

The burden on my shoulders pressed harder. "Kind of. I mean, just when I think he's out, he comes waltzing back in. His therapist says it's better to start any romantic relationships over fresh. He said most relationships don't survive a brain injury like his."

Trace slowed the pace he was downing his food. "Is he progressing?"

I remembered when I'd seen Riley in January at a local community theater production. It had been nice to see him, but hard also—hard because it made me realize everything I'd lost, all because of a senseless act of violence. "He seems to be."

"You still care about him, don't you?"

I shrugged, staring out the window a moment at a truck that pulled up and the cowboy who stepped out. "I think I'll always love Riley. The question is: How can I love him and move on?"

"Why do you have to?"

"Because moving on is what everyone keeps telling me to do. They make it sound like it's as easy as buying a new car. Like it's something you just get done and over with. It hasn't been that easy in my life."

"Moving on is something that has to happen organically. You have to give it time, give yourself space and mercy, stay positive about the future. Getting a dog usually helps, too." He flashed a grin.

"I suppose you're right."

"Sometimes, moving on isn't exactly what we envision it's going to be. Sometimes it's getting to a place where we're okay with the future, whatever it holds."

"You're pretty smart, you know that?"

He blew on his fingers and rubbed them on his chambray shirt. "I like to think so. They do pay me to wax philosophical about life and love, preferably with a touch of twang on the side."

I smiled. "What about you? What happens if we don't find Skye?"

His expression turned serious. "I'm not sure. I can't move on from the fact that she may have been hurt because of me."

"Because of *Georgia*," I corrected.

He nodded. "Because of Georgia."

"I'm hoping I can find you some closure, Trace."

"I'm hoping you get some closure yourself, Gabby."

I dropped Trace off at the warehouse where they were rehearsing and then programmed Georgia's address into my phone's GPS. As I moseyed down the road, I replayed last night in my mind, and a fire lit in my gut.

Levi Stone was not going to dictate my life for me. Nor would I let all the setbacks define me. It was time I dusted off my boots and took some initiative for myself. I knew I had what it took to succeed in forensics. And now was the time that I was going to do something about it.

I dialed Margo Grayson's number. I'd met her at a fund-raising gala a few months ago. She was the CEO of Grayson Technologies, a manufacturer of the supplies used to collect evidence at crime scenes. I had her number programmed into my phone.

I couldn't believe it when I was actually patched through to her. I really should have planned what to say a little more. "Mrs. Grayson, this is Gabby St. Claire. I'm a friend of Garrett Mercer's, and we met—"

"Yes, I remember you. We met in Cincinnati."

That gave me a little more courage to go on. "Yes, that's correct. You'd mentioned when we met that I should talk to you sometime if I ever wanted to work as a representative for you. I'm interested."

"Really? Well, that's wonderful to hear. I have to say, though, that we're not looking for any representatives right now. I filled that spot a couple of months ago."

My heart sank. "I understand."

"But I am looking for another trainer. It's only part-time and requires some travel."

"I'd love to hear more."

"Of course. Basically, the person will travel to various seminars and police departments to train people there on how to properly use equipment. You obviously have experience."

"That sounds like something I'd definitely be interested in."

"I'd love to do an interview with you. Maybe sometime next week?"

My heart sped with excitement. "That would be great."

"I'll let my secretary set something up then. We can do it over the phone. Send us your resume and a letter of interest, via email, beforehand."

After I talked to Mrs. Grayson's secretary, I put the phone down and smiled. Maybe the whole fiasco with Levi wasn't entirely terrible. It had given me the push I needed to take some initiative.

Thirty minutes later, I pulled up to an apartment complex on the outskirts of Oklahoma City.

I'd assumed Georgia was on the run or in hiding. But assumptions were dangerous things. I needed to know for sure if she was here, living her life as normal, or if her normal routines had been disrupted. It was probably one of the first places I should have started, but Dud's death had caused me to kick my investigation up a notch.

I went to the door marked 298 and knocked. No one answered, which wasn't surprising. On a whim, I knocked on the two doors on either side of apartment 298. Again, no one answered. I supposed everyone was at work. However, I really didn't want to come all the way out here for nothing.

With that in mind, I went down to the apartment manager's office. A woman with short, poofy blonde hair answered the door after I buzzed. Her apartment reeked of cigarette smoke and cat hair.

"Interested in an apartment application?"

I shook my head. "I'm actually a PI, and I'm trying to locate one of your residents."

She started to shut the door. "If it doesn't make me money, I'm not interested."

"This is a matter of life or death," I told her.

That made her pause. "Life or death?"

"It's about Georgia Dalton."

"Is Georgia in some kind of trouble?"

"You could say that."

She studied me a moment. "You say you're a PI?"

I nodded. "That's correct. It's of vital importance that I locate Georgia. Any help you can give me would be great."

"I don't know what I can tell you." She crossed her bony arms over her blue velvet housecoat.

"When you saw her last, for starters."

"Two weeks ago. Her rent was due, she never paid, and I haven't seen her since."

"Does she work?"

The woman sighed and turned. I thought she was finished talking to me, but then she opened a file drawer and began rifling through it. I stepped inside, and a moment later, she pulled out some papers and shuffled through them.

"Hair Kingdom. It's in downtown Lawton." She scanned some more papers and then looked back up at me. "She was always a bit peculiar. I hate to think of something happening to her."

I stopped myself from saying that she wasn't *in* danger, but she was *the* danger. I'd keep that to myself until I had more proof. I pulled out an outdated business card. It had Squeaky Clean at the top, but I hoped she might ignore that and focus solely on my name and phone number. "If you think of anything else, will you call me?"

"I suppose."

Once back in the truck, I pulled out my phone and found the number for Hair Kingdom. I asked for an appointment with Georgia.

"I'm sorry. She no longer works here."

I bit on my lip for a minute, not willing to let my one and only lead slip away. "How about her friend who works there? I forget her name, but I know Georgia recommended her as a last-minute backup."

"You mean Poppy?"

Bingo! "Yes, Poppy. That sounds right. Does she have any free time today?"

Silence stretched for a minute, and I heard computer keys tapping. "How fast can you get here?"

I took a stab at it. "Thirty minutes, probably."

"Then she can squeeze you in, if it's nothing complicated."

"I just need my hair fixed for an event I have tonight."

"Great. We'll see you in thirty."

CHAPTER
SIXTEEN

I ARRIVED five minutes early for my appointment and walked into a trendy-looking salon filled with workers with trendy clothes and trendy hair in a shop located in a—you guessed it—trendy-looking shopping center. A woman at the desk greeted me and immediately led me to a station in the corner and introduced me to Poppy.

Poppy had black hair that was cut into a blunt wedge. She was tall with sharp features and well-tanned skin. Her clothes were all too tight, and tattoos peeked out from every available spot—beneath her sleeves, on her midriff, up her neck.

She popped the gum in her mouth. "What can I do for you?"

She stood behind me and started picking at pieces

of my hair as she stared at me in the mirror with a cool detachment.

I stared at my reflection in the mirror and realized how tired I looked and what a huge mistake it had been to forget my styling gel when I packed. "I'd like a blowout."

She sulked. "With these curls? It's going to take some time to straight iron these."

"That's why I pay someone else to do it. I have no patience to do it myself." I flashed a smile.

"Let's get you shampooed, then."

I tried to be long-suffering as she washed my hair, because that was no time to strike up a conversation. I also tried to persevere as she blow-dried my hair, tugging mercilessly at my strands. That was also a terrible time to try and talk.

All of that said, I realized my time was whittling away and I should have probably chosen something simpler like just a haircut. Then I would have had plenty of time to try and get information out of her.

Finally, she put the hair dryer down and picked up the flat iron. It was just in time, too, because my hair right now looked like Bozo's right after he stuck his finger in a light socket.

"So, Georgia usually does my hair. Did I hear she's not here anymore?" I tried to sound casual.

She shrugged. "Yeah, she's gone. No one really knows what happened to her."

"She didn't turn in her notice or anything?"

She shrugged again. "Maybe she went to another salon. It's not usual. She probably tried to take her clients with her, which we sign a clause saying we're not going to do. Maybe quitting without explanation was the easiest way to get around it. Of course, I guess this means she didn't contact you." She raised her eyebrows as if to say, "Too bad, too sad."

I ignored the look. "Did anyone ever think it was suspicious she didn't come back?"

She raised an eyebrow. "You know something I don't?"

"I mean, if she went on her own, I'm totally offended that she didn't contact me. I considered myself to be a loyal client."

That seemed to appease her, because she shrugged. Still, she said nothing.

"I always get suspicious when people drop off the radar," I continued. "My cousin did that once. Turned out she ran off with her boyfriend, who was a drug addict. She's had a horrible life ever since then."

"Girls are so stupid like that sometimes. The things they do for men. I hope I'm never like that. Georgia . . . well, she might have had those tendencies. Call it daddy issues or whatever; she seemed to think she needed a man in her life in order to feel valued."

"That can be dangerous." I hoped I wasn't like

that, but something about her words struck me. It seemed like I always had a guy in my life. This was the first time in a long time that I was alone, and I wanted to appreciate just being me, without someone by my side. Despite that, I refused to think that Georgia and I were alike.

"Tell me about it." Poppy sprayed my hair. "If she didn't leave for another salon, then she probably dropped everything to become a Trace Ryan groupie."

Something buzzed through my blood. Now we were getting somewhere! "She was obsessed with his music, wasn't she? Even I realized that, and I was just a client."

"*Obsessed* is an understatement, and it wasn't just about his music. She was obsessed with Trace himself. Even claimed to go out on a date with him once." She rolled her eyes.

I stored away that information. Had she told people there was more to their relationship? Certainly there wasn't any truth to her words . . . right? Trace would have told me if there was. "You don't believe it?"

She shook her head. "No, I don't. Believe me, she would have pictures if she did."

"Was she like . . ." I struggled to find the appropriate words. "Stalker-like obsessed with him?"

Poppy froze. "You're really asking me that? Because it seems random."

"I've been accused of being random before."

"I guess I'm okay with random."

"Besides, I just read this article in *People* magazine about celebrities and the danger they're in because of the paparazzi and our celebrity-obsessed culture. It's really gotten me thinking."

"Sounds like you think a lot. That can be a bad thing." She continued spraying down my tresses. "Anyway, I don't think she would take it that far. Groupie, yes. Stalker, no."

"What makes you so sure? I mean, where are those lines exactly?" I shrugged. "It's something I've always wondered."

She paused and eyed me suspiciously. "It almost sounds like you're the one stalking Georgia."

I cringed, realizing I'd gone too far. I tried to shrug, hoping I didn't look guilty. "I'm just the curious sort."

"Curious, yes." She said it like an insult. Despite that, she went on to say, "Look, I like Georgia. I want to believe she's decent and doing okay for herself. But she was acting strangely in the week or two before she disappeared."

I knew I was pushing it, but I couldn't stop asking questions. I needed to know more. I needed to hear

Poppy's interpretation of all of this. "Why do you think that was?"

"I have no idea. I asked her about it once, and she nearly jumped out of her skin. She said she just had a lot going on." She flat ironed another section of my hair before twirling my chair back toward the mirror. "What do you think?"

I stared at my reflection, hardly recognizing myself. The smooth hair softened my features and made me look less spunky and more . . . pretty, I supposed. "I like it."

"It gives you an entirely different look." She took the cape off and walked me toward the front counter.

The receptionist quoted me the price, and I gaped. It was more than my monthly cell phone bill. I hoped it was worth both my time and my money. However, even if it wasn't, at least I had good hair for a day.

By the time I left Hair Kingdom and grabbed a burger at a local fast food joint, I had just enough time to swing past the residence of Quinton McLe-witz. Trace had gotten his information from Jono. He'd then texted me the man's name and address while I was getting my hair done. He was the guard who'd supposedly been on duty at the tent where Dud had died. I had a few questions for him.

Quinton lived in a townhouse about thirty minutes from Lawton. A car was parked on the cracked concrete driveway out front, so I hoped that was a good sign. Feeling more confident than usual thanks to my smooth new hair, I approached the door, saw a piece of duct tape over the doorbell, and decided to knock. I was observant like that.

A few seconds later, the door opened and there stood Quinton. He looked different without his uniform. He wore a stained T-shirt and old jeans and had some food stuck in his scruff. "Can I help you?" he asked.

Obviously, he didn't recognize me yet. Maybe it was the hair.

"I wanted to ask you a few questions about Dud Larson," I started.

His face paled, and he stepped back, waving his hands in the air like an air traffic controller saying, "Don't approach!"—only more frantically. "I don't have anything to say."

"Please. I'm not with the police or the media. I'm just asking as a friend."

He paused and viewed me as one might stare at a pit bull, wondering if the dog was going to attack. "You were at the scene that day. You were with the police."

"But I'm not the police," I told him. "Truth be told, I'm a crime scene cleaner."

That was the one advantage to my job—knowing I was a blue-collar worker seemed to make certain people trust me more quickly. Whether I liked it or not, there were just some people out there who didn't like law enforcement officials for one reason or another.

"What do you want to know?"

"Who'd you let into the tent with Dud?" I held my breath, waiting to see how he'd respond.

"Excuse me? I've already been through this. I didn't let anyone in. Nor did I see anyone go in. End of story." He stepped back again, his hand on the door and his scrawny face scrunched up in frustration.

"Listen, this is just between you and me. But I think you know more. You're claiming that you were probably talking to a pretty girl and he slipped inside. But I know you play the guitar."

I didn't know that until a few minutes ago when I spotted an old Fender inside his place. He didn't have to know that, though.

"What's that have to do with anything?" He looked at me like I was a pit bull again.

"It's just a hunch. But did you ever talk to Dud about music?"

He hesitated before rolling one shoulder back and raising his chin. "Maybe once or twice."

"Getting to know someone like Dud—getting in

his good graces—that might help open up some doors for you."

"Anyone would tell you that." He clucked his tongue as he nodded.

"What I'm wondering is if Dud made you some kind of promise in exchange for you letting him into the tent with a girl."

He rubbed his beard and remained silent for a moment. "That's a pretty big accusation for such a little girl."

His words made me abrasive. "We can do this the easy way. You can talk to me, and I'll use that information to benefit my investigation. Or we can do it the hard way, and I can report to the police that you know more than you're letting on. What's it going to be?"

He raised his hands in innocence. "I don't want any trouble. I had no idea what was going to happen that night. I just thought Dud was trying to impress a girl. You can't blame a guy for that."

"So he did ask you if he could go into the tent?"

"Yeah, he asked me. Said he was going to introduce me to some friend of his who was looking for a guitarist. He told me I could go hang out with the band at Wentworth's ranch sometimes and Trace would give me some pointers."

"Really?" It sounded like quite the deal.

"Yes, really. He insisted he wasn't going to cause any trouble. He just needed some privacy."

"Did Dud and this woman act like they were a couple?"

Quinton shrugged. "Hard to say. They weren't holding hands or anything. There was some tension between them. I couldn't tell if it was romantic or angry. All I cared about was that gig Dud had for me. I've been playing for years, hoping the right door would open for me. I thought it could be my in."

That was all fine and dandy, but his future was the least of my worries at the moment.

"Describe the girl again."

He looked off into the distance and pressed his lips together in thought. "I don't know. She had dark hair. Really dark. She was medium height. Thin. Kind of quiet. She seemed kind of eager about something, but she didn't really say a lot."

Had Georgia disguised herself as Skye and blackmailed Dud into meeting with her? Or maybe they'd had a romantic relationship? Since Trace wasn't interested, had she moved on to Dud? But, if that were the case, why had she killed Dud? I still had so many questions.

"So, spell out for me what happened that night. You were guarding the tent because there was expensive sound equipment inside. As you were at the door, Dud came up and whispered this little arrangement to you. You agreed. How much longer was it before we discovered Dud's dead body?"

"About thirty minutes, I suppose."

"You didn't hear any gunfire?"

He shook his head. "The music coming from the other tent was loud. I didn't hear a thing. I've felt terrible about all of this since it happened."

"But not terrible enough to go to the police?"

He leaned toward me. "Look, I've got a son. I've got to pay child support. I can't afford to lose this job. Are you going to tell the police?"

I stared at him a moment, contemplating my answer. Finally, I shook my head. "No, I'll keep this quiet—unless it becomes crucial to the investigation. I'll do whatever I can to protect you, though."

"Thank you."

I nodded, needing to let this new information sink in.

After talking to Quinton, I made my way back to the warehouse where the band was rehearsing. It took me nearly two hours. Rush hour was in full swing, and I was tenser than a cat on a tightrope over water by the time I parked and walked inside.

For the first time today, I wondered what I'd missed at my conference. I hated to pay the money for it and then not show up. But it had been good to dig into the investigation and get my hands dirty.

It had also been good to avoid Dr. Levi Stone.

I frowned at the mere thought of him. I'd had him up on a pedestal that he never deserved to be on. His fall had squashed me but didn't affect him at all. Arrogance was like that—it made people oblivious.

I leaned against the back wall and listened to the band. It just wasn't the same onstage without Dud. There was another drummer, but the band kept stopping in order to talk about how songs should be played. I could see the frustration and grief on Trace's face.

"They're almost finished," someone said.

I looked over and saw Jono standing beside me, his arms crossed as he watched the band finish rehearsing.

"I'll just wait," I told him.

"If you can't tell, they're trying out a new drummer."

"That's gotta be hard."

He shrugged. "You have to do what you have to do. They can't afford to lose any momentum right now. It's a hard reality, but reality can be like that. They'll have plenty of time to mourn once this tour is over."

"That seems harsh."

He scowled at me. "What can I say? Timing is

everything. Stopping the tour right now would be a huge mistake. I'm not sure if the band would recover. I've been trying to ready Trace all day for a press conference. He needs to seem sad yet hopeful. Our A&R guy has been rehearsing with him all morning."

Nothing I'd say would change Jono's mind about how insensitive he was being, so I just leaned against the wall to wait for Trace to finish. I needed to give his truck back, plus I was going to update him.

Jono shook his head beside me. "Next week at this time, they'll be off on a 150-city tour. But it's going to take a lot of work before then. They're making a lot of mistakes today."

I listened to the band and I didn't notice anything. "You mean the drummer is making a lot of mistakes?"

He let out a long sigh. "I know it doesn't look like anything is choreographed onstage, but everything is planned and on purpose. There's a science to being a good performer. Rule number one is that you have to make it look like you haven't practiced. Everyone's off their game today."

"Considering what happened, that's not surprising. All of this sounds complicated."

"It is complicated. That's why so many people fail in this business. They can be the most talented person musically, but if they don't have that 'it' factor, they're not going to succeed. This isn't the music business it was fifty years ago, when just talent alone could get you by."

I crossed my arms, talking louder than usual in order to be heard over the music. "You think Trace has the 'it' factor?"

He scoffed. "Think it? I know it. That's the only reason I agreed to manage the band. Trace has the talent, the look, and everything else in between. I know a sure bet when I see one."

Since Jono was being chatty, I decided to seize the moment. "I heard Lenny was pretty upset when you swooped in and took over."

"I hardly swooped in. I was hired." He rolled his eyes.

"Didn't you pursue them?" No one had directly said that, but I could see Jono as the type to go after potential clients.

"Nothing wrong with going after what you want. I saw potential in Trace." He pushed his glasses up higher. "Lenny just wasn't cutting it. He was holding the band back instead of moving them forward."

"I'm sure there were some hard feelings there."

"You know what I say: all's fair in love and music."

I glanced at him, narrowing my eyes. "Is that what they say?"

He shrugged, a small smile curling the corners of his lips. "That's what I say."

"You and Lenny ever have any confrontations about this? I could see where he might think you'd stolen his job. There's a lot of potential for negative feelings."

"He's got to be a big boy and grow up. I don't know what else I can say."

"I see."

"How's your investigation going?"

"I haven't found as many answers as I would have liked. I'm not ready to give up yet, though."

He glanced at me with his beady, high-strung eyes. "Look, I want all of this cleared up just as much as anyone, but sometimes I think Trace is just being dramatic."

His words threw me off guard. "She's done some disturbing things. In fact, I thought I saw her spying on me when I was at Trace's place."

Jono shook his head and flipped his hand in the air in a nonchalant manner. "Trace led her on, and she didn't know how to accept his rejection. End of story. I just wish Trace would get over this. It's really getting old."

"Why would you say Trace led her on?"

"He gave her some attention and then started to brush her off. She thought it was more than he did. Same old story that's happened since dating began." He rattled it off like it was a grocery list or something.

I didn't like Jono's reaction to what had happened. How could he be so flippant about everything?

Unless Trace hadn't shared with him everything that had occurred with Georgia.

It was the only thing I could think of.

"You've heard about everything that's happened?" I was trying to give him the benefit of the doubt. Really. I mean, Jono was the one who'd assembled that folder full of information. I thought he was invested in this.

"He's reading too much into things. He has a flare for drama. It helps with his charisma factor, but he's going to have to get used to women wanting to be groupies. He can't yell 'fire' every time." He shook his head. "I can't tell Trace that, though. Stars have to be treated very carefully."

"I'm sorry, but did you say there's been another occasion?"

Jono nodded. "Yeah, there has been. I wasn't his manager then, but apparently a year ago he thought another woman was following him everywhere. He even thought she broke into his house. There was never any proof. If you ask me, it's because it never happened."

I absorbed the information. Before I could ask any more questions, Trace spoke into his microphone. "I'm going to be running late, Gabby. It's probably going to be another hour or two. You good with that?"

Truth was that I was exhausted, and I was mad at myself for not having a car right now. Make that, I was mad at Levi, since he was the reason I didn't have a car.

I waved to him, and he took it as a sign I was okay. He ran his pick across his guitar strings again and began tuning a wayward string.

I turned to Jono. "I'm going to get a cab. I'd really like to get back. Could you give Trace his keys back and let him know?"

He offered a tight smile. "Of course. Anything for Trace's future stepsister."

But I had a feeling he couldn't wait for me to get out of town. He was determined not to let anything ruin Trace's tour. I wondered if he thought of me as a liability also.

SEVENTEEN

I STEPPED OUTSIDE of the warehouse just as a faded old yellow sedan pulled up. I eyed the passengers stuffed inside for a moment. Finally, the window rolled down and a college-aged girl with glossy auburn hair and wide, dancing eyes stuck her head out.

"Is this where Trace Ryan rehearses?"

I wanted to deny it, but Trace could clearly be heard singing in the background. "Maybe."

A car full of squeals sounded. "I knew this was it, girls! I knew it. We found him!"

Another round of squeals emerged.

Groupies, I realized. This was my chance to find out some more information about Georgia.

I pulled up Psycho Woman's picture on my phone, knowing I needed to make the most of this opportunity. Wasn't that where success happened? Where preparation and opportunity met? Those self-help books might pay off after all.

"Have any of you ever seen this woman?" I asked.

My phone got passed around.

"Why do you want to know?" the driver finally asked, not so much with hostility as curiosity.

"We're worried something happened to her," I responded. "She was a die-hard fan; that's why I thought one of you might recognize her."

"Who are you?" The driver's voice was still light, like she was storing the information away to embellish later when she got back to campus or when she wrote her next killer Facebook post.

"I'm an investigator who's searching for her. Anyone leading us to information that helps us find this woman will have the opportunity to meet Trace Ryan and get backstage passes."

Another round of squeals. I hadn't confirmed that, but I felt sure Trace would be willing. I hoped so, at least.

"I've seen her before. My name is Bridgette, and I can give you my phone number," a brunette in the back said, rolling down her window.

"Tell me more," I pushed.

"She was named after a state. Savannah, maybe?" Bridgette scrunched her pert little nose.

"Savannah's not a state, idiot!" the girl sitting beside her said, swatting her friend on the arm.

"Ouch. Whatever. I just got confused." She rolled her eyes.

"I think it was Georgia," the driver said. "Yeah, we've seen her around. We go to every concert. She's always there. She always acted entitled to be near Trace, you know what I mean? She'd give us dirty looks like we were beneath her and she was the deserving one."

That was obviously the ultimate insult to these fan girls, because they acted like the homecoming queen was trying to steal their collective boyfriend.

"When was the last time you saw her?" I asked.

They all looked at each other, as if they had to confer before answering.

"Probably a couple of weeks ago. At that concert in Austin," the driver said.

"Austin, Texas?" I clarified.

She nodded. "That's right. If it's within a certain driving distance, we try to make it. Austin was kind of pushing it, but it was a great concert, wasn't it?"

Her gaggle of friends agreed.

"Anytime we see Trace Ryan, it's great," the back-seat girl who thought Savannah was a state said.

"Did she ever say anything about herself? This girl." I raised my phone, thinking a couple of them might need additional clarification.

They all glanced at each other and shrugged.

"Not really," the driver said. "Everything was about Trace. Where he was playing next. How good he looked in his jeans. How his voice made her swoon."

"Did anything else ever strike you as odd about her?" I asked. "Other than her obsession with Trace."

"I heard her say one time that she knew she and Trace would end up together one day," Driver Girl said. "I thought that was weird. I mean, really? I'd never even seen Trace talk to her. She seemed to think they were going to get married or something."

"Oh, and I think I heard her mention that she'd started a fan page," Backseat Savannah said. "She said she was talking to the drummer—or was it the guitar player?—about getting some more information, maybe some never-seen-before photos. Apparently, she wasn't above using people to get what she wanted."

Interesting. Maybe Georgia really was that scheming. Which really meant that this case was becoming more dangerous all the time.

As I rode back in the cab, my mind turned over what I'd learned today. Based on what Jono had told me about another potential stalker, was Trace one who liked to cry wolf? Was Georgia innocent here and Trace just exaggerating? I found that hard to believe. Besides, I'd seen that woman peering into Trace's house.

Then there was Skye. Maybe she was just a gypsy who didn't like to stay in one place for too long, and maybe all my investigating was for nothing. It was a possibility I needed to face. I'd be foolish if I didn't.

And what about the information Fan Girls had given me? Had Georgia manipulated another band member into helping her? Had she manipulated *Dud* into helping her? Perhaps she'd gotten close to him, just so she could be nearer to Trace.

I shook my head. I just didn't know.

Just as I pulled into OKC, Trace texted me and asked if I wanted to meet tonight to hang out. He said he'd come out to my part of town and meet me.

I thought about it a moment. Why not? Even though I was tired, I'd still like to ask him a few more questions.

The cab driver dropped me off in front of the convention center hotel, I handed over nearly all my cash, and then I started toward the front door. I noticed the same sidewalk prophet standing on the corner, holding signs about the end being near.

Maybe that's what I needed to do to proclaim my faith. Stand on the city streets and yell at everyone who passed. That just wasn't my way of spreading the gospel message, though, and I didn't think it would ever be.

"Ma'am!"

I paused, knowing good and well who was talking to me. I slowly turned toward the Willie Nelson lookalike. "Yes?"

"She's watching you," he said, his eyes so wide the whites were visible. He jabbed a finger toward me and stared.

I shuddered, though I wasn't sure if it was because of how he looked or what he said. Maybe both. "What?"

He nodded, his skin vibrating at the intensity of the motion. "Danger lurks close."

I tried to brush off his words as those of a crazy man. That had to be it. Right? It wasn't like the man was really a prophet. Not even a psychic. At the most, the man had mental problems. At the least, he was just passionate about proselytizing. But still, I felt a little rattled.

I hurried inside, desperate to get away from the craziness. I had no idea what I'd do tonight, but at least I'd have the freedom to set my own schedule and not rely on anyone else for transportation.

Much to my dismay, the first person I saw when I walked into the building was Evie. She stood with a phone to her ear near the front door, wearing almost all black again.

Winona Ryder, I decided. That's who she reminded me of, only with less expression and more of a goth vibe.

As soon as she saw me, she put away her phone and approached me. "There are better ways to get ahead, you know."

I stopped and gave her my best no-nonsense stare. "What?"

She looked down at me, her eyes full of challenge. "You don't have to sleep with Dr. Stone to advance your career."

My arms went to my hips as fire heated my blood. "What in the world are you talking about? Are you on drugs or something?"

"I saw you leave with him yesterday. And now you're wearing the same thing as you were last night. I can put things together, Gabby. I'm not a member of Mensa for nothing."

"You're making a lot of assumptions."

She twisted her head. "Am I?"

"I may have had a lapse in judgment, but you've got all of this wrong. Dr. Stone is a first-class jerk. But I'm not the type to use people to get ahead. Get that through your Mensa-sized brain. I've worked for everything—everything—I've got in this life. It may not be much, but I've earned it all through tears, sweat, and hard work. So, why don't you go pick on someone else?" Anger singed my voice. She'd obviously hit a soft spot. But I was really tired of people assuming things.

I started to walk away, to storm back to my room, for that matter, when Evie called me. "I'm sorry, Gabby."

Her voice sounded soft, sincere.

After drawing in a deep breath, I slowly turned. I needed mercy in my life. That meant I needed to offer it to other people also, even people who didn't deserve it. "But are you?"

She cut her eyes to the left and right and then stepped closer. "I was up for a position in Chicago. It was between me and another woman. The other woman was 'friends' with Dr. Stone, who just happened to be working there at the time. Needless to say, the other woman ended up getting the position, even though I was more qualified. I guess you could say I'm still bitter."

"I had no idea that Dr. Stone had this kind of reputation."

She nodded coldly. "He does. It makes me sick. He's a narcissist. And yes, that is my official opinion."

I shook my head and decided to explain even more. "I had to get a ride home last night, and one thing had snowballed into another. That's why I'm just getting back."

She stared at me another minute, her dark eyes

obviously calculating something. "Have you had dinner yet?"

"No, I haven't."

"Want to grab something?"

"I'd love to." Even though some solitude in my hotel room was calling me, Evie had me intrigued. I wanted to know more about Dr. Stone, and she seemed to be just the person to ask. "But it will have to be close. As you reminded me, I'm still wearing what I wore yesterday."

"There's a place right down the street where I've been hanging out after the conference. We can walk there."

We talked about Evie's career as we walked the three blocks to this restaurant she was sure I'd love. She had big dreams of essentially doing what Dr. Stone did now. She wanted to write books, consult, speak, and head up national forensic organizations. She sounded smart enough to do just that.

I pulled my coat tighter as I listened to her speak. For a moment, I felt jealous. She'd seen what she'd wanted in life and gone after it. That was more than I could say for myself.

"Hi, Evie!" A man with a bright, silly smile on his face approached us on the sidewalk.

I studied him as he got closer. He was of average height, thin, and had thick dark hair and wire-framed glasses. He wasn't classically handsome, but instead studiously nerdy. I'd seen him in one of the classes I'd attended.

"Oh, no," Evie muttered. Louder, she said, "Hi, Sherman."

He stopped beside us. "What a coincidence we ran into each other. Do you know what the probability of that is? It's like 2.34 out of more than a thousand. It's pretty crazy."

Evie grunted, looking uninterested.

"You two just heading out?" Sherman continued, his puppy-dog-like gaze volleying between the two of us.

Evie nodded. "That's right. We're grabbing some supper."

"I'd love to grab a meal together sometime while we're here. I mean, if you're available. Not, like, *available* available, just if your schedule is free." Every inch of visible skin on his face turned bright red.

"I'll check and see," she said coolly before starting to walk again. "Good running into you."

"You too!" he called, a little too brightly and eagerly.

I flashed him a smile, hoping to reassure him not to take Evie personally, before continuing down the street. The poor guy had it bad. "I think he likes you."

She scowled. "He's been following me around like a lovesick teenager all week."

"Do you work together?"

"No, he's a computer forensic scientist from Kansas. We actually know each other from Mensa. He's a know-it-all, and he's always quoting off-the-wall facts. Who really cares about the probability of us running into each other? And, for that matter, his statistics didn't sound anywhere close to correct. We're at the same conference, for goodness' sakes. That increases the likelihood exponentially."

I hid my smile. "Not interested?"

"I prefer to be married to my career. Relationships will only fail me. My career won't."

Her words surprised me. "You really feel that way?"

"Yes, really. I don't have time for games or dating or people who try to toy with my emotions. I have a lot to do in this life and only one chance to get it right."

I felt the same way about the time I'd been given here on this earth, but I tended to put more emphasis on relationships in that aspect. In a way, her words were true, though. I'd given up a lot for my relationships, starting when my mom was diagnosed with cancer. I'd dropped out of college to help out. Then I'd put my job search on hold to take care of Riley.

Did I regret those things? I knew I didn't. But life would be different right now if I'd made other choices. Maybe Dr. Stone was right. I hated to admit it, but maybe I needed to really buckle down.

I didn't believe in only looking out for myself. There was no fulfillment in that. But maybe how I'd been living wasn't the best choice either. One way or another, I really needed to think long and hard about my future.

"Since you're not interested in Dr. Stone, is there anyone else in your life? A boyfriend back home?"

I shook my head. And, yet again, I found myself pouring out the story about Riley. All of it.

"You really should give him time, you know," she said.

I blanched. "What?" I was not used to hearing that. I was used to hearing people telling me that enough was enough.

"Yeah, traumatic brain injury is difficult. I know everyone says that relationships always suffer afterward, but the truth is that they change more than they suffer. I think the statistics are overblown."

I paused on the sidewalk. "What are you saying?"

She shrugged. "It's your life. I'm just saying that as a psychologist, I can attest to what all the professionals have told your ex. I can also tell that you still care about this guy, and that's half of the battle. Give him time."

"You're the first person who hasn't told me to move on."

"Sometimes moving on isn't about making drastic changes. Sometimes moving on just means being sure of who you are; that way you know that whatever the future holds, you'll be okay."

Before I could fully absorb her words, we stopped.

"Here we are," Evie said, pulling open the door to a corner restaurant called Barbarians.

Much to my surprise, it looked like a cave inside. Not only that, but all the servers were dressed like cavemen and -women. The smell of steak and other sizzling meats made my stomach grumble like any true meat eater's would.

"Cool, huh? I discovered it by accident on the first night when I was walking around."

"Interesting." Probably not my first choice of a relaxing place to hang out, but I went with it. Besides, now that she'd mentioned food, I was starving.

We were seated at a chunky wooden table, and I ordered a petite sirloin with a baked potato and broccoli. Apparently, all the food was what might be served during prehistoric times. It was a fun twist on the whole-foods trend that most of my friends were embracing.

"So, what happened with Dr. Stone?" Evie asked, picking at a dinner roll.

As last night flashed back into my mind, I frowned. "He wanted more than I could give. I had no idea he had that reputation." I shook my head. "I'm really not naïve. I guess I just had him up on a pedestal."

"A lot of people do, but he's full of himself. He's let all his success go to his head, and people have let him. Honestly, he thinks he's better than he is."

"You really don't think highly of him, do you?" I took a long sip of water, not realizing how parched I was.

She stared at me a moment. "Can you blame me?"

I shook my head. "No, not at all."

"Apparently, that's why his wife left him. She couldn't take his little trysts on the side anymore."

"The more I hear, the more I think he's a horrible person."

Evie eyed me a moment, her jaw twitching. Finally, she shared the thoughts that had been brewing in her mind. "I have to warn you. A couple of other conferees saw the two of you leave together yesterday. The rumor mill may have already started up."

"*May* have? Is there something you're not telling

me?" I braced myself for her response, worst-case scenarios rushing through my mind.

"I try not to gossip, but the doctor has a reputation for having his flavors of the week at conferences like this."

I sighed and leaned back. "This is what I get for being out of the loop, I suppose."

"No woman deserves to be treated like this, in or out of the loop, no matter what she's done or what's happened to her to lead her to this point. Men like Dr. Stone disgust me."

I decided to nibble on the roll some more, even though my appetite was leaving me. "Thank you."

I could read between the lines, though. Most likely, I'd be wearing my scarlet letter for the rest of the week.

Silence fell for a moment, but I could tell that Evie was still thinking.

Evie slathered some butter on another roll. "So, where did you go after the good doctor made a pass at you?"

"I had to call my future stepbrother. I spent the rest of the day investigating a new case."

"A new case? While you're here, off work, in Oklahoma? Tell me more."

Since she offered, I did. I told her everything about Georgia and Skye and Dud. I even added my new doubts that maybe Lenny had something to do with this or even Jono.

"Sounds intriguing."

I nodded. "The problem is that I don't have much time. My plane leaves on Saturday, and I'm not planning on coming back out here again after that."

"That makes things more complicated."

"This case seems bigger than what can be done in the interim."

"Do you think the cases are connected?" She took a bite of her roll.

"I can't see how."

Evie stared at me. "I don't believe in coincidences. Two crimes surrounding the same group of people within a one-month time period? It would be worth investigating to see if there are any other links."

I nodded. "You're right. I should see if there are any connections."

"You really should look into getting your doctorate, Gabby. I think you could go really far."

"You really think so?"

She nodded. "I do. It's a competitive job market out there. Anything you can do to give yourself an edge."

"You're the second person who's told me that."

"Then it's a sign."

As our food came, I nodded. "You know, I will think about it."

EVIE and I walked back to the hotel. I had to admit that it had been surprisingly fun talking with her. I didn't know if we could ever be best buddies or anything, but being with someone who was like-minded was refreshing—even if her IQ was chutes and ladders above mine.

We said goodbye in the lobby, and she headed up to the sixth floor while I headed to my first-floor room. Just as I pulled out my key card, I heard a foot-fall behind me. Before I could turn and see who was coming, someone grabbed my arm and pressed into me.

I twirled around, ready to fight, when Dr. Stone came into view.

"Get your hands off me," I growled. I jerked away from him.

"Where have you been?" he growled.

"Don't you remember? You left me on my own and made me fend for myself when it came to getting a ride back from your place. I'm sorry I was such an inconvenience." I lowered my voice when I saw some conferees go past. They sent glances our way. Great. Evie was right. Dr. Stone and I were going to be fuel in the gossip lovers' wildfire.

"Keep your voice down," Dr. Stone warned.

"I'll speak as loud as I want to speak. And what kind of foolishness are you engaging in? Did you cut the electricity at your place when you went to bed or something? Do you get a kick out of shaking women up?"

"What are you talking about?" His eyebrows scrunched together, and he looked truly confused.

"I tried to turn the lights on in the hallway. There was no power, which only added to the little creep show going on in your place."

"In the hallway? The bulb burned out, Sherlock, and I haven't had the chance to change it."

His breath was hot on my face, which reminded me that he was still standing close. His spearmint scent turned my stomach.

I crossed my arms, speechless. Finally, I blurted, "You would say that." I couldn't own up to the fact that I'd had an airhead moment, thinking in terms of paranoid malice instead of logic. "You're still a jerk."

"I don't know what to say."

"How about 'sorry'? And how about loosening your grip on me before I report you to security?"

He glanced at his hand and finally let go of me. "I don't have time for this. You had your chance to make something of yourself."

Fury flared in me. "Why, you little—"

Before I could finish, he slapped something in my hands. "Glad you're okay. The last thing I need is someone disappearing with their last known location being at my house."

He turned and walked away.

I was fuming mad. Like, madder-than-I'd-been-in-a-long-time mad.

The nerve of some people.

As soon as Dr. Stone was out of sight, I glanced down at my hands. He'd given me pictures of shoe prints in the dirt. What in the world?

I shook my head and let myself into my room. I checked the locks several times before sinking into my bed. As soon as my back hit the pillows I'd arranged behind me, my muscles thanked me.

I rubbed my eyes a moment and then tried to focus on the photographs Dr. Stone had handed me. Was this a classroom assignment I'd missed? What did he want me to do with them?

I glanced down at the bottom of one of the photos and saw a label with an address on it.

That's when it hit me.

These were the crime scene photos from Skye Flores's house.

I had no idea why someone as heartless as Levi Stone would find it in himself to help me after everything that had happened between us, but I didn't argue. I'd asked him if his friend might let me see the evidence, and he'd obviously checked for me.

I put the pictures down beside me for a moment, my mind racing.

What had Levi said before he stormed away? Something about how he didn't want his house to be the last known location for a missing girl. The statement sparked something in me. I wondered exactly where Georgia's last known location was.

I pulled out my notepad. From what I'd gathered, she disappeared nearly two weeks ago to the day. That was the last time her apartment manager had seen her. My guess would be that rent was due on the fifteenth. I checked online, and an information section of the website confirmed my theory.

Poppy at Hair Kingdom also said that Georgia had left about two weeks ago.

Trace had said he hadn't seen her in a month, which took me to the fifteenth again.

What had happened leading up to that date to make Georgia lose it?

Skye, on the other hand, had disappeared a month ago. Had Georgia taken her, tried to resume her life while taking care of Skye, only to finally give up and run? Poppy had said that in the two weeks before Georgia disappeared, she'd been acting strangely. Maybe that was because she was trying to figure out what to do with Skye.

For all I knew, maybe I'd been the last one to see her. After all, someone had lured me into that bull pasture. My bets, at the moment, were on Georgia.

I sighed and leaned back into my pillows, not realizing just how tired I was.

Just as my mind began to replay facts and events, my phone buzzed. I looked down and saw I had a familiar number on my screen. Riley.

I remembered what Evie had told me, that sometimes moving on didn't mean leaving everything behind. Sometimes it just meant trusting in the person you'd become and being ready to face the future, whatever it held.

I smiled as the words replayed in my mind before answering. "Hey, Riley."

"Gabby. I wondered if you were going to pick up."

Just hearing his voice did something that should be considered illegal to my heart. I forced myself to speak and not just stand there in a stupor. "I just got back to my hotel room a few minutes ago."

"How's the conference? Sierra told me where you went. It sounds like a great opportunity."

"So far, so good." I leaned back into the bed, realizing just how good it was to hear his voice. His voice felt like home, a realization that was bittersweet.

"I just wanted to let you know that I've been thinking about you," Riley continued, his voice sobering. "I'm sorry I missed you when I came down."

I wasn't sure how to respond. There was so much I wanted to say. Yet I kept most of my thoughts to myself, fearing I'd hamper his recovery. I cared about him too much to do that. His health was the most important thing right now.

I cleared my throat, feeling unusually jittery. "What brought you down to Norfolk?"

"You, of course."

"Me?" I couldn't contain the surprise in my voice.

"I just—" He started to talk again, but sighed instead. "I just wanted to see how you were doing. You've been on my mind a lot lately."

"I'm doing okay."

He paused for a moment. "That's great. You deserve good things in your life, Gabby."

He was the one good thing I'd wanted in my life, and that hadn't worked out very well, now had it?

It's just another setback, Gabby. Setbacks are made for launching forward. Two steps forward, one step back. Like a rock in a slingshot being pulled back before being released and soaring into the air.

I may or may not have been reading self-help books lately. I was trying to learn the art of positive thinking.

But moving on doesn't always mean leaving everything in your past behind.

I was starting to like Evie's advice more than those twelve-step plans I'd read.

"Listen, maybe we can talk sometime when you get back," Riley said. "There are some things I'd really like to share with you."

Talk? He wanted to talk? About what? It didn't matter. Of *course* I'd talk to Riley. He was my weakness, my kryptonite. "That sounds great."

Relief was evident in the softening of his voice. "I was hoping you'd say that. I'll give you a call early next week, then. Sound good? Maybe I can come down and we can have dinner."

"It's a date. I mean, not a date. But a get-together. A hangout. It's on my calendar." I scolded myself for sounding like a bumbling fool.

He paused and mercifully didn't seem to notice my fumble. "My therapist says I'm progressing quickly, Gabby. I know it seems slow. It seems slow for me. But I feel like I'm finally seeing some light at the end of the tunnel."

I felt like there was something he wanted to tell me, a deeper meaning behind his words. But I didn't ask, nor would I allow myself to speculate or hope. He'd tell me in his own time.

"I'm glad things are looking up for you," I told him. "We'll talk more soon, okay?"

"Good night, Gabby."

"Good night, Riley."

As I leaned back in bed, my phone slid out of my hands and onto the floor. I told myself I wouldn't speculate, but a seed of hope felt like it had been planted in my heart. It was dangerous territory I was toying with entering, and I had to stop myself.

I sighed, too tired to think. I needed to retrieve my phone and get some sleep.

When I glanced down at the floor, my phone was nowhere in sight. It must have bounced under the bed, out of sight. With a sigh, I climbed off the comfy mattress and crouched on the carpet. I lifted the covers to retrieve my cell, when I spotted something.

Daisy petals.

I remembered what Colorado Caitlyn had said. Crazy Georgia had left flower petals wherever she went. This couldn't be a coincidence. It just couldn't be.

CHAPTER
NINETEEN

HOW HAD someone gotten into my room? My mind raced with the possibilities. The windows appeared to be the kind that didn't open. There was an adjoining door.

Out of curiosity, I jiggled the handle. It was definitely locked.

Strange.

I was supposed to meet Trace and Wentworth in a few minutes. But first I went to the front desk. The same young man who'd been working there when I checked in smiled at me. Jeffrey, his name tag told me, was twenty-something with an overeager smile and a certain smarminess about him.

"How can I help you?"

"I'm curious . . . is the room next to mine available? I'm in 1026, and I'm interested in the room with the adjoining door."

He stared at me a moment.

I needed something more.

"I'm a little paranoid sometimes, and I'm interested in the other room just to give myself peace of mind."

He shrugged but typed something into the computer anyway. "There's no one in the room. It's been empty all week."

Before I had to explain any more, Trace and Wentworth walked in. I had the information I needed, but it didn't make sense. If the room was empty, how had someone gotten in? Had they somehow come in through my door? I had both of my key cards, so I knew no one had swiped one. Strange.

"Hey, sis." Trace tugged at my hair. "I like the new look."

"Thank you. And thanks for coming. I know my phone call was a little last minute, but there are a couple of things that I wanted to ask you about in person."

"No problem. We were just finishing up rehearsal and on our way to relax a little."

"How's the new drummer working out?"

Trace's face went from jolly to somber. "He's okay. I mean, he's actually really good. But he's not Dud, you know?"

I nodded.

Trace glanced at Wentworth. "We were thinking about trying this place that has some live music. What do you think? I know it's not the quietest venue, but I'm hoping we can still talk."

"That's fine with me."

Before we reached the door, two women rushed over from the bar. "Are you Trace Ryan?" one starry-eyed one asked.

Trace smiled, though it didn't reach his eyes. It was like he hit an "on" switch and went into performance mode. "I am."

"I'm your biggest fan!" the woman squealed.

He talked to her a minute, and I stepped back to listen. I had to admit—if this was the life of a celebrity, I was quite content to live my own life. Could Trace ever let down his guard? And, if he did, would it be the one minute the media was waiting and could slam him for being "real"?

After several minutes of schmoozing, I looped my arm through Trace's. "We really do need to run, Trace."

He said goodbye as I pulled him away.

"Thank you," he whispered.

"I don't know how you do it."

"I was flattered at first. Now I feel exhausted. But if there's one thing you don't want to do, it's tick off your fans. So I just keep smiling."

"Oh, come on, Trace. You know you love it," Wentworth chided with a grin.

"Now, Wentworth here. He does love it."

Did he love it enough to somehow conspire with Georgia? Had Georgia convinced him to help her out in her scheme for some kind of benefit? He wouldn't be the first man who'd fallen under the spell of a beautiful woman.

Twenty minutes later we reached the restaurant. The band blared in the background, which would make talking difficult. Trace requested a corner table, and the waitress found one for us. I didn't know if it had to do with Trace's reputation and or just plain luck. Either way, I was happy to be away from the loud music for a minute.

I waited until after Trace and Wentworth had ordered burgers and fries before talking.

"I found daisy petals under my bed," I started, getting right to the point.

"Daisy petals?" Trace asked.

"Colorado Caitlyn said that Georgia left a flower trail wherever she went."

Realization dawned on his face. "I guess that's true. I mean, she never said she liked them—not to me, at least—but you're right. Petals did show up in the aftermath of every 'event.' But how did they get in your hotel room?"

I shrugged, uneasy at all the conclusions I drew. "That's what I want to know."

He swung his head back and forth. "Man, Gabby. I sure don't know. But I sure didn't mean to pull you into any of the craziness."

"What if Georgia thinks the two of you are dating?" Wentworth said.

Trace and I glanced at each other, but said nothing.

"What?" He raised his hands, palms up, looking almost offended that we didn't immediately agree. "It makes sense. She probably doesn't know you're about to be stepsiblings. You're both single and attractive. It's a natural assumption that you could be together."

"So you're thinking I'm her next target?" I mumbled.

"I think it's a rather good theory." Wentworth stood. "And, with that said and everyone feeling totally awkward now, I see an old friend over there. I'm going to say hi."

As he sauntered off, I turned to Trace, grateful that I had a moment alone with him. "I have another question. I was talking to Jono tonight, and he seems to think you're exaggerating about Georgia's stalker-like tendencies."

Trace sighed and readjusted his hat. "Jono has a way of putting a positive spin on anything. Plus, he's desperate not to do anything that might ruin the launch of this album. He's a manager but also a PR genius."

"He said you thought someone else was stalking you a few months ago."

He blinked. "Wow, he was really running his mouth, wasn't he?" Trace leaned back. "Look, there was another girl who freaked me out for a while. She wasn't as bad as Georgia, but she did follow me around everywhere. Eventually, she left me alone. She wasn't scary like Georgia is scary, if you know what I mean."

I nodded. "I see. Can I ask another question?"

"Please do. I want you to get everything out in the open, because I don't have anything to hide."

Despite his willingness, I hesitated a moment before responding. "One person I talked to thought it was strange that you didn't do more to find Skye when she disappeared. Why didn't you plead to your fans or go online to inquire about her disappearance?"

He let out a long, heavy breath. "I thought about it. But I have these doubts in my mind. There's evidence that seems to say she left on her own free will. The police think that. I don't want to make a mountain out of a molehill. That's why I asked you to help. I'm still doing something, but it's subtle. If you discover evidence that there is foul play involved, I'll do whatever I can to find her—especially if she disappeared because of her relationship with me."

I believed him. Maybe I shouldn't. Maybe I was being naïve. But he seemed sincere, and I thought his words made sense.

I pressed my lips together, hoping to properly measure my words. "Trace, I've been asking a lot of questions and talking to a lot of people. A couple of folks said that you actually led Georgia on."

As soon as the question left my lips, Wentworth showed back up and slid into the booth beside me.

Trace pulled his head back in revulsion. "Absolutely not. Look, since you outright asked me, I have to tell you that she's not even my type. I like brunettes with brown eyes. Georgia was a blue-eyed blonde. I like reserved girls who are kind of mysterious. Georgia was clingy and loud and brassy."

Wentworth nodded. "He's telling the truth. Georgia wasn't his type."

I traced a line of condensation on my glass with my finger. "The last time I can pinpoint that someone saw Georgia was two weeks ago to the day. After that, she seems to have disappeared. I've already talked to her landlord and coworker. Aside from that, she seems to have no life."

"That's probably about right. Seriously, she followed the band everywhere," Wentworth said.

"Kind of like a Dead Head?" Was there any crazier group than the one who'd followed around the Grateful Dead? *I think not.*

"Exactly."

"Did she ever give any indication of where she was from?"

"I did ask her about that once. I was trying to make polite conversation, like I always do when people want to talk to us. It was a generic question, but I remember her answer was strange. She said she was from Georgia. She also said she'd run away when she was sixteen and hadn't been back since then."

"Was she exaggerating or telling the truth?"

"I never looked into it. But she had that lost look about her, you know? Like a person without roots."

"Sounds like a new song," Wentworth said.

The band finished playing and Trace looked over, making eye contact with the lead singer, who waved him toward the stage.

"Excuse me for a minute." Trace sauntered off in the distance to talk to the band.

Wentworth smiled. "Trace is legendary around these here parts. He's the American dream. He started with nothing and worked his way up to a record contract and radio hit."

"It's good to see someone who has everything going for them."

Wentworth leaned toward me. "So, what do you think happened to Dud?"

I shook my head. "I can't help but think that the cases are connected."

"You think Georgia abducted Skye and killed Dud?"

I nibbled on my lip for a moment. "I think there's a link there. I'm just not sure what the link is."

"Between you and me, can I tell you something?"

Like I'd say no. "I guess."

He leaned closer, his voice just above a whisper. "I heard that there was bad blood between Dud and Jono."

"Really?" It was news to me. Very interesting news.

Wentworth nodded. "It's true. Dud hasn't been a part of the band for that long. Not even a year. You heard about our first drummer, right?"

"He died."

He nodded. "Committed suicide. Sad stuff. Anyway, when Jono came on board, he really wanted us to hire this other guy, but Trace wasn't willing to let Dud go. He'd worked with him in the past and really liked him. Jono was pretty mad."

"You think he was mad enough to kill Dud?"

Wentworth stared at me, and I knew the answer even though he hadn't said a word.

It seemed like a lame reason for murder, but people had killed for far less compelling motivations.

"I don't like to say anything about it in front of Trace. He gets a little worked up over it all. Jono wants us to keep everything even for Trace."

"Why?" As the waitress set some onion rings on the table, I couldn't help but snitch one. I wasn't even hungry, but they were so hard to resist.

"You know how us creative types are. We're either on top of the world or in the depths of despair. Trace swings between those two easily. The last thing we need for this part of the tour—the launching of our career—is for Trace to not want to get out of bed. It's happened before."

I soaked in the new information. Before I could ask any more questions, Trace reappeared. So did the food.

As the guys dug in, I let my questions simmer. When the time was right, if I needed to address them, I would.

My gaze traveled across the restaurant, and I spotted a familiar face. Seeing this person here couldn't be a coincidence. I had to go find out more information.

"IF YOU'LL both excuse me a minute while you eat," I murmured. "I see someone I recognize across the room."

Trace and Wentworth were already involved in a deep conversation about sound equipment, so I eased out of the booth and walked to the other side of the restaurant.

I almost hadn't spotted him, but there in the shadows, I'd caught a glimpse of good old Lenny. Before he could object, I slid into the booth across from him. There was a glass in front of him, filled with beer, if I had to guess. He wore a black T-shirt, and his red eyes made him seem like he was struggling and tired and had had too much to drink.

His eyes widened as he tried to place me. "Can I help you?"

"I hope so. I'm working for Trace Ryan, investigating some strange incidents that have been occurring lately."

His face fell. "What's that have to do with me?"

I laced my fingers together on the table, the picture of cool, calm, and in control. "I understand you were his manager?"

He picked at the paper napkin in his hands, every few seconds his gaze sweeping to the band playing in the corner. "That's no secret. Half of the people in this room could have told you that."

"I heard you were devastated when he fired you."

His lips quirked up in aggravation. "*Devastated* would be a strong word. I was surprised. Taken off guard. Shocked. We were a team for five years, and I'd slaved endless hours to see that Trace succeeded. I thought we had more than a business relationship. I thought we were family. Still, *devastated* would be overstating it."

I stared at him, trying to detect any tics, anything that would be a clue as to if he was telling the truth or not. He overall seemed nervous and on edge, so it was hard to tell. "You've heard about everything going on with Trace?"

"You mean, his record contract and yearlong tour, complete with a bus?"

"That, and the death of his drummer."

He nodded, some of the contempt disappearing

in favor of sympathy. He swept the remnants of his napkin into his hand and made a pile on the table. "Of course I heard. The world of country music is smaller than you might think it is. We're all mourning Dud. The police have any idea who killed him yet?"

"I was hoping you might have some ideas."

He let out a quick breath. "Me? I have no idea. Maybe you should talk to Jono." He said the man's name like it was a bad word.

"Why would Jono know?"

"Apparently, the man walks on water. Maybe he reads minds, too."

I ignored the jab. "What do you know about him?"

If there was anyone who'd be willing to air Jono's dirty laundry, it would be Lenny. I didn't like alcohol, but sometimes having too many drinks could help things to work in my favor. It gave some people loose lips.

"Jono is a shark. He'll do anything to get ahead. And he's a passive-aggressive control freak." He paused suddenly and tilted his head. "Anything else?"

"You know anyone who had any beefs with Dud?"

He offered a half shrug. "I heard he and Jono were arguing."

I knew I had to take anything he said with the clichéd "grain of salt." The man obviously had a grudge. "Oh, really? About what?"

"Between you and me, Jono promised another drummer from an old band he used to manage a spot on Trace's tour."

Interesting. He was telling me the same thing that Wentworth just had. I wanted to hear his version of it, though. "How do you know that?"

A smile started to curl the corner of his lips. "I get around."

"Tell me more."

"Why should I?" He raised an eyebrow before downing the last of his drink and setting it on the table with a clunk.

"Because otherwise you'll remain at the top of my suspect list."

His mouth dropped open and he pointed to himself. "I'm on your suspect list? Me? Lenny Williamson? That's preposterous."

"You were at the band's release party—yet no one knew you were going to be there. I find that suspicious. Maybe you were trying to sabotage something. Maybe you were the reason they were having all those technical glitches. I heard you were a master sound tech." I actually hadn't heard that at all, but I took a chance on it.

He pointed to himself again. "I am one of the best

sound techs around. Anyone would tell you that. But I did not sabotage anything. That's not my MO. If I have a grievance with someone, I tell them to their face."

"Then why were you there at the release party?"

He shrugged and stared off into space for a minute. "What can I say? I was curious. I felt like the guys were my friends. We'd been together for a long time. I wanted to hear how they sounded. Feel the reaction of the crowds. Find out what had changed."

"Or you wanted to see them fail? Isn't that the ultimate revenge?"

"Look, I just signed with a new band. I think they're going to skyrocket, much more than Trace Ryan. He's only going to be a flash in the pan. That's what Jono does. He's good at quick, short-lived successes. I want to build long-term careers."

"You don't sound like you think highly of him."

He leaned close. "Here's the other side of the story: he tried to buy Dud off in exchange for him leaving the band."

"Why would he do that?" Certainly I hadn't heard him correctly. The other stuff, I could believe. But buying him off? That was a big deal.

"He promised the other guy that he was going to get the spot. But Trace wouldn't budge. He insisted on Dud. Trace doesn't like too much change. He likes being around people he can depend on. There wasn't a chance he'd fire Dud for Jono's guy."

"But you're making it sound like Jono was determined?"

"He's very manipulative. He likes to get his way. That's all I'm saying."

"He likes to get his way enough to murder someone?"

Lenny's eyes lit. "I didn't say that, but I think it's a possibility worth exploring."

I went back to the table, still chewing on what Lenny had said. Could Jono be guilty? It seemed like a long shot that he would have anything to do with this. But, to stay objective, I had to consider that someone other than Georgia may have abducted Skye and someone else may have killed Dud.

Where did that leave me now?

Georgia was the most obvious suspect, at least when it came to Skye's disappearance. I supposed there was always the chance that maybe she'd disappeared too, that maybe she'd been the victim of foul play. It was a possibility worth considering.

Then there was Jono. Could he really be that manipulative?

How about Lenny? He was nursing a grudge. Was it worth killing over, though?

Quinton, the security guard, seemed to be in the wrong place at the wrong time. But what if there was something he wasn't telling me?

So many possibilities raced around in my mind that my head started to spin.

"Everything okay?" Trace asked.

I nodded. "Just fine. Thanks."

The singer onstage began talking into the microphone. "I have a good friend I'd like to call up onstage right now. He started with me in this crazy business, and I'm proud to say now that he's landed himself a contract. He'll be leaving on tour soon. Would you welcome Trace Ryan?"

Trace grinned and stood, waving to the crowds around him like a true showman. He hopped onstage, shook hands with his friend, and then strapped a guitar on.

"I didn't come up here trying to steal the show, but I do want to thank my friend Jim—Slim Jim, as I always called him—for inviting me up."

The crowd cheered.

"I was hoping to play you one of the first little ditties I ever wrote. It's called 'Love Along the Way.'"

He strummed the guitar. I sat back and listened as he crooned about a girl and boy who'd loved each other since they were eight. They grew up and got married, faced hard times, and loved each other through it all.

Something about the lyrics brought tears to my eyes. I wanted a love like the one Trace sang about. I could try to deny it as much as I wanted, but deep inside, I wanted to share my life with someone.

Riley. I wanted that someone to be Riley. I'd been willing to marry the man, to give up everything for him.

But I had to be okay with whatever the future held. My plan for my life didn't always equate to being God's plan for my life. I was willing to take God's hand and let Him lead me into the unknown.

"You okay there?" Wentworth asked.

I wiped away a stray tear. "Yeah, I'm going to be just fine."

He tilted his head. "You sure about that?"

I nodded. "Yeah, I'm sure. I only see a few feet in front of me. God can see the big picture. I need to hold on to that knowledge, even when it doesn't feel true, even when I desperately want to take things into my own hands."

"What happens when you leave here?"

"I'm interviewing for a new job, applying to get my master's, and learning to roll with the punches." Now that I thought about it, it couldn't be a coincidence that punches usually hurt.

"Who's the guy?" Wentworth asked.

"What guy?"

He gave me a knowing look. "I can see it in your eyes. You're in love with someone."

My lips parted. "Really? Am I that transparent?"

He nodded. "Yeah, you are. He's a lucky guy."

If he only knew. I wasn't going to get into it now, though.

A few minutes later, I heard Trace on the stage.

". . . when I think about all the sacrifices I've made to get to where I am today, I realize it's all worth it. Whether I'm playing in front of a crowd of one hundred or thousands, the music is what's important. That's what's in my heart. Thank you for letting me share with you this evening."

The crowd roared with applause as he took the guitar off and came back to the table.

"You've got a God-given talent," I told him.

He grinned and tugged at his hat. "Why, thank you, Gabby. It doesn't feel right playing without Taylor, though."

"Taylor?" Someone else I hadn't heard about?

"My guitar," Trace said.

"He's in love with his guitar, that's what I keep telling him," Wentworth joked. "I mean, he named it, for goodness' sakes."

"My granddad gave it to me. What can I say? He peddled it off someone when he was working at a truck stop. When I developed an interest in music, he decided the guitar should be mine. It's what I learned to play on."

"Well, regardless of the guitar you're using, you tell stories with your words. And you keep managing to choke me up. Not a lot of people can do that." I drew in a deep breath, feeling like things had turned too serious and it was all my fault. "So . . . what's going on tomorrow with you guys?"

"We're actually shooting part of a music video," Trace said. "Should be fun. We'll be in OKC, not terribly far from you."

"Exciting."

"On Friday, some of us are heading out to my ranch," Wentworth said. "We're going to cut loose one last time before the tour. You should come."

"Really?" I asked.

He nodded. "Yeah, really. We'll have horseback riding and maybe a bonfire."

"I'll tell you what. If I find either Skye or Georgia before that, I'll come. If not, I'm going to keep investigating until the very end."

"A determined woman. Who doesn't love that?" Wentworth asked.

He grinned.

CHAPTER
TWENTY-ONE

I EMERGED from my hotel room the next morning and walked into the atrium. To my surprise, I saw Lenny standing by the bar, staring right at me. Before I could approach him, Wentworth walked toward me from the front desk. Quinton was by his side.

What in the world was going on?

As I turned, I saw Trace standing on top of the grand piano and singing. Even stranger, Jono played the drums, and Georgia and Skye sang backup.

Suddenly, I jerked my head up.

What in the world?

I blinked a couple of times, and then realized there was a small puddle of drool on my arm. Gross.

I was in class. Everyone was leaving. Except me.

Had I really fallen asleep? It was bad enough that I'd gotten here late. Even worse that the teacher had a monotone voice. But how many people had seen me snoozing?

One thing was for sure—I wasn't cut out to live the life of a musician. Up all night, sleeping during the day. That schedule wasn't for me.

I hadn't gotten back last night until nearly two. All night, as I'd tried to sleep, I'd turned over thoughts about the conversation I'd had with Wentworth. More facts kept coming to light, but I had to figure out what to make of them.

I grabbed my notebook and shoved it into my bag. Then I stood, taking heavy steps toward my next session.

I noticed some strange looks as I stepped out into the hallway. They must have seen me snoozing in class. Not very professional on my end, but I couldn't do anything about it now.

Someone inched up beside me. "What happened to you?"

Evie. She stared at my face. Did I have lines on it from where I'd leaned against my spiral notebook? That would just be lovely.

"I fell asleep," I muttered.

"I can tell."

"I had a long night."

"Gabby, you need to go to the bathroom."

"No, I think I'm fine."

She stopped me, a no-nonsense look in her eyes. "No, really. You need to go look in the mirror."

My goodness, I must really look bad. I shrugged and veered from the hallway into the women's restroom. A couple of women snickered as they passed me, and a feeling of dread crept into my psyche.

As soon as I saw myself in the mirror, I knew exactly what everyone was gawking at.

Someone had drawn a curlicue mustache on my upper lip.

"What?"

Evie frowned. "I think this is where I'm supposed to say something compassionate that makes you feel better."

"Why would someone do this?" I continued, rubbing in vain at my new marker-mustache accessory.

"I told you there had been rumors."

"About me and Dr. Stone?" I realized my voice was climbing and immediately lowered my volume before I drew a crowd. "Nothing happened!"

"I know that, but everyone else doesn't. People get bitter over stuff like this. People who've gone to Harvard and feel like others get jobs over them because of how far you're willing to go with someone higher up."

"That's the most ridiculous thing I've ever

heard." I grabbed a paper towel, wet it, and began to scrub my face. "Great. This is permanent marker."

"It sure is."

I sighed and turned to Evie. "What am I going to do?"

"I'd suggest keeping your head up, going to your room, doing whatever you can to clean up, and then going back to class. Show everyone that what they think about you doesn't matter. You know the truth. Isn't that what we believe? That the truth will prevail?"

"That's what I like to believe. It's not always reality, however."

"You've got this." She paused. "That was kind of motivational and sympathetic, right?"

I let out a half sigh, half smile and nodded. I wished Evie's lack of social skills was my biggest concern at the moment.

But it wasn't. Not by a long shot.

I wished I felt as certain as she did.

I did exactly what Evie had advised. I could still see the faint outline of the mustache, and now my face was also red and raw from scrubbing. It was all just . . . peachy.

But I refused to let anyone know just how upset I

felt about the whole incident. I kept my chin up and made sure I volunteered first to answer questions in the remaining sessions.

I did steal out of class early, and I escaped back to my room to make a phone call. While in one of the main sessions on DNA testing, I'd searched missing person reports for the past eight years. I hit the jackpot when I found a picture of a woman from Georgia named Georgia Clements who disappeared ten years ago. She looked like the same Georgia I was looking for.

I sat at the little walnut desk in my bedroom, and after a quick Internet search, I had the family's phone number. I knew I had to handle this situation very delicately, and I prayed that I'd have the right words. Tact wasn't always my strong suit.

I braced my elbows on the desktop and propped the phone to my ear as I listened to the call go through. A man answered on the fourth ring.

"I'm looking for Mr. Clements," I started.

"Speaking."

"Mr. Clements, my name is Gabby St. Claire. I'm investigating a case out here in Oklahoma, and I came across the information about your daughter, Georgia."

"Georgia? Did you find her?" His voice turned urgent.

My heart lurched. I couldn't tell the man that I

suspected that his daughter might be a psycho. "I'm not sure. I don't want to get your hopes up. But I wondered if I could ask you a few questions."

"Of course. If it might help me find Georgia. Everyone else has given up on finding her. But not me and my wife. We still hold on to the hope that we'll see her again one day."

I swallowed hard, looking away from my reflection in the mirror in front of me. I feared I might see the hollow eyes of someone who understood his loss. Having a brother who was kidnapped when we were children had made a permanent stain on my life, even now that he was found. I'd never forget how difficult those days were. I'd never forget the questions that had haunted me through many sleepless nights.

I kept my voice soft. "I know this is difficult, but could you tell me a little bit about her? It was ten years ago, and I wasn't able to find as much on the Internet about her disappearance as I'd hoped."

"Things weren't as viral back then as they are today, I suppose. What do you want to know?"

"Is it true that the last time you saw her, she was sixteen?"

"That's right." His voice caught. "She'd gotten in with the wrong crowd. She was doing some drugs and partying a lot. We felt like we were losing our little girl. We tried to tighten our boundaries—we gave her more rules, hoping that would reel her in. It seemed to do the opposite. She pushed even harder."

I heard the grief in his voice, and my heart panged with compassion. "If this is too difficult for you—"

"No, I can do this." He cleared his throat. "My wife and I woke up on the morning of March 9. We didn't hear Georgia stirring, but that wasn't unusual. We had to drag her out of bed for school every morning. We went into her room, but she was gone. Her bed was made. Clothes were missing."

I closed my eyes, understanding the horrible feeling he'd experienced that day. "Did you think she was abducted?"

"No, I felt rather certain she'd run away. It fit with the train wreck we feared might be coming." His voice trailed, and it was obvious the years hadn't diminished his pain.

"What did you do?"

"First, we called her. Our messages went straight to voice mail. Then we called her friends. They claimed to know nothing. When she wasn't home by dinner, we called the police. They did their best to find her, but she seemed to disappear without a trace."

I opened my eyes again and tapped the hotel pen against the pad of paper left there as a courtesy by the housecleaning staff. "There were no leads?"

"No leads. There were a couple of people who thought they'd sighted her at a bus stop in Atlanta, another one in a grocery store near Nashville. But there was nothing firm. Georgia was like that. She was sneaky. She knew when to be quiet and blend in. She also knew how to be the life of the party."

"That must have been extremely difficult."

He let out a long, shaky breath. "It was. I feared she may have gotten involved in prostitution or drug running or any of those crazy things kids do trying to support themselves. They think making it on their own is so easy. But the cold, hard reality is that life is difficult, especially when you try to do it alone."

"Just curious—what did Georgia want to do with her life? Was there any particular career she wanted?"

"She wanted to be a hairstylist."

TWENTY-TWO

I COULDN'T STOP THINKING about my conversation with Mr. Clements. This had to be the same Georgia. Before I'd gotten off the phone with him, I'd told him that I was looking at someone who fit Georgia's description. I also told him my lead was out of Lawton, Oklahoma, and promised to give him any updates. I already dreaded that potential phone call, though. Was it better not to know the truth when the truth was devastating and painful?

My own brother had been missing for years, so I had to say the answer was no. It was better to know and deal with it than to always wonder. That didn't make my job any easier, though.

I stood, stretched my legs, and then decided to grab a bite to eat. Maybe while having dinner I could figure out my next move. Sometimes time offered the best answers.

As soon as I stepped out of my room, I ran into Evie.

"I was coming to check on you," she said. "What are you doing tonight?"

I shrugged. "Not sure."

"Come eat with me. The conference is almost over, and then I can go back to being antisocial. In the meantime, I think you could use a listening ear as well."

A listening ear did sound great, especially from someone with credentials like Evie. She was esteemed and intelligent. Strange and awkward. Dark and mysterious.

"Let me guess—you want to go to the cave place again?"

"It's quickly become one of my favorites. Besides, we can walk there. I'd rather not fight this traffic in my car."

"Why not?" I pulled my purse up higher. "Ready to go now?"

"Sure thing. We'll get there before the crowds."

We started walking down the plush hall together, and I filled her in on my conversation with Georgia's dad.

We stepped outside, and the day was briskly cool.

I couldn't get used to the wind in the area. It seemed to cut through right to the bone.

The sidewalks were full with people just getting off work. The sun was low in the sky, casting an amber glow over the tops of the buildings.

It was hard to believe that in a couple of days I would leave Oklahoma and head back to Norfolk. For the first time since I had arrived, I was looking forward to the changes that would await me once I arrived back in Virginia. I could sense changes were coming—good changes. I was ready to do what was necessary to walk forward in faith. God had led me to the place where I was right now, and He certainly wasn't going to leave me now.

Life was always changing, always fluid. I was ready to navigate my way downstream.

On the corner, I spotted the homeless-looking man preaching again. I wanted to turn and walk the other way, but I didn't. His eerie words to me earlier continued to echo in my head. *She's watching you. Danger lurks close.*

He was just crazy. That was all there was to it.

"Someone's watching." He turned to me, his eyes as wide and crazy as ever.

Evie took my arm and tried to steer me away. But the man wouldn't be deterred.

"No one knows the day or the hour. Keep your eyes open to the evil around you."

His words caused a chill to start at my heart and work its way outward, cracking with each frosty expansion.

Crazy. He was just crazy. He had no idea what he was talking about.

"You!" he said with a raspy conviction that made me pause.

I knew he was talking about me.

I turned and glanced at him, despite the fact that Evie tried to tug me away. "Yes?"

"You're being watched."

"By whom?"

He turned down the street and pointed. A brunette hurried away, looking back before quickening her steps.

Georgia?

"Come on!" I grabbed Evie, and we started running toward the woman.

As soon as we spotted her, the woman took off in a run.

"What are we doing?" Evie shouted.

"That's the crazy lady I've been looking for. I can't lose her!"

At the curb, the light turned green and cars cascaded from the side street. We stopped in our tracks. My muscles tightened as I watched the woman flee in the distance.

"Forget this," I muttered. I darted into traffic,

dodging cars. A truck slammed on brakes, and the driver shouted something out the window at me.

"What are you doing?"

I looked behind me and saw that Evie had followed. "I can't let her get away. I just can't."

All those times when I'd felt like someone was watching me, and someone actually *had* been watching me.

I reached the sidewalk and pushed through the crowd waiting at the crosswalk for its signal to go. Several people gave me dirty looks, some looked like I was crazy, others had no idea what was going on because they were staring at their phones and oblivious.

Evie kept up with me as my feet pounded the pavement. I wasn't a fast runner, but I was gaining ground on Georgia. Every time she glanced over her shoulder at me, she temporarily slowed only to sprint again.

She veered off the sidewalk and climbed into a sedan. A feeling of defeat started to grow in my gut.

On foot, I had a fighting chance. But there was no way I could get my car in time to continue tracking her. By the time I got to the garage, Georgia would be long gone. Short of throwing myself on top of the car hood, there was little I could do to stop her.

A surge of frustration rose in me, and I wanted to kick something.

As the car squealed away from the curb, the driver cast a glance at me. I swung my fist in the air in frustration.

"What now?" Evie asked, panting for breath.

"I wish I knew."

Just then, another car pulled up to the sidewalk. "You guys need a ride?"

I stared at the face of Sherman. Evie and I glanced at each other.

"How fortuitous," she muttered.

Without wasting any more time, we hopped in the back of his twenty-year-old luxury sedan, also known as a boat on wheels.

"Follow that red sedan!" I told him, pointing straight ahead. Thankfully, I could still see it, but I wasn't sure for how much longer that would be true.

I had to give Sherman credit—he put the pedal to the metal and took off down the busy downtown street. The light ahead of us turned yellow.

Please don't slow down, I pleaded silently.

To my delight, he accelerated. To my relief, no one got hurt in the process. Thank God.

The red car turned to the right at the next block. We had to gain some time and distance here. But in the middle of rush hour, it was difficult. There were too many pedestrians, too much traffic. It made no sense if we hurt someone else on our way to rescue another person.

But my adrenaline was pumping through my blood, and I was so close to answers, I could practically taste them.

"What were you doing? You just happened to be driving past?" Evie asked, clinging to the bench seat in front of her.

"Just taking an evening drive." He glanced at Evie and flinched. "What? There's nothing weird about that."

"Whatever." She shrugged.

My eyes were fixated on the light ahead. It turned red, and there were two cars in front of us. Anxiety built in me. I was so close. So close.

Was she going to slip away now?

"Breathe. Just breathe, Gabby," Evie said.

I shook my head. "I just can't believe this. I feel so helpless."

I tapped my foot impatiently, digging my hands into the vinyl upholstery of the seat.

The light turned green, and the cars in front us couldn't move fast enough. "Go, go, go!"

Finally, we surged forward. I blinked in surprise when I saw the red sedan stopped at the next light. There was hope!

Just as we got closer, the light turned. The road led out of downtown and onto a highway headed south, toward Lawton.

I had to admit—Sherman surprised me. He was

pretty good at the whole car chase thing.

I thought Evie was impressed by it. She seemed to have a new respect in her eyes as Sherman wove in and out of traffic, trying to keep up with the red sedan.

"Do we want her to know we're following her? Or are we trying to be more subtle?" he asked.

I chewed on the thought for a minute. "Subtle," I decided. I needed to see where she was going.

Thirty minutes later, we still stayed behind her. Did she not realize that we'd gotten in the sedan and followed her? There was a chance she'd missed that. I mean, who would be able to anticipate such great timing? I couldn't have planned it better if I'd tried.

Around us, the landscape grew barren. The sun set in the distance, smearing orange and pink across the sky. It would have been a breathtaking scene if we weren't in pursuit of a dangerous, psychotic criminal.

"Where is she going?"

"Toward the Wichita Mountains, it looks like," Sherman said.

"There are mountains out here? I need to study my geography more." I'd always pictured Oklahoma as flat. Maybe that was because I'd watched the movie *Oklahoma* too many times.

"The Wichita range is beautiful and made of red-and-black igneous rocks, light-colored sedimentary rocks, and boulder conglomerates," Sherman said. "It's also dangerous and rugged. They aren't my favorite roads to be driving on at night."

The tension in my shoulders pulled harder. What exactly was going on here?

Sure enough, in the distance, the ground rose. Mountains. I sucked in a deep breath at the beauty of it all.

"So, who is this person we're following?" Sherman asked as we settled into a subtle pace.

"I think she may have abducted someone," I said.

His eyes widened, and he pushed his glasses up on his nose. "I see. I've always wanted to do field work. Mostly, I'm stuck behind a computer."

"I prefer field work," Evie said. "Not because it allows me to interact with people, but because being inside all day makes me feel suffocated."

Sherman glanced in the rearview mirror. "How about you?"

"I prefer working period," I mumbled.

"What?"

I shook my head, not in the mood to explain. "Never mind."

We rounded a bend in the road, and suddenly the red sedan was gone. The highway was empty in front of us.

"What?" Sherman muttered.

"The car couldn't have just disappeared," Evie said.

"So where did she go?" I asked, leaning forward.

"Uh, guys . . ." Sherman said, just as the car lurched. "We have bigger problems."

"What's that?" Evie asked.

"We're almost out of gas."

"What?" Evie screeched.

"In my defense, I had no idea I'd be driving an hour and a half away, and there was no good time to stop and fill up."

I moaned. I'd come this far only for this?

The car sputtered again and then rolled to a stop on the side of the road.

All my hopes of finding Georgia and Skye disappeared faster than the fuel in Sherman's car.

CHAPTER
TWENTY-THREE

WE CLIMBED out of Sherman's car and looked around. Mountains surrounded us. Mountains complete with massive boulders, red dirt, and very few trees.

"Don't people die like this every year? Stranded on isolated roads with absolutely no supplies?" Evie said.

"You're correct. Rural roads are actually much more dangerous than—" Sherman started.

"Enough!" Evie said, slicing her hand through the air.

Sherman sighed. "Look, I'm sorry. I'll figure out something."

Evie stared at her cell phone. "No signal out here, either. We're too far out. Great. It looks like we're going to have to walk."

"We should be careful of snakes," Sherman said. "There are an abundance of rattlesnakes in this area. There are also some coyotes and other predators—"

"Okay, I've heard enough!" Evie said, slicing her hands through the air. "The last way I want to die is at the hands of a wild animal."

"Wild animals actually don't have hands—" Sherman started.

"I don't care!" Evie said. "I just don't want to die out there."

Sherman pushed up his glasses. "Understood."

I shivered, the air out here much cooler than I'd anticipated. The jacket I wore was perfect for a brisk walk, but terrible for staying warm in the arid climate here.

Just as the thought entered my mind, the sun slipped behind a mountain to the west, leaving us in a dim gray wilderness.

"We should walk back to the main road," Evie said.

"It's twenty minutes," I told her. "I think we should keep moving ahead and see what we can find. You never know, there could be a store or a gas station or who knows what else just a little farther up."

"Or we could be walking into a death trap," Evie argued. "There could be barren roads for miles and miles, and towering mountains that will continue to block our signal."

"We're definitely safer staying together than we would be splitting up, so we should come to some kind of agreement," Sherman said. "Statistics have found that groups that stay together in a situation like this, or when lost in the woods, have a 50 percent better chance of surviving when they stick together."

We both turned toward him.

"I guess you're the deciding vote," Evie said, crossing her arms. "What do you think we should do, Sherman?"

"Me . . . me?" He pointed toward himself, suddenly looking even more out of sorts. "I don't know."

"We should keep walking," I told him.

"You just want to see if you can find that red car," Evie said.

I shook my head. "It's long gone. I know that. But look, daylight is fading, I'm freezing, and we need to make a decision. I'm going this way." I started walking toward the west, on the road not yet traveled—by us, anyway.

"Fine, but if we die, it's your fault," Evie said. She scrambled to keep up with me.

I wasn't confident at all, but I figured this was our best shot. If nothing else, maybe we could climb one of the mountains or boulders and get a cell signal. All hope wasn't lost . . . not yet, at least.

The area was narrow, almost making me think we were walking through something that had been a canyon at one time or carved out by powerful currents. Large rock formations rose on both sides of us, and a small river trickled by on the other side of the road.

"You know what water means? It means wild animals," Evie said. "Water is a commodity out here. And now it's dusk, which also means feeding time in the animal world."

She traipsed behind in her heels. I kept moving forward, trying not to think about the what-ifs. There were enough uncertainties without me letting my mind go to worst-case scenarios.

Besides, I was getting a little creeped out. This was so out of my territory, out of my comfort zone. The wind kept sweeping through the landscape, and each time my chills intensified.

"There's a road right here." Sherman pointed ahead to a little lane that cut through the dirt. "I wonder where it leads."

It seemed like a good starting point for any horror film ever made. Walk down an abandoned road in the middle of nowhere and hope for the best. I was certain everyone else would agree with me.

Evie bent down. "There are tire tracks turning

here. They look fresh. The dirt is so powdery here that if they'd been here for too long, the wind would have swept them away."

"So you think that's our best bet?" I asked.

"I think it's our only bet."

I didn't argue, because I had no better ideas at the moment. Besides, her words were true. At least we knew someone had been down this way in the recent past.

"Would this be a good time for a rendition of 'Home on the Range'?" I asked, a hint of mischief in my voice.

"No!" Evie said.

Sherman almost looked like he was going to affirm my idea until he heard Evie's displeasure. Then he shrugged.

The canyon-like rock formations around us began to fade as the road opened up before us.

"It's the mesa," Sherman said.

I pointed. "Is that a house over there?"

"If that's what you want to call it," Evie mumbled. "It looks abandoned."

"Maybe we'll have cell reception up here," Sherman said. He stared at his phone screen. "Bingo! I do. Who should I call?"

All three of us looked at each other. None of us knew anyone out here, except for each other.

Sherman looked at me. "Dr. Stone . . . ?"

Anger rose in me. "It's not like that—"

Evie cut me off. "Don't you have a stepbrother out here?"

I took a deep breath. "That's right. I can try him."

Trace answered on the first ring. "I was wondering if you were going to call today."

"Listen, Trace. I need your help." I gave him a rundown on what had happened and basic directions to find us. "I hate to bother you, but I have no one else to call."

"It's no problem, sis. Except we're filming that music video."

I shook my head. "You know what? Don't worry about it. We'll figure something out."

"I'll send Jono. How would that be?"

"Better than no one."

"I'll do that. He may be grumpy, but he'll do it."

I gave the phone back to Sherman. "Someone is coming. Maybe we could wait at that house. It might block the wind."

"It is called Tornado Alley around here. The wind isn't surprising in that sense. The wind truly does come sweeping down the plains. Sometimes without end, it seems." Sherman continued to walk, talking on and on about the winds.

I tuned him out.

Why had Georgia been following me? Did she

really think Trace and I were dating? Was she going to try and destroy me also?

I paused as we got closer to the abandoned-looking house in the distance. It wasn't the old plantation style that caught my eye, nor was it the peeling white paint or cracked windows, or the skeletal trees beside it.

No, what stopped me was the peek of red I saw.

Georgia's car was parked behind the house.

It looked like I'd just hit the jackpot.

TWENTY-FOUR

"WHAT DO WE DO?" Sherman asked.

"We approach carefully," I said.

"What if she has a gun?" Evie asked.

"Okay, first we call the police," I conceded. "Then we carefully check out what's happening inside. I mean, what if she's trying to kill Skye? What if she thinks we're onto her and wants to destroy evidence? There are so many things that can go wrong here."

"I agree with the 'so many things that can go wrong' part," Evie said.

"Rule number one of being in the field: keep a cool head," I reminded.

Evie sighed. "Let's just get this over with."

I felt like we should be less conspicuous as we approached, but there was nothing but open space around us. There was no way to hide our arrival.

Sherman called the police as we walked. Meanwhile, fire sizzled through my blood. Was this it? Could this possibly hold the answers I'd been looking for?

We ducked under the windows as we got closer to the house. Evie motioned for us to be quiet. So we were. We listened.

And heard nothing.

But a strange scent filled my nostrils.

Gasoline, I realized.

This whole house was about to go up in flames.

"I've got to see if Skye is inside," I whispered.

"It's too dangerous!" Evie said.

"What other choice do I have?"

"You don't even know if she's in there!" Evie said.

"I need to check."

Before I could take a step, I saw the first flame. Dread filled me. No. Not a fire.

It came from the second floor. I knew in a house this old, the whole thing would go down fast.

"I'm going to check. Don't come after me." I took off toward the front steps. I'd just check the first floor. I'd get out before the blaze could consume me. At least, that was my plan.

The scent of smoke became stronger as soon as I stepped in the front door. I heard a crack above me.

The ceiling could come down at any minute, I realized.

Was it worth it to risk my life for a stranger? I couldn't live with myself if I didn't.

I pulled my shirt up over my mouth and nose and tried to protect my lungs from the suffocating fumes and the hazy smoke. My eyes burned and my heart pounded out of control.

I tried not to think about everything that could go wrong. But there was so much that could go wrong in here.

I darted past the stairway and saw orange and yellow licking at the edges of the walls there. I rushed through the kitchen and dining room.

They were empty.

I kept pushing myself forward, knowing I couldn't slow down. I staggered into the living room, my breaths not coming as easily anymore. It was hard to see, hard to find air.

The house was getting hotter, and more ceiling beams cracked above me. At any minute, the entire second floor could come crashing down.

Lord, help me. Watch over me. Protect me.

I reached for a doorknob. Before I touched it, I pulled my sleeve over my hand and turned. Just as I'd thought—the metal was already hot. I twisted it, and plumes of smoke rushed out.

Water ran from my eyes. If the fire didn't kill me, the smoke inhalation would. I'd need to check this room and get out.

An old bedroom came into view. At least, that's what I thought it was based on the dresser beside me. I pushed inside the room, knowing my time was limited. I'd search the perimeter.

I coughed, the sound deep and achy. I had to feel my way around the room.

Another crack sounded above me. I glanced up and saw the wood was moving. Orange began to slither through the cracks there.

I turned to go back when I spotted something.

Feet.

Could it be . . . ?

I ran toward the opposite wall and sucked in a breath. A woman lay there, moaning and dazed. A gag was around her mouth, her legs, her arms.

I pushed a mop of brown hair from her face.

It was Skye. I'd found Skye!

I helped her sit upright and pulled the gag down. "Come on. I'm going to get you out of here."

Before I could help her to her feet, the ceiling cracked and burning embers crashed into the room, right in front of the door.

TWENTY-FIVE

I QUICKLY PULLED at the binds around her feet. With a few tries, I got them loosened and pulled the rope off. "We need a plan B," I told her.

She nodded, seeming out of sorts. Her eyes were glazed and tired.

I had to think, and fast.

The windows. Of course.

I ran to the nearest one and pushed on it. It was stuck.

I pushed harder.

It didn't budge.

There was more than one way to open a window.

I grabbed a lamp from the table and swung it like a baseball bat. The window shattered. Using the edge of my sweatshirt, I brushed aside any remaining glass. As I did so, I saw Evie and Sherman standing there.

"I found Skye!" I shouted over the roar of the fire.

The flames came closer, licking at my heels, reminding me too much of the first case I'd ever investigated. I'd almost died in that house too. But I hadn't. And I wasn't going to die here either.

"Help her out, okay?"

Evie and Sherman nodded.

I turned to Skye. "Legs first. They'll catch you."

She nodded lethargically and did as I told her. She slipped down to the ground, down into the waiting arms of Evie and Sherman. Down to safety.

Now it was my turn. Just as I put my leg out, an explosion sounded behind me and I was thrown outside.

***

"Gabby? Gabby? Are you okay?"

I opened my eyes and saw Evie, Sherman, and two strange men staring at me. I nodded and tried to push myself up, but my head throbbed so badly that all I wanted was to lie back down.

Then I felt the heat.

I blinked and spotted the house. Only, I was no longer right outside the window. I'd been moved— based on the marks in the dirt, I'd been dragged—

away from it. Now, firefighters surrounded it, trying to douse the flames.

"Skye . . . ?"

"The other paramedics have her right now. She's going to be fine," Evie said. "Thanks to you. You didn't have to go into that house, you know."

A paramedic stuck a stethoscope on my chest.

"I'm fine," I muttered, pushing him back. "How long was I out?"

"Just long enough for us to pull you away from the house," Sherman said.

"I pulled you," Evie said. "Sherman helped Skye."

"Did they catch Georgia?" I asked.

Evie and Sherman looked at each other and shook their heads. "She's gone," Evie said.

"What do you mean gone? Her car was here. She set the house on fire. How can she be gone?"

"We don't know exactly. We think that maybe she had another car waiting in the barn back there. I have a feeling she was gone by the time we got here. It's hard to know for sure."

I craned my neck, despite its ache, toward a sound in the distance. I looked over and saw another car coming down the dirt lane, kicking up clouds of dust behind it. The vehicle screeched to a stop, and Jono rushed out.

He ran over toward me, a bundle of nervous, type

A energy. "What happened? I got here as soon as I could."

"We found Skye," I told him as the paramedics helped me to my feet.

"What? That's great. Maybe Trace can finally relax and enjoy himself. After Georgia is caught, that is." He scowled. "You heard what she did today, right?"

"She did something today?"

"Smashed his guitar. Guitars are kind of like favorite sweaters—they fit just the way they're supposed to. This is just one more setback for Trace."

Georgia had been downtown today. Trace had been rehearsing only fifteen minutes from the hotel. She very well could have sneaked in and wreaked some more chaos.

The biggest question, however, was: Where had she gone, and what was she planning next?

Jono leered at me. "By the way, what's that on your face?"

I touched my upper lip, knowing it was more than soot and ashes he was talking about. Then I scowled. "Long story."

TWENTY-SIX

I ENDED up at the hospital, despite my protests. The doctor said I was fine, just a little bruised, which I already knew. While I was there, not only did I give my statement to the local police, but Detective Brooks also drove in and questioned me. I told officials from both police departments everything I knew, and they took notes and got my contact information.

"May I ask a question?"

The other detective—I thought his name was Bartowski—stared at me. "You can always ask."

"Did you run the plates on that car that was parked beside the house?"

He stared at me for a moment before nodding. "I did."

"Were they Georgia's? Did the car belong to her?"

"I'm not at liberty to say."

I frowned. I'd expected that answer, but it was still disappointing.

"By the way, Skye would like to speak with you," the detective said.

I instantly perked. "Really? I'd love to talk to her."

He led me to another room. Skye lay in a hospital bed there with a blanket over her. Her dark hair was fanned out behind her on the pillow, and her thin frame looked like the hospital bed had swallowed it. Her skin, tanned in her pictures, now looked pale, and her eyes were red, as if she'd been crying. She had an IV and several scrapes and bruises. But she was alive and safe.

She started to sit up when she spotted me, but I gently nudged her back down. "Please, take it easy. You've been through a lot."

She offered a weak smile. "I can't thank you enough for what you did for me. I would have died if you hadn't found me."

"I'm just sorry that you went through everything you did." I squeezed her arm.

"Yeah, me too." She frowned. "It's been a nightmare. I thought I would never get away."

I shifted. "Listen, I hate to ask you this, but do you have any idea where Georgia escaped to?"

She shook her head back and forth on the pillow. "I have no idea. She came and went. She was at the house about ten minutes before you came. She'd rushed inside, spread the gasoline, and then left. I'm pretty sure she had a motorcycle parked in the barn out back."

"I don't suppose you have any guesses where she went?"

"No idea. I just know that she's obsessed with Trace. It wouldn't surprise me if she went after him next. That girl is crazy. I think she was on drugs and maybe had some type of impulse control problem. Who knows?"

"Really? Why do you think that?"

"Just the way she acted." She stared straight ahead for a moment, and I feared she might fall asleep midsentence. Finally, she spoke again. "I have a feeling someone who worked with Trace was selling the drugs to her. Maybe one of his security guards?"

Interesting. That could shed some new light onto this whole situation. Was Quinton somehow involved in this? Had he been Georgia's wingman, so to speak? If he was selling drugs to a woman who'd abducted another woman, they'd have every reason in the world to lie about what happened the day Dud died.

"Is there anything else Georgia said that gave you any clue as to where she was staying or what she was planning next?"

Skye shook her head again. "She brought me food once a day. But otherwise, she kept me locked up in a closet at that house. She said very little, though she did mutter under her breath quite a bit. I was thankful every day that she didn't kill me."

"Why did she let you out today? Not to sound callous, but why not just leave you in the closet, where you were harder to find?"

Skye shrugged, her eyelids drooping. "I have no idea. Unless her plan all along was for you to follow her. Maybe she was hoping you'd die in that fire as well. What's the saying? She could kill two birds with one stone. Literally."

That thought wasn't comforting. But if Georgia had been in OKC today, ruining Trace's treasured guitar as Jono had said, then she could have swung by the conference center, as well. Maybe she was *that* conniving.

"Anything else?"

"Right before she left, she said she was finally going to put an end to all of this. I'm not sure how helpful that is. I'm assuming she meant that killing me would end it."

I shuddered at the eerie message.

The detective hovered by the door, and I knew

my time was up. I stood and patted Skye's arm again. "If you need anything, let me know. Have you talked to Trace yet?"

"No, not yet."

"I'll be by to check on you soon."

She nodded, though her eyes looked sad. "I'm looking forward to seeing him as well."

As I stepped out the door, the detective stopped me. "You're staying at the conference hotel, right?"

I nodded.

He handed me a key card. "I think you dropped this in the explosion. We found it outside the house."

"Thanks." I took the key card and slipped it into my back pocket.

On my way out of the hospital with Evie and Sherman, I ran into Trace.

He grasped my arms, and concern was written all over his features. "I heard what happened. Are you okay?"

I nodded. "I'm fine. Just a few cuts and scrapes and bruises. It's all in a day's work."

"I'm thanking my lucky stars that everyone is okay. My knees were knocking when I heard what happened."

"Thanks for sending Jono."

"He did show up?"

I nodded. "He did. It was probably about twenty minutes after I called you."

Trace's eyebrows knit together. "That's weird. I called him, and he said he was in Oklahoma City. He should have at least been an hour and a half away."

That was interesting. Just where had Jono been that he'd arrived so quickly?

Trace took another step toward the hospital. "You think they'll let me see Skye?"

"It can't hurt to ask," I told him. "I know she'd like to see you."

He leaned closer, staring at my face, his eyes narrowing with confusion.

I frowned. "Oh, for goodness' sakes! Yes, some very immature colleagues of mine decided to be funny today and draw a mustache on my upper lip, and no, I can't get it all off."

He shrugged. "I wasn't going to say anything."

"Sure you weren't." I narrowed my eyes at him this time.

His eyes twinkled as he tipped his hat. "I'll call you later, okay?"

I nodded. "Sounds good."

As he walked away, Sherman turned to me. His eyes looked wide and starstruck. "Was that Trace Ryan?"

I nodded. "The one and only."

His gaze volleyed from Evie back to me. "I want to hang out with you two all the time. I haven't had this much excitement in years. Maybe ever."

Evie and I shared a smile before climbing into Sherman's car, which had been refilled with gas. It was time to go back to the hotel. One worry was over: Skye had been found. But with Georgia still on the loose, not all my concerns had vanished.

CHAPTER
TWENTY-SEVEN

AS SOON AS we got back to the hotel, I expected Evie and Sherman to rush back to their rooms and unwind. Instead, Evie turned to me. "I'm so glad we can finally talk. I didn't feel like we could do it in front of that rookie cop who drove us back. Can we go to your room?" she asked me.

I shrugged, all thoughts of a shower and a clean set of clothes vanishing. "Sure. What's on your mind?"

"We'll talk in your room. I don't know who to trust."

I slogged down the hall and pulled out my key card. I swiped it across the door, but nothing happened except that a red light flashed. "What?"

I tried again and the same thing happened. Strange.

"My card's not working," I muttered.

"Weird. Maybe the fire melted something and messed up the encoding," Sherman said. "Did you know it's just an urban legend that those cards contain any other personal information? There's actually an algorithm—"

"Sherman," Evie warned.

He quieted.

I stared at the card in my hands and shook my head. "It's weird, because I don't know how I lost it. I usually kept the card in my bag, which was in the car."

Out of curiosity, I searched through my bag and found . . . another key card. I swiped this one over my door, and the light turned green.

I glanced over at Evie and Sherman. "Did either of you lose this card?" I held up the one the detective had handed me.

They pulled out their own cards.

"So, who does this belong to?" I asked.

We all stared at each other a moment, something unspoken passing between us.

I decided to voice my thought aloud, no matter how crazy it might sound. "What if someone else was at the crime scene who has a room at this hotel?"

"What are you getting at?" Sherman asked.

"What if Georgia is staying at the hotel? What if

that's one of the reasons she was able to sneak into my room?"

"What makes you think she snuck into your room?" Evie asked.

"Because I found daisy petals under my bed last night." I explained to petals to them, and their interest in what I was saying seemed to grow.

I glanced down the hallway. "We could see if there's a door this card works on."

Sherman's eyes widened. "You realize how long that would take? There are approximately one hundred rooms per floor, if my calculations are correct. There are also six floors to this hotel, bringing us to a grand total of—"

"Six hundred rooms," I finished. "I know, it's a long shot."

"It's more than a long shot," Evie said. "Even if we had the time to check every room on every floor, don't you think we'd be caught red-handed in the meantime?"

I leaned against my door in thought. "But let's think this through. Let's say this is Georgia's card. If she were here at the hotel, it would be because of me, right? And if she checked in here to keep an eye on me"—that was putting it nicely—"then she'd probably want a room that was close to mine. That makes sense, right?"

They both nodded sluggishly.

"So, I say we check a few down this hall. What could it hurt? If it doesn't work, I'll give the card to the detective and see if he can figure something out, especially given the nature of these crimes."

"Anytime I can try to avoid confronting a psychopath, I try to do that." Evie crossed her arms.

"That is a great life rule. I'd stick to it, whenever possible." The humor faded from my voice. "If you don't want to do this, you don't have to. I'm not trying to drag either of you into something you want no part of. But I need answers for myself."

"Why?" Sherman said.

I sighed. "Maybe it has something to do with Dr. Stone. He really put me in my place. I thought he believed in me, and all along he really wanted something else. Maybe I feel the need to prove to myself that I'm competent and capable."

"You shouldn't feel like you have to prove yourself to anyone," Evie reminded me.

"I know." I pointed to the faint outline of the mustache. "Believe me, any pride I had left is now gone. Long gone."

"I'm with you, Gabby," Evie said. "At least, for this part, I am. I'm not going to risk going to jail or anything, though."

"Understood." I glanced at Sherman. "You taking off?"

He shook his head. "No, I meant it when I said

this was the most fun I'd had in years. I'm here, and I'm in."

"Great." I glanced down the hallway and saw the long row of rooms ahead of me. "Let's get started. Sherman, can you keep a lookout? If someone is coming, can you let us know?"

"Let you know how?"

I shook my head, trying to come up with a great idea. Did I have to have all the great ideas? "I don't know. You could whistle. Sing. Drop something."

"Just say hello to the person who's approaching. We'll hear you and know," Evie said, her voice dry and her tone sure of herself.

Her idea made the most sense. "Do what she said. I was being too creative, obviously."

He wandered down to the beginning of the hall-way, right by the elevators. He leaned against the wall and pulled out his phone, making it look like he was checking his emails. Perfect!

I decided to start on the far side of my room, the one closest to the outside exit. I figured the one beside me was my best bet. I held the card over the sensor and held my breath.

The light turned red.

Disappointment bit at me. But I kept going. I continued down the row, but every door was a red light. Could my theory have been wrong? There was no way I'd be able to check every room at this hotel. Sherman was right about that.

But I'd hoped for some kind of answer. Maybe this was just another humbling moment in my life. Maybe I really did need to learn to leave things to the police instead of taking matters into my own hands. I would have thought I'd have learned that lesson by now, especially considering everything I'd been through.

"There are the doors on the other side of your room, toward Sherman," Evie said after we reached the end of the hallway.

I nodded. "It can't hurt to try, I guess. Sixty down. Five hundred and forty more to go."

I held up the card on the room on the other side of mine. Each door I'd tried had lessened my enthusiasm until I questioned myself. This had all been a whim. I should have given the card to the detective and told him it wasn't mine.

To my surprise, the light turned green.

I looked at Evie, and both of our faces registered surprise. This hadn't been a wild goose chase after all.

"What now?" Evie whispered.

I stared at the green light on the door handle, a tremble raking through me as I pictured what I might find on the other side. "Now I need to figure out if anyone is inside, I guess."

"What if it's Georgia?"

I didn't have time to think too much. Instead, I rapped on the door and waited.

No one answered.

Evie nodded at me, so I swiped the card again. When the light turned green, I turned the handle. Slowly, I pushed the door open.

Inside, the lights were out and the shades drawn. We stepped inside and closed the door before turning on the lights. I blinked as the room came into focus.

From where I stood now, the suite looked just like mine. Except it was freezing cold. Colder than it would be simply if the heat had been turned off. It almost felt like the AC had been turned on.

I crept through the front room, noting that there were no personal effects here anywhere. No suitcases or clothes or papers. It almost looked like no one had been here.

The tension continued to grow between my shoulder blades as I approached the bedroom. Would Georgia be waiting there? Had she been camped out beside me this whole time, and I'd been clueless?

The thought wasn't comforting.

Evie trailed behind me as I pushed open the door. I found the light switch and flipped it on.

The room was empty.

I nodded toward the bathroom. It was the last place we needed to check.

With a touch of reservation, I pulled the door open.

I sucked in a breath when I saw Georgia sprawled on the floor against the toilet.

A gun lay beside her hands, and blood was all over this place.

By all appearances, she was . . . dead.

TWENTY-EIGHT

EVIE RUSHED toward Georgia and put her hand at her neck. "She still has a pulse," she said. "Call 911. Now."

I pulled out my phone just as someone knocked at the door.

"Guys, it's me. Sherman."

I darted across the room, let him in, and stuck my phone in his hand. "Talk to dispatch for me. Tell them we found a woman with a gunshot wound and she's barely hanging on."

I grabbed the towel from the shelf and placed it over Georgia's chest wound. It was improbable that we were going to be able to save her. She needed blood. A lot of blood, based on the amount on the floor. But maybe she'd hold on until the paramedics got here.

I knew Georgia was not a good person, but that didn't stop me from wanting to help.

Lord, help her. Help us know what to do here!

I kept the blanket over the wound, trying to stop her from losing any more blood. Beneath my hands I could feel the faint beat of her heart. Evie knelt on the other side of me and propped Georgia's head up.

I glanced down at Georgia's face. Somehow, in the pallor of near death, Georgia didn't look as scary. She looked like a young woman who'd run away from home and gotten really confused on how to live life. Her hair was dyed a dark brown. Her lips were purple.

Beyond the putrid smell of blood, I also caught a whiff of something else. Body odor, maybe? Her jeans did look dingy. Surprisingly, however, I didn't smell gasoline.

What had she been doing here at the hotel?

Had she gotten this room for the sole purpose of spying on me? The thought made me shudder. Who knew what else this woman had been up to. I didn't even want to think about what she may have been plotting here with only a wall between us. The thought was terrifying.

"The ambulance should be here any minute now," Sherman said. He paused in the doorway, soaking the scene in for the first time. "It doesn't make sense. Why would she shoot herself?"

"Maybe she knew she couldn't get away with everything she'd done and decided suicide was an easier option." I glanced at the blood on the floor. Something didn't settle in my gut. "Look at this, guys. The blood is already starting to coagulate."

"So?" Sherman said. "Blood can congeal in fifteen minutes."

"This blood has coagulated in full. In fifteen minutes, the outer edges might turn to gel. But this entire puddle is thick, and it's already drying on the edges."

"The cooler temp in the room may have sped up the process," Evie said.

I shook my head. "The time line doesn't add up. The earliest she could have gotten back to the hotel would maybe be a couple of hours ago. The blood is solid, so it has been sitting for longer than that."

"So you think that someone tried to kill her?" Sherman asked.

I pointed to the wall. "Look at this blood spatter. She was shot and she struggled. This transfer stain leads out the door. Look at the direction of this swipe."

"It's like someone left and wiped their hand into the back spatter that spurted out from the entrance wound," Evie uttered. "I think you're onto something."

"By all appearances, it's a suicide," Sherman

continued. "I found this letter tucked under a pillow while I was talking with 911."

"There's no doubt that the woman was unstable," I said, keeping my hand on her chest as air expelled from her chest, resulting in a small moan. I lowered my voice out of respect, not that I thought she could hear me. "There's no doubt she was unbalanced. But she wouldn't have killed herself without reaching out to Trace first."

"Uh, guys. Look at this." Sherman held up a slip of paper he'd found on the floor.

I took it from him. It was Jono's business card. Interesting.

Just then, the paramedics rushed in, and we were shoved out of the way. But we certainly had a lot to think about. Maybe too much.

"So, how exactly did you discover Ms. Dalton in someone else's hotel room again?" Detective Farmer asked after Georgia had been taken to the hospital.

Detectives from all the different municipalities in Oklahoma were starting to know me on a first-name basis. Though I should be horrified, I was halfway flattered.

"It's a long story." And the least of my worries at

the moment. Couldn't he see there were more urgent matters at hand?

He crossed his arms, obviously not in a hurry. I sighed and launched into my explanation. When I finished, he continued to stare at me like I'd just lied.

"So, you just thought you'd see what room here at the hotel that key card worked on?" he repeated.

I sighed. "I know it sounds . . . unconventional. But I did what I thought was best for the case. I didn't want to cry wolf and call you out here for nothing."

The shadow suddenly blocked the light. I frowned when I saw Levi Stone standing there.

"Levi, thanks for coming," the detective said.

"No problem, John." Dr. Stone's gaze lingered on me for a moment, and I scowled. He turned his snakelike eyes back onto the detective. "What can I do for you?"

They were on a first-name basis, so they must be chummy. I hoped that didn't work against me.

"I was wondering if you'd take a look at this scene for me?" Detective Farmer said.

"Of course. Whatever I can do to help." With one last smoldering glance, Levi stepped under the crime scene tape.

I glanced back at Evie and Sherman and shook my head. They'd also been questioned by the detective, and I was pretty sure they shared my sentiment and felt like a group of adolescents instead of professionals.

Dr. Stone stepped out a few minutes later. I heard him through the doorway. "It looks like an attempted suicide to me. Plus, you said there was a note, right? I'd check the video footage here at the hotel to confirm it, but I think this is pretty cut and dry."

My mouth gaped open, and I lunged inside the room. "You said investigators are better off not knowing the details of the case before looking at the evidence. If you were objective, you'd realize this was not a suicide."

"I might have had a clearer view of the evidence if you and your friends hadn't trampled through the scene."

"I was trying to save her life. You're the one being hypocritical."

"And you're being idealistic."

I seriously wanted to punch him right in his smug little face.

"Ms. St. Claire, you're free to go now," Detective Farmer said. "If we need anything, we'll give you a call. In the meantime, stay out of any room you're not invited into."

I frowned and nodded. I waved to Evie and Sherman, figuring it would be in our best interest to go separate ways. The last thing I wanted was to get them in more trouble.

But this case did not feel over yet. Not in the least.

TWENTY-NINE

THREE HOURS LATER, I was back to my room. Alone. Exhausted. Angry.

I scrubbed the blood off my hands and turned everything over in my head. Why would Jono's card be in the room? If someone had tried to kill Georgia, then who had it been? Jono?

I plopped back on my bed and decided to give Trace a call. He answered on the first ring.

"What's going on?" he asked.

"Are you still at the hospital?"

"No, they kicked me out. They're keeping Skye overnight for observation, but I think she's going to be okay."

"Listen, have you seen Jono?"

"No, why?"

"Because we found Georgia tonight."

"What?" His voice rose with emotion.

I explained to him what happened.

"Wow. I never expected to hear that," Trace said.

"But Trace, we found Jono's card at the scene."

"Why would his card be there?"

"That's what I want to know. You said he was supposed to be in OKC earlier, but he'd arrived early at the scene to help us, correct?"

"Yeah, it should have taken at least an hour, probably more."

"Where did he say he was going?"

"He said he had to get some things in order before the tour started. He wanted to meet with Dud's family also. The memorial service is on Sunday after church, and the band is going to play a tribute to him. Jono's handling that for us."

I picked at a string on the comforter as my thoughts solidified. "What about your guitar? I heard it got smashed today."

"That's right. We broke for lunch, and when we came back, my guitar was in pieces."

"Any idea how that happened?"

"No idea. We were filming a scene for a video and we'd left, but the place was secure."

"Jono could get in, though. Correct?" Everything seemed to be pointing back to him.

"Gabby, you think Jono was in cahoots with Georgia?"

I nibbled on my lip for a moment. "I don't know, Trace. I really don't. But until we figure everything out, be careful, okay?"

"Gabby, Skye is safe and Georgia is in police custody. I don't know how Jono's card was in Georgia's possession, but, as far as I'm concerned, this is the first night in a long time that I can actually sleep easy."

"Just be careful, okay? Even if everything is tied up now, I want to be certain before you get too comfortable."

I went to two classes on Friday morning, but I decided to cut out early for the day. I was tired of people giving me strange looks behind my back. Enough was enough.

I escaped to a corner to call Detective Brooks for an update that I was sure he wouldn't give me. I pulled out a stack of business cards, shuffled through several other police departments, and finally found Detective Brooks's number.

"How's Georgia?" I started. I both wanted her to be okay and wanted her to wake up so the police could get some answers.

"She's still unconscious. Her family is flying in right now. Thanks for that tip about her."

"Are you still claiming this was a suicide attempt?"

"We have video surveillance that shows Georgia entering the hotel room alone that evening. No one else. Just Georgia. No one left the room between the time she entered and the time you and your little merry band of misfits broke in."

What? I couldn't believe it. "Can I see that video?"

"Of course not."

"You're sure it was Georgia?"

"It's grainy, but it looks like her. Her credit card was also used to reserve the room. The case isn't closed yet, Gabby, but there's no evidence that Georgia was assaulted by anyone but herself."

I hung up and frowned. When I looked up, Sherman was walking toward me. An idea hit me. It was a long shot, but it just might work. If only it didn't require something illegal.

"How are you today?" he asked.

I shrugged. "Still bothered. Listen, I have a question for you. However, I don't want to pull you into anything that will get you in trouble."

"Are you kidding? I haven't had this much fun . . . well, ever. What do you need?"

"Do you think you can hack into the hotel's security system?"

He raised his eyebrows. "Really?"

I nodded.

"Of course I can. But why?"

I explained to him what the detective had told me about the video and Georgia being the only one who entered the room.

"You want to see the video?" he whispered.

I nodded. "I *need* to see it. Something's not adding up, and we're the only ones who see it."

He rubbed his lips together a moment, a fine layer of sweat already covering his face. "I'll see what I can do. No guarantees, though."

"Can you do it without being discovered?"

He snorted. "Of course. Gabby, I know what I'm doing."

I thanked him and then started toward the parking garage. I hoped to make it back in time for the closing ceremony tonight, even though I'd heard a rumor that Dr. Stone was receiving the Kirsh Award. The thought of it turned my stomach.

I supposed if I separated his personal life from his professional life, then he deserved the honor. It was factually possible for a person to live a double life. But a person's character and integrity couldn't change identity like that. Either he was upright or he wasn't. I knew what my vote was for.

In the meantime, I was going to take Wentworth up on his offer and head out to his ranch for a little while. After all, when would I be back in Oklahoma again? I might as well enjoy a bit of the Oklahoma I'd always envisioned—one filled with farmers and cowmen, all being friends. Besides, I wanted to ask some more questions about Jono.

The ranch, like nearly every place I'd visited here so far, was about an hour away. As I drove northwest, I tried to relax, but I couldn't.

I knew I should be relieved and feel closure now that both Skye and Georgia had been found. But I didn't, no matter what anyone else said.

Skye had said that Georgia's last words were that she was going to put an end to things. Could she have meant her life? I just couldn't believe that.

I still hung on to the idea that someone else may have been working with Georgia. What if that person had become angered and tried to kill off Georgia?

My number one suspect at this point would be Jono. Had he hired Georgia to ensure Dud was out of the band and then killed her off to keep her silent? Was that a strong enough motive?

Quinton, the security guard, seemed to be looking for a way to get ahead. He liked female attention. How far would he go, though?

Or how about Lenny? Was he nursing a serious grudge—one worth murdering someone for?

I wasn't sure, but my gut told me that something was amiss. As much as I wanted to celebrate the end of this madness, I didn't feel settled.

After a few more turns, I pulled up to an old ranch-style house, surrounded by a wooden fence with stables and a barn in the background, along with several grazing horses. I spotted Trace's truck right away, and I knew I was in the right place.

I climbed out, sporting my cowboy hat, and before I even reached the door, Wentworth threw it open. "You found us."

"Nice spread of land you have here."

"This used to be my grandparents' property, actually." He started walking toward the backyard. "Anyway, like I said earlier, we're doing horseback riding and maybe having a bonfire later. We're celebrating, and it's all because of you."

"I don't know about that."

"Don't be humble. We can finally go on tour and have some closure, you know? No more unanswered questions haunting us. And it was a happy ending—for everyone except Georgia, I suppose."

"Moving on is a good thing." Wasn't that what God was trying to teach me lately? Sometimes I had to be hit over the head with things.

He flashed a grin. "Isn't it, though? Come on. Let's get saddled up."

"SO, just to give you a heads-up, Skye is here," Wentworth said as we walked across the vast expanse of lawn toward the barn.

"Really? So soon?" I figured she'd either stay in the hospital longer or go somewhere else to recover. It was great that she was jumping back into things so quickly. Maybe she needed that.

"That's right. Doctor released her. I guess Georgia took good care of her, so to speak. I mean, other than some mental anguish and probably years of counseling, she should be fine." He offered a half smile, half frown.

His words were true. She had a lot to deal with. Of course, some people might have said the same things about me after Scum had abducted me. Those weren't thoughts I wanted to address right now.

Right now, I was going to combine business with a little pleasure.

I spotted the stable ahead, a faded wooden structure that looked sturdy but old. The scent of horses and hay saturated the air around me. I could hear the neigh of one of the animals and the gentle chatter of two people talking.

"I have to admit, I haven't ridden a horse in years," I told Wentworth.

"It's like riding a bike."

I wasn't so sure about that.

As soon as I stepped inside the stables, I spotted Trace and Skye talking quietly in the corner. When Skye spotted me, she headed toward me and pulled me into a hug. "How can I say thank you?"

"You just did."

"You risked your life to save me. If you hadn't found me . . ." She shuddered.

I studied her a moment. She had gauze across her wrist and a Band-Aid on her forehead. She looked thin—maybe she'd always been thin?—and still a little pale. But today her eyes sparkled with new life, new hope. "I'm just glad you're okay, Skye."

Wentworth cleared his throat. "I don't want to break anything up here, because this moment is touching, to say the least. But we should get going."

Wentworth let me ride a mare named Annabelle. She was gentle and sweet, and she seemed to like me well enough. I gripped the reins, feeling as giddy as a girl on Christmas at the prospect of riding today.

I followed the rest of the gang out into the open field. There were miles and miles of nothing out here. The nearest house was probably half a mile away, at least. It was barely visible on the horizon.

"So, are you guys ready to go on tour?" I asked. "Everything's going well with the new drummer?"

"We're as ready as we can be," Trace said. "The drummer is doing well. But he's not Dud. However, I think everything will come together."

"That's good to hear."

"I'll race you to the other side of the pasture," Skye suddenly said.

"I'm game," Wentworth said.

As Skye and Wentworth—who were much more skilled than me—began to race, I trotted up beside Trace.

"This is appropriate, huh? Back in the saddle again," Trace said. "I think that's true for both of our lives. We fall down, but we get back up again. That's what makes us stronger."

"You're right. Absolutely right." I smiled and glanced across the field at Skye. "So, what's going on with you two? Are you picking up where you left off?"

He shrugged, his gaze switching from light-hearted to heavy faster than a rookie bull rider getting thrown. "I'm hoping we can take some time to figure everything out."

"A little hard when you'll be doing 150 concerts this year."

"You're telling me. But where there's a will, there's a way. Isn't that what they say?"

I glanced over at Skye as she smiled, looking like a natural in the saddle. "She seems like she's doing okay, especially with all things considered."

"Yeah, she does, doesn't she? That can only be by the grace of God. I can't even imagine what she went through. What you went through, for that matter. It's like Skye said—I can't thank you enough."

"It was nothing." I waved my hand in the air, brushing him off.

"No, you're wrong. It was everything."

Just then, Skye and Wentworth joined us. We all rode side by side for a while, shooting the breeze and acting like everything was normal. I knew that nothing was normal, though.

While Trace and Wentworth went to check out a section of fence that needed repair, I grabbed a moment alone with Skye. "So, how are you really, Skye?"

She shrugged, looking off into the distance. She looked so wholesome, like a small-town beauty with her long hair and unblemished features. "I guess I'm okay. I'm sure everything will hit me later, you know? Right now it just seems surreal."

"Can I ask you a question?" I approached the subject carefully, with hesitation in my voice.

"Sure. What's on your mind?"

"Skye, do you feel like Georgia had anyone helping her? Did you ever hear her talking to someone else?"

She glanced down at the saddle for a moment before glancing at me. "I did hear her bring someone back to that old shack one time. I'm not sure if he knew I was there or not. They were in the other room."

"You said *he*?"

She nodded. "That's right. It was definitely a male."

"Would you recognize the voice?"

She shook her head. "No, probably not. I'm sorry, but there was a wall between us. I couldn't hear anything that was being said."

"What's next for you, Skye? Are you going back to your old job? Staying in this area?"

She shrugged. "I don't know. Trace offered me a place on his tour. He said merchandising is always looking for additional help."

"So you're thinking about it?"

She halfheartedly seemed to nod. "Maybe. It's all soon, though, you know? If the tour was another month away, maybe. I feel like I need to pull myself together first. Then again, maybe I can pull myself together on the road. It's all kind of complicated."

"I can imagine."

A huge gust of wind nearly knocked me off my horse. I grabbed my hat and held tight. Just as I raised my face, I spotted the storm clouds on the horizon.

"We should get back to the stables," I mumbled.

I nudged my horse, and Annabelle started at a slow trot. I held on tightly to the reins. Wentworth and Trace followed us in.

Just as we got inside, the wind gusted hard again. The horses seemed to sense the severe weather and started pacing.

"You think they know something we don't?" I asked.

Suddenly Annabelle reared. The motion sent Skye flying back into the wall with surprise. Wentworth grabbed Annabelle's reins and pulled her down. He whispered something to her, and the mare seemed to calm.

Trace rushed toward Skye.

"Are you okay?" Trace asked.

She nodded, her eyes looking dazed and her hands trembling as Trace helped her stand. "I think so. Just shaken."

The small bandage on her forehead had come off,

and her old wound had busted open. She was going to need to clean that up before it got infected.

"I'm sorry about that, Skye," Wentworth said, examining her cut. "I don't know what got into her. Let me get you something for that wound."

"Let me go," Trace volunteered.

"I would, but you'll never find my first-aid kit. It's a miracle I even have one. Can you take care of the horses until we get back?"

"Of course," Trace said.

"I'm going with you," Skye said, her voice trembling. "I'm feeling all out of sorts right now. I'd feel better if I were inside. Maybe it was too soon to rejoin the living."

"Of course." Wentworth looked back at Trace. "Keep an eye on the skies. If you see anything, get to the storm shelter."

"You don't have to tell me twice."

Skye walked with Wentworth toward the house, her hair whipping in the wind.

With some prodding, Trace and I managed to get the horses back into their stalls. They all seemed anxious, though, which caused more unease to slosh in my gut.

"I'm going to go secure the gates," Trace told me. "Stay with the horses, okay?"

I nodded and crossed my arms as I wondered what to do with myself. Certainly there were other things that needed to be done, but I didn't know what. I only prayed that the weather didn't get any more serious than a rain shower.

As I paced the dusty ground, something buzzed in the distance.

I pivoted, trying to find the source, and spotted Trace's cell phone. He must have taken it out of his pocket when he'd been trying to wrangle the horses.

Out of curiosity, I glanced at the phone. Jono's name was on the screen. I'd been wanting to talk to him again.

I second-guessed myself for a split second before grabbing the phone and answering.

"Gabby?" Jono asked.

"It's me. Trace is a little busy, so I'm taking his messages."

"I guess you're out at Wentworth's ranch. How cozy."

I ignored whatever he was trying to get at. "I have a question for you, Jono. Where were you yesterday when you were supposed to be in Oklahoma City? How'd you get to the mountains so fast when I was stranded?"

"What? You think I'm behind some of these things that happened around here?" When I didn't say anything, he gasped. "You've got to be kidding me!"

"I'm not kidding. Where were you?"

"I was looking for a new guitar for Trace, if you must know. He was so upset about his. I knew I had to cheer him up. There's this used-guitar shop about an hour from Oklahoma City. I was there. Ask the owner and he'll confirm it."

"Why was your business card found on Georgia?"

"Aren't you smart? The police already talked to me about it. I did give Georgia my card, but it was a couple of months ago. I was trying to convince her to leave Trace alone. I told her there could be incentives for her cooperation. She never responded."

I frowned as a better picture of Jono formed in my mind. "You like trying to pay people off, don't you?"

"Money talks. That's all I'm saying. I know what language most people speak, and it's cash. Anyway, please tell Trace that I called. Goodbye!"

I hung up the phone and set it back where I found it.

Jono was a manipulator. Just how far would he go to get what he wanted, though?

Before I could dwell on it too long, my phone rang. I pulled it out and saw that Sherman had texted me a video.

Bingo!

I pulled it up. Sure enough, at 6:07 yesterday, a woman whose hair and frame matched Georgia's entered the room next to mine. I continued to watch, waiting for someone to emerge. No one did.

At 6:24, the door to my room opened. I walked out, and instead of walking toward the atrium as I always did, I walked in the opposite direction, my back toward the camera.

The only problem was that I'd been at the fire during that time. Someone else had dressed up like me and snuck into my room! Someone must have managed to unlock the adjoining door.

Could it have been Jono? He was thin enough and not that tall. What if he put a wig on? Could he pass for me on a grainy video? I didn't know.

Trace came running in through the door and pointed outside. "I have a feeling we are in for quite a storm."

I followed his gaze and frowned. "Those clouds look fierce."

He nodded solemnly. "They appear to be. Don't be alarmed. It might not mean anything yet."

I swallowed hard. "Or it could mean everything."

THIRTY-ONE

"I'VE BEEN THROUGH HURRICANES, TRACE." A gust of wind swept inside the stables and propelled strands of my hair into my eyes. "But not tornadoes."

He grabbed my arm. "We need to get to a storm shelter."

"What about the horses? We can't leave them." I couldn't let these animals fend for themselves. It just didn't seem right.

"Horses have good instincts. We'll leave the door to the stable open so they'll be able to get out if they need to. They're smart animals."

Hesitantly, I nodded and started at a slow jog toward the outside.

As we stepped outside, a smattering of rain hit us.

A new voice cut through the air. "You've got to help. I think Wentworth is going crazy!"

Skye ran toward us. Her eyes were wide and darting madly about. Did she have some posttraumatic stress kicking in right now? Why else would she look like that? Why else would she say Wentworth was going crazy?

"What do you mean?" Trace met her in five strides.

"We were inside, and he just started throwing things. I thought he was going to kill me! The look in his eyes was just . . ." She shuddered. "What should we do?"

Wentworth was Georgia's right-hand man? He couldn't be. Not Wentworth.

I glanced toward the dark clouds and saw that they'd begun to churn. And it was headed our way. "I don't know if this is the best place to be right now," I yelled.

"Come on. I've got to get you guys to safety," Trace said. "There's a storm shelter not far from the house. Our best bet is to wait it out there."

The wind gusted, nearly blowing me down. Debris flew in my face—dust and dirt and maybe even some sticks and leaves.

I held one of Trace's hands, and Skye held the other. We pushed through the wind until we reached the storm shelter doors. With some effort, Trace managed to open one. He ushered us inside and paused at the top of the steps.

"I've got to go back for Wentworth," he said.

"Trace . . ." I wanted to argue, yet I understood his urge to help his friend.

But what if Wentworth tried to kill him?

Just then, a loud bang sounded outside. I could only imagine what might be flying through the air.

"You guys are going to be okay down here," he said. "I'll be back."

"Please be careful!" I called to him.

He shoved on the door. "What?"

He pushed harder, but nothing happened.

"Maybe something fell on it. There was a pile of wood and debris not far from the door," I said.

He sighed and ran a hand through his hair. "I don't know. I just know we're not getting out of here right now."

I reached the bottom and shivered. The space was cold and dark, with only two small windows at the top of one wall. I assumed they were there for airflow in case people were to get trapped down here.

I imagined Wentworth emerging from the shadows. We'd be goners down here, stuck with no escape. There was a ladder, an old armoire, a table, and some chairs. The ground was cold and gritty—

either packed dirt or filthy cement, I couldn't tell which. The lights flickered above us, and I wasn't sure if it was my imagination or if the whole place was rocking.

"We'll wait it out here," he said, starting down the steps.

"Is this normal?" I asked, feeling the pressure around me drop.

"Tornadoes in Oklahoma?" Trace asked, joining Skye and me as we hunkered by the wall. "They're about as normal as worms in an apple. You know they happen; you just hope you don't taste them."

The wind kicked up, and the lights flickered again. My ears started popping.

Skye pulled her knees to her chest while Trace stood and began pacing. The tight set of his shoulders and his rigid jawline told me that he was worried also.

The intensity of sound outside strengthened. The funnel cloud must be getting closer. I closed my eyes, imagining the destruction.

Lord, protect us. Protect everyone in this storm's path. Oh, and please help us to find some answers, give us closure.

"We're just going to have to wait this out," Trace said, his hands on his hips.

"I'm so bad at waiting." I paused. Had I said that out loud?

"Sometimes, waiting is all you can do," Trace said. "There's no other choice but to hold tight until things calm down."

As I lowered myself to the floor, I thought about all the ways that could apply to my life. Half of the time, I waited too long and missed opportunities. The other half, I pushed ahead before I should. Life was such a delicate balance sometimes, and I often tilted the scales too quickly in one direction or the other.

The ground began to shake, the walls vibrating from the pressure and wind outside.

"Get under these tables!" Trace yelled.

Skye ducked under a small table beside her while Trace and I huddled under an old, farm-style kitchen table.

My heart pounded hard in my chest. My ears continued to pop. My throat tightened.

I wanted to look outside. I wanted to see what was coming. But sometimes we didn't have that luxury. In life *and* in tornadoes.

I put my head between my knees and waited.

And waited.

I tried to brace myself, prepare myself, for the walls to be ripped away. For flying debris to assault us. For winds strong enough to suck us into the sky.

My blood rushed through my ears, nearly drowning the sound of the tornado.

The house shook harder.

The wind howled.

Hail slammed into the ventilation window.

Then there was quiet.

Stillness.

The wind died.

The atmosphere calmed.

I raised my head and glanced at Trace. "Is it over?"

"Sounds like it," he said. "It appeared quickly and now it's gone."

I let out a breath of relief. Thank goodness. "Can we come out?"

"Stay put for a few more minutes, just in case," Trace said. "I'm going to try that door one more time."

I glanced over at Skye. She stretched her legs out. The bottom of her boots stared back at me, and I spotted a little flower emblem on the bottom. My heart shuddered a beat.

I'd seen those same boots in the picture of Skye, the one with . . . daisies on the table behind her. Why hadn't I thought of that before?

Those footprints I'd seen after Dud was shot—the ones that matched the set outside of the window at Skye's place—I'd assumed they were Georgia's. I'd assumed they were the evidence that tied both crimes together, that connected Georgia with them.

But what if I'd tied the wrong person to both crimes?

I sucked in a deep breath as the implications of my thought washed over me.

THIRTY-TWO

I SHOOK MY HEAD. No, I wasn't thinking clearly. That had to be it.

Why would Skye stage her own abduction? Why would she kill Dud? And, even if she did, why was she back here with us now? Unless . . .

I couldn't even finish my thought.

I glanced up at her. She stared at me with a dark, foreboding look in her eyes. Did she know that I knew? That I suspected something? More facts collided in my head.

The security guard, Quinton, had said he'd seen a dark-haired woman with Dud before he died. I'd assumed that Georgia had changed her look again, since people said that's what she did.

What if that woman was Skye and not Georgia, though?

Trace stomped back down the steps, shaking his head. "Bad news—the door still won't budge. It looks like we're stuck down here for a while, at least until someone comes to check on us."

I swallowed hard. That wasn't good. "Are you sure?"

"Positive. Something must be on top of those storm doors." Trace pulled out his cell phone.

"Stephen used to love storms, you know," Skye said.

Trace paused, the phone still in his hands but his fingers no longer moving.

"Who's Stephen?" I asked, an idea loosely circling around in my brain. I watched Skye carefully, trying to get a read on her, trying to anticipate what she might be thinking.

"My brother," Skye said.

"The one who died, right?" I questioned, realizing I sounded callous. However, if my theory was right, then this was no time to be polite.

She nodded. "Suicide."

I glanced at Trace and saw a wrinkle form between his eyes. He was beginning to put everything together. The fact that all along he'd been the real target here. Not Georgia. Not Skye. Not Dud.

Trace.

"Stephen was your brother?" Trace asked.

"Half-brother, actually. That's why we had

different last names." Her eyes looked colder and darker by the moment.

Trace continued to stare at Skye, his face taut and slightly bewildered. "But he was my drummer. Before Dud."

He seemed to be processing everything out loud.

I remembered what he'd told me before. Stephen —I hadn't known his name until now—had done drugs and acted irrationally. Trace had to let him go from the band, and shortly after that he'd taken his own life.

As realizations continued to hit me, my gut churned.

Was Skye trying to avenge her brother's death? Had she killed Dud to ruin Trace?

But what about Georgia? How had Stalker Girl been involved with all of this?

"His death was always your fault, you know." Skye stood, suddenly looking less like an innocent victim and more like a vicious, conniving killer. All her focus was on Trace.

"What are you talking about?" Trace asked.

"You got too big for your britches. You thought you were better than him. That he was expendable. So when the going got tough, you cut Stephen out of the band. Right in the time when he needed you guys the most. You turned your back on him."

Trace raised his hands as he pleaded his case.

"That's not true, Skye. Stephen had a lot of problems. We tried to get him help. We gave him a lot of opportunities to change. We thought the only thing that could help him was hitting rock bottom. None of our pleas got through to him."

"Liar!" Her voice rose and became coarser, angrier. "You didn't want him to hold the band back. You were afraid he'd bring all of you down."

"Stephen had a lot of issues, Skye. A lot of issues. He needed help."

"So you kicked him to the curb? How loving of you." Bitterness dripped from her words. She reached behind her and emerged with a gun. "Now you're going to pay."

"Skye . . . no." Trace's eyes widened, and he stepped back.

Skye's nostrils flared as she stepped toward him. "Stephen killed himself. Meanwhile, the person responsible—that would be you—is as happy as can be. You're living your dreams, doing what you love, raking in money, adored by so many. If they only knew the real you."

"Skye, I mourned for your brother when he died. I hoped he would get his life together and never anticipated things would end as they did. I still miss him."

I glanced around, knowing I had to do something. I had to time my moves carefully, though. All Skye had to have was one knee-jerk reaction and someone could die.

Reaching behind me, I tried to pull my phone out and dial 911.

"I want to see your hands, Gabby St. Claire," Skye said, jerking the gun toward me. "You're too clever for your own good. You were never supposed to be involved here. You ruined everything!"

I pulled my hands forward and set my phone on the table. "I saved your life."

"I would have gotten myself out of that house before it burned down."

"So, this whole thing was a setup?" I asked. "You made me believe that you were Georgia, got me to follow you out to that house. Was I supposed to die?"

She smirked. "It would have been nice."

"Why? Why did you go through all that trouble?"

"Can't you see? Everything was on purpose. I never liked country music. I knew Trace liked to check out that old music store, so I made sure I was there one day when he was. The meeting wasn't chance at all. I moved here just so I could make Trace realize everything that I'd lost because of him."

Suddenly, the wind started whipping up outside again. My already tight nerves tightened even more.

"Let me guess: Georgia was your scapegoat."

"I saw her following Trace around everywhere like a little lost puppy dog. I knew an easy mark when I saw one. I was actually holding *her* hostage. She was so unstable that everyone easily believed she was the guilty one. My plan worked like a charm."

"You tried to kill her, though, and make it look like a suicide."

"I did. Yesterday was the perfect day. I swung by the hotel, finished off Georgia, and then went to the video shoot. As soon as I had the chance, I sweet-talked the guy at the front desk and smashed your precious guitar. After that, I stood outside of the conference center until you emerged, and I made sure that you saw me, Gabby, and followed me to the house. As soon as I saw you walking down the road, I lit the gasoline and tied myself up."

I shook my head, trying to process all of that. "You're the one who lured me into the bull pasture?"

She shrugged. "Well, at that time I thought you might be dating Trace. I had no idea you were going to be stepsiblings."

"You had this whole plan worked out, didn't you? And Georgia was the perfect victim."

"She was. I planted Georgia in that hotel room knowing she'd look guilty. I even used her credit card. It all worked just as it was supposed to."

"But video surveillance shows a girl who looks like Georgia entering that hotel room around six last night," I said. "Georgia was in that hotel room dead before that. Who was she?"

Skye shrugged. "Just some dumb teenager who'd do anything for fifty bucks. I told her to keep her head down, go in the room, and exit from the adjoining room a few minutes later. I gave her a wig to put on before she exited so she'd look like you."

"You're clever. But how did you get the key card to my room?"

She smiled. "Haven't you ever heard of womanly charms? Some guys—even professionals working at the front desk of hotels—will do anything for a pretty girl with an innocent smile."

I needed to keep her talking. "So, why not let everyone think she was guilty and that you got away with it? Why ruin everything by pulling out a gun now? You were home free."

"And Trace is still going on tour, still happy. He still hasn't learned his lesson." She sent a scathing scowl his way. "That's unacceptable. There are consequences to our actions, Trace. That's what I always told my students. Theirs usually involved extra homework." Her scowl turned into a malevolent smile as she took a step toward Trace. "Yours will be a little harsher than that, unfortunately."

I braced myself to fight for my life and Trace's.

TRACE RAISED HIS HANDS AGAIN. "It doesn't have to end this way, Skye."

She shrugged. "I was hoping the tornado might just finish you off. I wasn't that lucky."

"What did you do to Wentworth?" I asked.

"I just knocked him out. He'll be fine. If the storm didn't get to him." By her smirk, it looked like that was exactly what she was hoping.

The wind swept into the shelter again. What exactly was going on outside? And how was I going to get out of this storm shelter? Who knew we were here?

This wasn't looking good.

I glanced around the room, trying to determine what my options were. There was an old table, nothing on it. Some tools. One of them could work, if

I could get to them. There was also an old lamp, a refrigerator, and cans of paint.

She'd shoot me before I could get over to any of those items, though.

Maybe I just needed to keep her talking until help arrived.

But what if help didn't arrive? Who knew what kind of damage the storm had done outside?

I was going to go with talking my way out of this one. It probably wouldn't work, but what other choice did I have at the moment?

"You don't have to let this ruin your life, Skye. There's still so much you can do. You can turn this tragedy around." That's what I hoped to do with my own life.

She snorted. "I don't even have the desire to try. The only thing that brings me any possible joy is the thought of Trace suffering."

I glanced over at Trace and noticed he'd gone pale. No one would blame him for that.

But right now Skye was focused on me, obviously trying to prove how much smarter she was than everyone else. I needed to use that to my advantage.

Make that, *Trace* needed to use this to his advantage.

Trace took a step back, his hand reaching for something.

Something rumbled outside, causing us all to pause. The ground moaned around us.

"Trace suffering isn't going to make you feel better," I continued. "Only for a minute. When that wears off, you're going to regret your choices."

"You wouldn't understand!" she snapped.

"My fiancé was shot by a man who should have been in prison," I told her. "We broke up. I've lived a lot of days in misery. But not anymore. If I can turn things around, then so can you."

Her nostrils flared. "Don't use this mumbo jumbo on me. You're only trying to delay the inevitable. We're all going to die down here. You need to face the facts."

I exchanged another glance with Trace. There were two of us and only one of her. If I could get the gun away from her, we might have a fighting chance.

Getting the gun away from her would be the challenge.

When the wind slammed into the building, I saw my opportunity.

I swung my leg toward her. Just as my foot connected with the gun, it discharged. I held my breath, praying the bullet hadn't hit anything, anyone.

Before I could gather myself, Trace grabbed the rope behind him. He circled it and, in one swoop, wrangled Skye. I scrambled on the ground and found the gun.

My hands no longer shook like they used to when I held a gun. This time, I aimed it at Skye, knowing good and well what I was doing with it.

Skye struggled, but Trace wrapped the rope around her and tied her up. She struggled against her binds.

My heart slowed finally.

"You're both crazy!" Skye sputtered, fighting her binds.

"We're crazy?" Trace said. "You killed Dud and tried to kill Georgia."

She spit at him. "You make me sick. This isn't done, you know."

Just then, the shelter doors opened. Two police officers peered down at us. "You okay down there?"

My heart finally slowed. Really slowed down. Help was here. Skye couldn't hurt us. And, apparently, the tornado had passed.

THIRTY-FOUR

"YOU HAVE the right to remain silent," an officer told Skye as he handcuffed her.

"How'd you know to come?" I asked yet another detective.

"Someone named Wentworth called," the detective said.

Wentworth! He was alive!

"Paramedics are treating him in the house right now. Apparently, he has a pretty nasty concussion," the detective said.

I took a deep breath, more than relieved that all of this was finally over. My gaze roamed the landscape around me and stopped at the stables. They were still standing, untouched by the storm!

The house behind me was still standing as well, but I could see a line of destruction farther away. It only appeared to be a tree, some fencing, and part of the old barn. A trash can, a toilet, and a water heater lay in the field. Who knew where they came from?

As I turned, I saw my rental car. It had been picked up and dropped by the storm. It now lay on its side.

Awesome.

Despite that, it could have been so much worse. So much worse.

Thank you, Lord!

Trace and I gave our statements, and three hours later, we were okayed to leave. Trace agreed to drive me back to the hotel before meeting Wentworth at the hospital.

"That was some evening, wasn't it?" I said, once we were in his truck.

"I just can't believe it." He shook his head, looking a little shell-shocked. "How did I not notice that Skye was related to Stephen?"

"They had different last names, different fathers, they probably didn't look alike, and she was deceitful. No one plans for something like this or knows in advance to keep their eyes open for shrewd relatives to show up with vengeance in their eyes."

He squeezed the skin between his eyes. "I feel horrible about Stephen."

I clutched his shoulder, wishing I could make him feel better. I knew the real healing would come with time, though. "People made bad choices, Trace. You tried to do what was best for him and for the band. You couldn't have him coming on tour with you with drug problems."

We rode silently for several minutes. I was going to miss Oklahoma. It was hard to believe I'd be on my way home first thing Saturday morning. My time here had flown by.

I pushed the CD into the player, ready for some music to cut the silence. Trace started to say something, but before the words could leave his mouth, his deep, crooning voice rang through the speaker.

It sounded raw and uncut, like he'd sat down with his guitar and recorded in his living room. But that wasn't what stood out to me. What stood out were the words of the ballad.

Move on
  Even when the past
  Tries to drag you back

Be strong
  Even when the road is long
  Even when sadness is your song

• • •

Just sing
> *Get back up*
> *Show the world that you're tough.*
> *But remember that moving on*
> *May not be what you thought.*

Something clutched my heart. I wasn't exactly sure what it was. Gratitude. Realization. Understanding.

"I wrote that for you, Gabby," Trace said. "It's rough, but I wanted to capture what I had so far. I didn't expect you to hear it yet."

"It's beautiful," I told him. "Really beautiful."

Finally, we pulled into the garage of the conference center. We parked and started toward the hotel.

"Thanks, Trace, for everything," I told him as we walked.

"Thank you!" he said, pausing at the door to the hotel. "I'm really glad we met, Gabby. I wasn't sure if I was going to have to fake being nice to you. But then I met you and realized you're the real deal. Genuine, smart, likable, and you've got spunk. I know we're a little old to become stepsiblings, but I'd be honored to have you as family."

Spontaneously, I threw my arms around him in a hug. "Thanks, Trace. I feel the same way. I hope we'll stay in touch."

"I have a message for you," a new voice said.

I turned and saw the sidewalk prophet who'd set up outside of the hotel this week. Immediately, I braced myself. The man was still out here at this hour? He was dedicated.

His gaze latched onto mine, determination written there. "God is going to bless you, young lady. Keep your eyes on Him, and He'll show you the way."

With that, the man disappeared down the sidewalk.

My heart slowed a moment as his words washed over me. I didn't know if that was a message from God or not, but I did know that the Christian life was blessed. It was still full of pain, but peace superseded the heartache when we put our trust in God.

"I think I second that motion, Gabby. I can't wait to see what God does through your life." He tilted his hat. "Let's stay in touch, okay?"

"You know it."

I stepped inside the hotel, hoping for the life of me I didn't run into anyone. My fellow conferees should all still be at the banquet. I glanced at my watch and saw that it was only 9:30. It felt like days had passed since I left this morning. So much had happened.

All I wanted was to go to my room, shower, and get a good night's rest. I looked down and saw that my jeans now had a rip in one knee and a dirt stain on the other. A couple of specks of blood stained my shirt. Without even looking, I knew my hair was wind tousled and a frizzy mess.

I took a step toward my room when someone called my name. All my muscles tightened as I turned and saw Evie running toward me.

She, of course, was decked out in a black dress with a pearl necklace and painfully high heels. She was a picture of cool poise and elegant detachment.

"I was hoping I'd catch you!" She looked me up and down. "You look terrible, by the way."

If she only knew.

"Thanks." I couldn't keep the sarcasm out of my voice.

"It doesn't matter. You need to come with me." She took my arm and tried to tug.

I didn't budge. My job here was over, and I didn't feel obligated to do anything else. I'd solved the mystery, completed my workshops, and met Trace. I could rest easy tonight.

"I'm not going anywhere."

She frowned. "You have to see this."

"See what?"

"Walk with me." Somehow, my feet slowly moved beside her. I would put on brakes again if she tried to take me near the banquet hall, though. "Get this. Rumor has it that Dr. Levi Stone is being sued for sexual harassment."

"What?"

Evie nodded. "It's true. A past employee of his has filed a lawsuit, saying she was fired when she didn't comply with his wishes outside of work."

"Ouch. That's gonna hurt." I had to admit that a touch of satisfaction coursed through me. Dr. Stone had gotten what was coming to him. He'd gotten the justice he'd deserved.

"Apparently she has one of the best law firms in the country representing her."

I remembered that letter from a law firm that I'd found in his desk. Had it been a legal notice of some sort? "Maybe this will teach him to play well with others."

"Maybe it will tarnish his reputation here among his colleagues. He shouldn't get away with treating people like that. No one should feel shamed for doing the right thing."

I jerked my head toward her as something in her voice made me think twice. "You're the woman, aren't you?"

She glanced at me, sadness in her eyes as she nodded. "I'm not *the* woman, but I'm one of them. Now you can see why I was so upset. First, he passed me over for a job. Then he later hired me. When I didn't give in to his advances, he called me nasty names and fired me. He said if I told anyone, he'd make my life miserable. I was humiliated. I almost didn't participate in the lawsuit, but after hearing what he did to you, I changed my mind."

"I can't imagine, Evie. I'm so sorry."

"Anyway, I'm sorry I started that rumor about you."

My mouth sagged open. "You started that?"

"Yes, and I regret it. However, I did not draw the mustache on you."

I shook my head, outraged. "How could you do that?"

"You're not who I thought you'd be, Gabby. You're pretty and smart. I thought you were the type who might do anything to get ahead." She sighed. "Anyway, the whole reason I'm telling you all of this is because Dr. Stone was supposed to receive the Kirsh Award tonight. The board changed their minds after they heard about the lawsuit. I guess there are five women total who are suing him."

Anger still coursed through me, but her last statement had been a nice distraction from my negative emotions. "I can't believe the nerve of some people." I was talking about Dr. Stone and Evie, unfortunately.

"The good news is that Sherman won the award in his place. Isn't that great?"

"Sherman did? That's wonderful."

The door to the banquet appeared ahead, and I shook my head, digging my heels into the carpet.

"Just step in here while I finish talking to you."

"I'd rather not. I look like a wreck."

"It's dark. No one will see us."

"Why can't we talk out here?"

"Because the president is supposed to make an announcement. I want to hear what she has to say."

I frowned. "If anyone sees me, so help me . . ." I made the idle threat, knowing nothing would come of it.

"Thank you." She wasted no time dragging me into the room. Thankfully, it was dark inside. Guests were seated at tables lit only by candlelight. On the stage at the front of the room, Dr. Gable, the head of the American Forensic Association, made her closing remarks. She had everyone's rapt attention.

"Finally, I'd like to announce the recipient of this year's First Time Attendee Award. The honoree who receives this distinction is someone who puts forensics and justice above themselves. It's someone who's committed, dedicated, and who's made positive strides at making a difference in the law enforcement community, although a bit unconventionally sometimes."

I crossed my arms, curious to see who would receive the award.

"It's my honor to present this award this year to . . ." She held up a certificate in one hand and a plaque in the other. "Gabby St. Claire."

I stared at her, certain I hadn't heard her correctly. Evie nudged me forward, but I still felt dazed. What was going on here?

"Ms. St. Claire has demonstrated great fortitude. Not only has she overcome some big obstacles in her life, she's also worked tirelessly to ensure that justice prevails. Many deserving people were nominated. But when Ms. St. Claire found a missing woman this week while off duty, it proved she was willing to go above and beyond."

Evie moved beside me toward the stage. If she let go of my arm, I was fairly certain I'd ended up just stopping and staring. Everything seemed hazy, and I still didn't feel like I'd understood a word of what was being said.

"Ms. St. Claire used her prowess and intellect, as well as her intuition, to ensure that every life counts." She turned toward me. "I'm pleased to see she's here tonight."

As I took a step closer, I noticed her grin flattened some. She was probably wondering what I'd been through. If she thought a tornado and nearly being killed by the very woman I'd supposedly saved earlier, she'd be correct. There'd be a time to give her the latest version of the story later.

"Gabby, please join me onstage."

I did as she asked, pulling a hair behind my ear and really wishing I'd gotten that shower in.

"We are so pleased that you joined us here this year for our conference. You've been an inspiration to us all as you've gone above and beyond, all for the sake of forensics. Can everyone please give her a round of applause?"

People in the banquet hall not only clapped, they rose to their feet.

My hands shook with surprise and shock. I'd had no clue this would happen. Not even an inkling.

"Gabby, would you like to say something?" Dr. Gable asked.

I took the plaque and certificate from her and stood awkwardly behind the podium. I stared out at my classmates, the same ones who'd acted like I'd been given a scarlet letter earlier. It was funny how people could change their opinions so quickly. One minute I'd been judged harshly, the next I was being praised.

Welcome to life in the real world. Not always fair. Not always right. But it was what it was.

"Thank you," I started, my voice shaky. "I'm nearly speechless. *Nearly* being the key word."

A chuckle washed through the crowd.

I drew in a deep breath, trying to collect my thoughts. "One of the most important things I've realized is that it doesn't make a difference where you are in life, what point you're at. Maybe you're testifying in court and in demand from lawyers and police departments. Maybe you're a lab tech or maybe even something as lowly as a crime scene cleaner."

A slight murmur ran through the room. I knew what they were saying: Who in their right mind would be a crime scene cleaner? After all, I was at a conference of trained professionals. I was also a trained professional, in more than one sense of the word.

"All the work we do is valuable. We look at the minute things, the things that most people don't see, and we make sense of it. We're putting the puzzle pieces together. We're making things make sense through the same details.

"There's a principle we all operate by called Locard's that professes that people leave bits of themselves wherever they go. I want to take that principle a step further. As investigators, we touch people's lives. We leave a trail of justice wherever we go. Though it's not always visible to the human eye, though we're not always recognized by the news or sometimes even by the victims, there are traces of the work we do all around us. We're all making a difference."

I shifted, wishing I was better at speaking in front of people. "With all of that said, I wanted to say thank you. This award means so much to me. My life right now isn't exactly how I envisioned it would be.

But I'm in a good place, and I'm ready to look to the future and to move forward. Thank you all for this honor. I'll never forget you."

Applause sounded again as I walked down from the stage. Evie met me and offered a huge thumbs-up. "I'm so proud of you."

"You knew about this?" I asked.

"Who do you think nominated you?" She looped her arm through mine.

"I thought you had to be a board member to nominate someone?"

"I *am* a board member."

"Then why are you attending this conference?" We continued out the door and into the hallway just as various faculty members were recognized.

"Even board members need new training sometimes."

"Thank you. It means a lot."

She smiled, one of the first smiles I ever remembered seeing on her. "You deserved it. When nominations were being accepted, I immediately thought of you. You've done some outstanding work. You've risked your life and gone above and beyond."

I smiled, satisfaction rising in me.

If the setbacks in my life hadn't happened, I probably never would have come here. I would probably not have a clear plan for my future. I didn't have all the answers, not by a long shot. But at least I was getting out of the rut I'd been in.

God certainly did use our greatest pain to form the most effective launching pads for our lives. I knew I had to continue helping people. I'd pursue more education, but in the meantime, I'd realized that crime scene cleaning wasn't all doom and gloom. God was using me through it.

I still had hope that I'd have resolution in certain areas of my life. But until then, I was going to make the most of things.

Just then, my phone buzzed. I glanced down and saw I had a text message from Sierra.

Guess what I just heard? Riley is moving back into his old apartment. Can you believe it?

My heart quickened. It looked like life was about to get even more interesting.

~~~

Thank you so much for reading **Broom and Gloom**. If you enjoyed this book, please consider leaving a review!

Keep reading for a preview of **Dust and Obey**.
~~~

An undercover assignment at a couples retreat
proves love—and housework—can be deadly.
SQUEAKY CLEAN MYSTERIES, BOOK 10
DUST AND OBEY
AWARD-WINNING AUTHOR
CHRISTY BARRITT

DUST AND OBEY: CHAPTER ONE

Finally my life was getting back on track. I was looking forward and not behind. I was pressing on. Running the race. Considering my trials pure joy.

Then my phone rang.

I climbed into my van, in a hurry to grab some lunch before I had to be back for the next training session for my new job, and glanced at the screen. When I saw Riley Thomas's phone number, my nerves ratcheted from a-day-at-the-beach calm to New York City crazy. He was my ex-fiancé, the man who'd crushed my heart, turned my life upside down, and left me wandering aimlessly for the past few months.

Why is he calling me?

I cranked the engine and let some air blow on me. Unfortunately, the air was still hot. Springtime was unreasonably muggy here in Raleigh, North Carolina, and I needed all the Freon possible to help me chill.

I stared at the phone another moment in contemplation. What possible reason could Riley have to call me? I already knew he was moving back home to Norfolk, taking up his former residence in the apartment across the hall from me. Just like old times. Not that *he'd* told me that little update.

My best friend, Sierra, had been the one to mention it. Not that I was bitter about it or anything.

Just when I thought I'd gotten over Riley and the way he'd broken my heart like a Greek engaging in some celebratory plate smashing, the man decided to reenter my life. Lucky me.

I sighed and, after a moment of hesitation, decided to get this conversation over with.

"Hey, Riley." I leaned back in my ripped seat, trying to deny the fact that my heart raced.

"Gabby." His voice sounded smooth and warm. "How are you?"

"I'm . . ." I almost said "hanging in," but that sounded weak.

Instead, I glanced out the bug-splattered windshield at the new facility where I'd spent the majority of my time the past two weeks. I was now working as a representative and instructor for Grayson Technologies, a leading provider of forensic equipment and supplies. I'd begun a new chapter in my life, and that should equate with hope.

"I'm doing great," I finally said.

"I'm glad to hear that. Listen, I know it's been a while, but I have a proposal for you."

"A proposal?" As soon as the words croaked out of my mouth, I wished they hadn't. I knew how Riley could interpret them, but my quip wasn't about a lingering desire to marry him or our broken engagement or me longing after him. I rubbed my forehead and wanted a redo.

"Yeah, you know, an idea." His voice didn't hold any judgment or even sarcasm, but instead he sounded earnest.

I released the breath I held. Thank goodness he'd been gracious enough to let that one slide, because it could have easily made it onto my top ten most embarrassing list—and I had some doozies up there. "Okay, shoot."

"I was going to wait until you were back in town, but I'm afraid it will be too late by then. This . . . *proposal*"—he seemed to hesitate before using the word—"actually involves this upcoming weekend. Sierra said you'd be back home tomorrow, so I'm hoping if you say yes, the timing will work out."

"I'm sorry. Our connection is lousy. Did you say you want to elope this weekend?" My words contained a slightly devious edge. This time I purposefully wanted to make him uncomfortable because I was immature like that sometimes in matters of the heart.

"Uh . . ." he started.

I heard him waffling around in agony, and I thought I'd get more pleasure from his discomfort. My negative feelings had really just risen to the surface over the past couple of weeks, and I wasn't sure why. I suppose it tied in with the stages of grief. I had been in denial for a long time, and now I was wafting back and forth between anger and acceptance.

I prayed that I was edging closer to acceptance, but some days I questioned whether that was true.

"I'm just kidding, Riley." I needed for him to know that I was over him and that his return to Norfolk wasn't going to affect my mental well-being in the slightest.

In theory, at least.

Riley let out a short, clipped laugh. Had I made him nervous?

I was more curious now than ever as to where this conversation was going. "Anyway, all joking aside, what's going on?"

"You know how I started working for the law firm up in DC? One of the law partners has a brother named Brad. Long story short, Brad and his wife were having some problems, and they went to therapy. In the middle of the process, Brad's wife died. The police have ruled it a suicide. Brad doesn't believe that's true."

"That sounds terrible and tragic, but what's this have to do with me?"

"Well, I just happened to be telling my friend about you."

Riley had been talking to his friend about me? Now *that* was interesting. But he'd probably just been telling a crazy ex-fiancée story. I'd given him a lot of material.

". . . and your investigations," Riley continued. "You've got a great track record for getting to the bottom of things and finding answers."

"Yes, I do." That was mostly because I was stubborn and sometimes foolhardy, so I really wasn't bragging on my brilliance or anything. I also had a talent for putting my foot in my mouth and looking foolish—in the end it was a wash.

"Brad wants to hire someone to investigate his wife's death. It will require going undercover at this retreat center. However, there's a catch."

"What's that?" I fanned my hand toward my face. What was wrong with my AC? Did I even have money to fix it? And was smooth sailing ever in my future?

"It's at a couples retreat center."

I let that sink in quickly. "So I need to be a part of

a couple? Who in their right mind is going to sign up to do that with me?"

"Obviously, you can't go alone to investigate. You'd need someone to go with you, since the program is for husbands and wives."

"So you volunteered yourself?" I said the words jokingly, fully expecting him to deny it.

"Maybe I did," he said, his voice surprisingly relaxed and at ease.

That only piqued my interest. It really didn't sound like Riley. At least not like the Riley I used to know. "Go on."

"When Brad and his wife had to . . . drop out of therapy, for lack of a better term, a spot opened up. Brad pulled some strings, and we can get in—under assumed identities, of course. The retreat takes place on the weekends at a place about an hour and a half from Norfolk."

"You're really up for doing this?" I had to make sure I understood correctly because it was so out of the realm of what I'd expected.

"I am. Are you game?"

I thought about it a moment. I was free this weekend. Sure, I'd started a new job, but it was part-time and I didn't have any work to do until Monday. And I was moonlighting as a crime-scene cleaner still, but since I'd given up ownership in the company, I was now free to accept or reject jobs as I pleased.

"You don't think that would be awkward? You and me working together? Pretending to *be* together?" I finally asked, curious as to how he'd respond. There were a lot of unspoken issues between us. Knowing Riley, he had to feel awkward to a certain extent about this. He was conscientious like that.

"I think we're both mature enough to handle it, Gabby."

Mature. That's right. Doing this could prove to Riley that I was over our breakup and that I was emotionally healthy enough to be around him. In other words, I was She-Ra.

"So, what do you say?" Riley asked. "Are you game?"

I was never one to turn down a challenge, even if it did require having my heart torn out and trampled. "I say . . . let's do it."

He let out a little breath. A sigh of relief, maybe? "It will be like old times."

I could hear the pleasure in his voice, and the sound sent a shiver up my spine.

Drats!

And it *wouldn't* be just like old times. In old times, we were a couple. Now we would be two people working together, *pretending* to be a couple. I had to keep that at the forefront of my mind as I went into "Operation Protect My Heart" mode. Failure was not an option here.

"So what do I need to know?" I forced myself to focus. My lunch break was quickly ending, and I'd had no food. I rolled down the window and let some fresh air waft inside, wishing it would offer nourishment and not just comfort.

"I'll fill you in on the way there tomorrow. We'll have an hour and a half to talk on the drive. What time will you be home?"

"Around eleven tomorrow. Does that work?"

"It's perfect. I'll meet you at the apartment at one. You'll need to pack for two days overnight. And dress to impress. Most people at this retreat center make an income in the high six figures."

Oh, I was going to fit in *so* easily there. Struggling to make ends meet came as naturally to me as walking did for most people.

I resisted a sigh. "It sounds like a plan."

But as I hung up, I wondered what exactly I'd gotten myself into.

I could hardly wait to find out.

Click here to continue reading.

ALSO BY CHRISTY BARRITT:

BOOKS IN THE SQUEAKY CLEAN UNIVERSE

On her way to completing a degree in forensic science, Gabby St. Claire drops out of school and starts her own crime-scene cleaning business. When a routine cleaning job uncovers a murder weapon the police overlooked, she realizes that the wrong person is in jail. She also realizes that crime scene cleaning might be the perfect career for utilizing her investigative skills.

SQUEAKY CLEAN MYSTERIES
#1 Hazardous Duty
Half Witted (Squeaky Clean In Between Mysteries
Book 1, novella)
#2 Suspicious Minds
#2.5 It Came Upon a Midnight Crime (novella)
#3 Organized Grime

<u>#4 Dirty Deeds</u>
<u>#5 The Scum of All Fears</u>
<u>#6 To Love, Honor and Perish</u>
<u>#7 Mucky Streak</u>
<u>#8 Foul Play</u>
<u>#9 Broom & Gloom</u>
<u>#10 Dust and Obey</u>
<u>#11 Thrill Squeaker</u>
<u>#11.5 Swept Away (novella)</u>
<u>#12 Cunning Attractions</u>
<u>#13 Cold Case: Clean Getaway</u>
<u>#14 Cold Case: Clean Sweep</u>
<u>#15 Cold Case: Clean Break</u>
<u>#16 Cleans to an End</u>
<u>While You Were Sweeping, A Riley Thomas Spinoff</u>

SQUEAKY CLEAN IN BETWEEN MYSTERIES
Half Witted
Half Truth

THE SIERRA FILES
#1 Pounced
#2 Hunted
#3 Pranced
#4 Rattled
#5 Caged (coming soon)

ABOUT THE AUTHOR

USA Today has called Christy Barritt's books "scary, funny, passionate, and quirky."

Christy writes both mystery and romantic suspense novels that are clean with underlying messages of faith. Her books have sold more than four million copies and have won the Daphne du Maurier Award for Excellence in Suspense and Mystery, have been twice nominated for the Romantic Times Reviewers' Choice Award, and have finaled for both a Carol Award and Foreword Magazine's Book of the Year.

She is married to her Prince Charming, a man who thinks she's hilarious—but only when she's not trying to be. Christy is a self-proclaimed klutz, an avid music lover who's known for spontaneously bursting into song, and a road trip aficionado.

When she's not working or spending time with her family, she enjoys singing, playing the guitar, and exploring small, unsuspecting towns where people have no idea how accident-prone she is.

Find Christy online at:
www.christybarritt.com
www.facebook.com/christybarritt
www.twitter.com/cbarritt

Sign up for Christy's newsletter to get information on all of her latest releases here: **www.christybarritt. com/newsletter-sign-up/**

facebook.com / AuthorChristyBarritt
twitter.com / christybarritt
instagram.com / cebarritt